To S

A Novel by Earl Thompson

Note for Librarians: a cataloguing record for this book that includes Dewey Decimal Classification and US Library of Congress numbers is available from the Library and Archives of Canada. The complete cataloguing record can be obtained from their online database at:
www.collectionscanada.ca/amicus/index-e.html
ISBN 1-4120-5118-5
Printed in Victoria, BC, Canada

TRAFFORD

Offices in Canada, USA, Ireland, UK and Spain
This book was published *on-demand* in cooperation with Trafford Publishing. On-demand publishing is a unique process and service of making a book available for retail sale to the public taking advantage of on-demand manufacturing and Internet marketing. On-demand publishing includes promotions, retail sales, manufacturing, order fulfilment, accounting and collecting royalties on behalf of the author.
Book sales for North America and international:
Trafford Publishing, 6E–2333 Government St.,
Victoria, BC v8t 4p4 CANADA
phone 250 383 6864 (toll-free 1 888 232 4444)
fax 250 383 6804; email to orders@trafford.com
Book sales in Europe:
Trafford Publishing (uk) Ltd., Enterprise House, Wistaston Road Business Centre, Wistaston Road, Crewe, Cheshire cw2 7rp UNITED KINGDOM
phone 01270 251 396 (local rate 0845 230 9601)
facsimile 01270 254 983; orders.uk@trafford.com
Order online at:
www.trafford.com/robots/04-0013.html

10 9 8 7 6 5 4 3 2 1

ACKNOWLEDGEMENTS

I grew up fearing and hating my father. His criticisms and fists made my prime objective in my young life, to stay as far away from him as I could. He once told me how fortunate I was that he only used his hands on me. In high school, I participated in every sport and found after-school practices a secret blessing as I wouldn't get home until after five o'clock, only in time to see my father drive off to work his afternoon shift. We never waved.

Then, in my senior year, he came to all of my games, and while he never praised me, he didn't criticize me either. From this grew a truce, which lasted for the rest of our lives…almost.

Dying of emphysema, a heavy smoker for most of his life, I was fortunate to spend hours each day at his bedside as he talked of his life until he could only whisper. He told me stories of the orphanage, growing up in Viking, farming life, and what life was like nearly a hundred years ago.

As he talked, the years pealed off and I found a boy. I also found a love for him—a love, it felt, like I had always had.

I took a shovel, and with the family, buried his ashes and planted a Lilac tree over them. We have it today.

I wept as I planted the flowers. There was so much we missed. There was so much we could have done…together.

It is with the greatest pleasure that I thank John Gordon, my son, who played out yet another generation of family history by joining me in the completion of this work.

Also thanks to Carolyn Hawes, Sue Thorne and William McAusland, who all came to my rescue.

This is my Dad's story.

To Tommy Thompson

PREFACE

"If you ain't tough, you ain't going to make it."
—Canadian Pioneer Credo

Many came to homestead this wild and formidable land. The tough ones lasted longer, but even those who never made it through their first winter played a part in the overall scheme of overcoming the hardships and in making the west the vibrant land it is today.

Our family came from Europe to the United States, then moved north into Canada soon after Clifford Sifton[1] advertised the splendours of the Canadian West. Year by year, they fought droughts that dried out the land, the winds that stripped it, and the cold that paralysed it. To top it all, when a good crop was to be had, eastern interests did their best to cheat, and if possible, steal as much of the profit as they could, leaving the western farmer once again in debt to the banks for the following year's planting. It wasn't quite all that the Ministry of the Interior's propaganda led you to believe.

This history in its primal form, that is, from father to son, was created in my father's dying days. I sat bedside for

---

[1] In 1896 the Liberals under Wilfrid Laurier came into power. Between 1896 and 1905 Clifford Sifton, the new Minister of the Interior, assumed responsibility for immigration and settlement in Canada. Sifton reorganized the previously inefficient immigration department and made it easier for immigrants to obtain homesteads in the West. The focus of Sifton's efforts was to populate the North West with farmers. Sifton saw a need for increased advertising of the West, and initiated a vigorous recruiting campaign aimed not only at the American farmer and British agriculturists, but at Central and Eastern European rural peasants.
Sifton viewed western Canada primarily as a commodity to be sold. 'Selling' the West was problematic as many people viewed the West as a cold and barren tundra. This image had to be seriously revised before serious settlement could occur. Sifton, therefore, urged advertising copywriters to use words like 'invigorating' and 'bracing' instead of 'freezing' and 'desolate' to describe western Canada. Sifton also banned publication of Manitoba temperatures abroad. Eventually, Sifton succeeded in forbidding all references to snow and cold in official publications, creating a more hospitable image of Canada's West.

periods of hours on many occasions listening to him relive his youth and recall his heritage. It wasn't until several years later, when I started to relate my father's history to my sons, that I realised it was I who was now the keeper of our heritage.

As my father knew it, this is as true a story as historians can scribe. Literary license has been taken to create cohesiveness between his stories. I have changed the names of the characters that grew up with the family, but not the family itself. This was done for any and all legal ramifications.

Earl Thompson

EDMONTON—1919

It was mostly familiar to me; the large room was actually an abandoned classroom, empty except for a desk. The four of us stood at attention in front of the desk, each with one foot placed in the penalty box, a small square painted on the well-oiled wooden floor.

My oldest brother, Bob, myself and Earl, the youngest, all knew that the desk contained a rule, cane and strap easily accessible to the Bitch. Even Gladys, the eldest, couldn't manage to escape the punishment by these items which were readily applied to our ears, backsides and hands at the Bitch's whim. That was mostly familiar to Bob and me. James had said to me on more than one occasion, 'pay in pain and pay ye must' – and so we did.

Outside, heavy black clouds gathered, darkening the room. They were visible as black patches through the scratched, whitewashed glass of the windows along one wall. A single light bulb, hanging in the centre of the room and covered by a Chinaman's hat, gave a sick yellow pallor to everything inside. I could catch a glimpse of the Union Jack as it rolled and trembled in the stiffening winds.

"Oh dear, it looks like we're in for a bad fall day," the Bitch said, as she turned from the windows and looked at our father. He was the one thing that wasn't familiar to me.

Our father, according to Bob, didn't 'art in heaven'. You couldn't prove it by me. I scarcely remembered him. I was barely five years old when he went to fight the Heinies. That was going on more than four years ago. At that moment, as he sat on a stool a short distance from the desk he looked, for all the world, like a giant bullfrog; a head with no neck buried into huge shoulders and large arms, bumpy with muscles, and visible under the rolled up sleeves of his army shirt. Great hands dwarfed the seat of the stool as he clutched it between his legs. His army boots, hooked on the rungs of the stool, splayed his legs and gave me the impression he was going to jump on the Bitch at any second.

The Bitch seemed to sense this as well, and while I was hoping this might be fearsome to her, she seemed to bubble over with more charm than I had ever seen, but not more than I had ever heard. I knew what she was up to.

"I wouldn't think you would want to take the children into these elements Mr. Thompson. I'm sure we can find you accommodations right here," she cooed, "and the children won't mind staying one more night, I'm sure," she turned to us smiling.

She looked so nice: her face pinked prettily, her lips painted red, her blue eyes sparkled, and for the first time in daylight, her dark hair was down. It almost covered the tops of her breasts which showed between the buttons of her dress – the last three she had forgotten to do up. She turned back to my father, her hand twisting the ends of her hair over the opening.

"I'm sure we could find room for a returning hero," she said in a soft, sing-song voice. "Couldn't we children?" she added, but didn't look back at us.

"We should go Pa," Bob blurted out. "Storm ain't nothin' and we're ready" he added, taking the words right out of my mouth.

"Nonsense," the Bitch said, her fingers had left her hair and two of them were hooked on the front of her dress. "You children can sleep in the dorm after your chores are done." That was an order.

In the silence that followed, Bob began pulling at my sleeve. I knew what he wanted, but I hated to lie.

"Ma'am?" Bob paused, and waited until she raised her head to look at him. "Tom and me, we met Mr. Schlicter in the hall coming up here and he wanted us to tell you he had to go across town and said you would know?" Bob finished, saving me the lie.

"Yeah, that's right," I added to Bob's lie. I was really impressed by the way Bob could pull that stuff off. Only the truth stopped me from half believing him myself.

I turned to Pa and took one look. He looked even more like a bullfrog than before, bulging eyes looking down the front of the Bitch's dress as she pulled at it trying to disentangle her fingers. I half expected a long tongue to come out of his head and fasten onto her body. I knew right then that our arguments were going to be ignored.

"Well, Robert, you and your brother, Thomas, can stoke the fire and leave it for the night, can't you?"

"We could meet you on the road, Pa," I said. "You just tell us where you're off to and we'll wait for you to catch up in the morning." It was desperation.

"Thomas, one more night won't hurt you." She turned to us with the familiar anger creasing her face. "Your pa is home from the war and we are going to have afternoon tea and supper here. Your pa deserves a night of comfort before you go out on the trail. Now away you go, all of you."

Just as we turned away, a gust of wind spattered heavy raindrops across the windows and the room lit up from lightning followed almost directly with the sound of thunder as it cracked and rolled into the distance.

"There, you see?" the Bitch crowed triumphantly.

Pa, grinning, just shrugged his shoulders.

I guess I couldn't blame him. I knew more than anyone in the room, except the Bitch herself, what he was in for.

The four of us left the room and started down the stairs to the main hall. Earl took off for the boys' dorm to tell his friends about meeting his father. Gladys stopped and sympathised with Bob's and my eagerness to leave the orphanage, even though she didn't have any idea why we were so desperate, and then left us for the girls' dorm.

"What the hell are we going to do?" Bob asked. "We're stuck here now. We have to be at least out of the city or they could come after us."

Bob was right. How do you keep a body silent for that length of time? Kill it? Hide it? Where? For how long? What if they never found him?

"Warren the Warlock," I said to Bob surmising, "the sonovabitch is as much trouble now as he was before we got him. We'll figure something out." I assured Bob, as I put my arm around his shoulder and together we headed back to the boiler room. Who would have thought a Schoolmaster would be such a problem.

EDMONTON—1915

The hard wooden seats bounced us as the wheels rocked over the wet cobblestones. Holes in the road caused the wagon to lurch, throwing us against each other as the wheels dropped into them. A particularly deep one jostled the big constable against Earl almost squeezing him onto the floor but he said nothing and continued to cry softly. Gladys sat upright on the other side of the constable and cried into her hanky. Bob and I sat opposite them, facing forward, neither of us spoke nor did we cry.

"Glory be, Rob! Isn't there to be any level piece to this road? You're bashin' these younguns aroun' warse then a dory in a tempest, man."

There was no answer, nor any change. The wind puffed the oilskin door covers in and along with the cold came the first snowflakes of winter. I caught glimpses of passing buildings through the flaps and was astonished. Each building had three levels of windows and was bigger than our school – the biggest building at home. There were so many, each time the flap lifted another was coming into view or leaving. And there were lamps on each corner, with no people around them. Yet I felt sure they were lit for people to meet at. They did that at prayer meetings at home. They must have had a lot of people saying their prayers here. The flap swayed in as a lamp was being passed and, for a second, light discovered the inside of the darkened wagon.

The fat policeman held Earl on the seat with a hand clasping his shoulder. His other hand braced his body by stretching his arm around behind Gladys's shoulders. He smelled like dirty laundry. My eyes caught the reflection of chain on the floor. I peered into the darkness as the light left and could make out metal circles that were at the ends of the chains and a great piece of iron attached to the middle of the floor which the chains passed through. Then I knew that this wagon was meant for bad people. There was a loneliness to being punished that I never liked. I wasn't sure what we had done wrong that we had to ride in the bad people's wagon, but I sure felt lonely. I bent forward and touched Earl's knee. His sorrowful eyes looked up and he tried to control his crying by gulping air for a few seconds, then looking away, he softly whimpered.

The sound of hoof beats rapidly approaching grew louder as a coach rumbled by. The hoof beats faded and disappeared and we were alone to our thoughts once again. A short time later, our horse's slow, plodding progress came to a stop. We sat for moment in silence. The wagon creaked and leaned as the driver got down from the cab, and opening the door, reached in and helped Gladys to her feet.

"All right wee-uns, mind your step," the fat one inside hissed as he grunted and squeezed his body out. He turned, and reaching for Earl, lifted him out.

"Come now, up the steps. Quickly now."

I was the last to get out and stood on a wooden walk in front of a large, darkened building. The street was deserted and closed in with swirling snow falling heavily passed the lights. A wide staircase made from stone, each one identical to the next, travelled up in front of us. A sign that stood on two posts beside the steps in white letters identified the building to passers-by: *"THE BENEVOLENT DAUGHTERS OF THE HOMESTEADERS ORPHANAGE"*

I stood and looked up at the building as the two policemen, one carrying Earl, swayed their way up to the darkened doorway, hidden under a large half circle that sunk into the middle of the building. It had two rows of windows up to the top; none on the street level. I'll never forget the strange shiver that shook me for a second. This must be the jail for bad kids, I thought, as I started up the stairs in obeyance to the big constable's summoning arm.

Gathering tightly in the doorway, our backs to the wind and snow pelting down, the driver seized a rope attached to a small wheel. Just inside the door we could hear a bell ringing in response to his pulls on the rope. After a short time, a light appeared in the glass over the door but it required a second pull on the bell before the heavy latch clacked and the large door opened in noisy screeching protests from the large iron hinges which travelled across its complete width.

A hand, holding a light, appeared from behind the door. Gladys entered and turned to whoever held the light followed by the constable who carried Earl and steered Bob in front of him. The driver closed the door behind me.

"You are?" the fat constable asked the man holding the lamp.

The man held the lamp up close to the constable's face. "To ye, just the doorman," he said in a defiant tone. "The Headmistress will be down shortly".

He limped forward past the driver to push the door firmly closed and the loud noise of the latch catching echoed throughout the hallway.

I could see, in the dim light, that the man was old with thick, white hair on top of a skinny, bent body, and it appeared he had only one foot. The other had something flat on the end of a stick that seemed to run up his pant leg. Bob noticed it, too.

Somewhere out of sight, a second door slammed, again echoing through the whole building and footsteps could be heard coming down the stairs, then walking towards us.

The old man who had let us in silently shuffled to the head of a wide set of stairs not far from where we were standing and began to go down them slowly, his head bobbing until it disappeared below. Signs above the staircase said '*boys*', with an arrow to one side, and '*girls*', to the other.

We all stood waiting as the footsteps approached along a darkened hallway somewhere to the boys' side of the building. They grew louder and then the body of a large lady, almost magically, appeared from around the corner. She wore a blue kerchief around her head and had on a white dress with tiny red dots all over it. She approached looking at each one of us with a scowl, then her features lost their hard look as she acknowledged the big dry constable who shuffled and spoke.

"Sorry to bother you so late Mrs. Haywood, but the Chief Constable figured there would be all hell, excuse me…heck to pay if these sprouts were to spend the night in the hooscow, after all…that's happened… you know," he finished. "Ah, these here are the Thompson wee-uns."

He pulled a black notebook from his inside pocket. He flipped quickly through the book and scowled. "Damn, uh darn me, I'm afraid I neglected to write their names down. Let's see, the wee-est is…"

"Earl." Gladys stepped up beside Earl. "Our mother told us to look after each other but I'm the oldest and I'll look after them ma'am." She reached out and pulled Earl close. "Earl is three comin' four soon. Then there's Tom," she gestured to me. "He's smart as a whip and can read and write, count to a thousand and can recite the alphabet ma'am, even backwards. He's five closin' the half tomorrow."

I smiled as I stepped forward. I was even prepared to give the alphabet backwards which, I thought, was a pretty good trick. But something on her face convinced me on the spot that maybe she'd like to wait for another time, and I stepped back and studied my shoes.

"And the oldest boy is Bob, he's seven. Oh, Tom is five," she added again. "Bob ain't much on his letters and numbers but to tell the truth he's strong, gettin' so's I can't fair beat him without putting trousers on."

That was a lie. I knew it. She could beat the living daylights out of both Bob and me any time she had a whim for the exercise. The constables, both wet and dry, chuckled and I laughed, maybe a little too loud. But that lady – the *headmistress*, as the old, limping man had said – she never moved a mite. She was the meanest looking lady I had ever seen in all my five years.

"And I am Gladys, ma'am." Gladys made a little weak kneed gesture. "I'm almost ten."

"Now there you be, missus." The dry constable smiled like he had just introduced his own family.

I looked up once again into the lady's face as she turned from Gladys and saw the meanness disappear and her mouth turn slightly upwards as she answered him. "You haven't been around to check the windows and doors for a long time, Constable."

Now, a smile on her face. The meanness had never been there. It couldn't have been.

"Yes, I, uh, think that is something I should do right now, but it takes such time and the place is to bed now."

"Tomorrow then? Say seven?"

"Oh I'm afraid not, missus. I report at seven. Seven is the beginning of the shift."

"Fine, eight it is. Good night, Constables."

She ushered them to the door.

They left in such a hurry that they didn't say goodbye. Closing the large door behind the retreating constables with a slam that echoed again throughout the empty hall, she turned to us with a heavy sigh. "Alright children, follow me," she ordered, and we began to shuffle after her large form.

We turned the corner into a huge, dimly lit hall and began to walk along it, passing several doors as we went. Out of the dimness appeared a set of wide wooden steps, which we climbed to the next floor. Still sniffling, Earl took my hand and we followed the others. At the top of the stairs we emerged into another hallway that looked identical to the one we had just left, except there were no further stairs to climb. On the top floor there were more doors in the hallway and the lady stopped at one and, fishing in her pocket, pulled out a large key ring. She held it up to the single light that hung halfway down the hallway, selected one, and placed it into the lock.

"It's late and for tonight," she said, as she pushed the door open, "you can stay in this room." Her voice trailed off as she entered the room. We followed but stayed near the doorway until a match was struck and put to a lamp. The light revealed a windowless room with a single, large bed and a nightstand close by. It looked like Momma's room. A figure of a man, arms outstretched, hung on the wall. Apart from that, the room was empty.

"There now, two sleep up at this end and two at the bottom. It will only be for the rest of the night. Tomorrow the three lads will be in the boys' dorm and you missy will be in the girls'."

"Thank you, ma'am," Gladys sat at the end of the bed, her hanky still clutched into a ball in her hand, "but you needn't trouble yourself about putting the boys away from me. You see, our mother…we made a promise. We must stay together, as a family. I will look after them. Perhaps if you could just get us one more bed we would be fine right here in this room."

"Now we must have you understand a few things right off, missy," the woman turned to Gladys and bent close to her face. "All the children in this place are in the same predicament you're in, and," her voice grew stern, "you will do exactly as I say, and without question, is that understood?" she demanded.

All of us stared at her in silence. The mean look was back like it had never left her face.

"You are here tonight because the house is asleep. Tomorrow's events will be just as I said. Now off with your wet things, and as you're willing to look after your brothers, you will see to their blankets." She pointed under the bed.

"And you," she turned to Earl, "please stop that irritating sniffling."

She turned and started out of the room. "When you're in bed, I trust you know how to turn the lamp out." The door closed behind her.

We stood in silence for a spell then Gladys went to Earl and helped him out of his clothes. Soon four piles of clothes lay on the floor and we all huddled together under the two blankets from under the bed. Gladys blew out the lamp and we started drifting off to sleep, only to have Earl's continued sniffling delay us, but just for a few minutes.

"I've got to pee."
Earl's whispered complaint reached me seconds before the sleep did. "Hold it," I said and drifted off. It was only in the morning that we were aware that he couldn't.

****

A loud bell sounded in the hall outside the room.

"Aw, no, Earl you wet the bed."

I heard Bob and then Gladys voice their dismay at the same discovery.

"I couldn't help it," Earl began to cry.

We tumbled out of the wet bed and onto the floor in the darkened room bumping into each other.

"Gladys, can you light the lamp?" Bob asked.

"I can't find any matches," she replied, as she finished groping around the nightstand.

Just then, the door flew open and a tall boy stood, silhouetted from the hall light.

"The Witch says to get dressed and come with me. Jesus, who pissed? Did you piss the bed? Christ, you're in for it now," he said to no one in particular.

"He couldn't help it," I answered the boy as he backed away from the doorway. "He's but a toddler."

It took us a few moments but we got into our still damp clothes and followed the boy into the hallway.

As we passed the room next to us we could see two girls placing tin plates on rows of tables with an awful clatter. The boy stopped and leaned into the doorway. "Pissed the bed," he announced, jerking his thumb over his shoulder to us.

From the look they gave as they stopped laying out the plates, I knew we were in for trouble.

"He's only a small child," I offered once again as Earl renewed his sobbing.

We followed the boy down the stairs, Earl holding my hand, then along the second floor to the big front door where we turned and went down the same stairs that the old man who answered the door last night had gone down. There, at the bottom, were two more signs, *boys* and *girls*, each at the entrance of a hall and heading in opposite directions.

He turned into a door marked again, *BOYS*, in big jumbo letters. "This is the lavatory, we call it the *lav*." Inside the room were two tiny rooms with one-holers and above them big glassy boxes. The boy said they were water closets. When you did *the big one* you pulled the chain. We gathered as close as we could to watch as he pulled the chain and the bowl chugged and gurgled as water rush down and out. "You're really from the sticks, ain't you?" he shook his head and grinned at us.

He moved through a second doorway to a larger room that held a big tub in the middle of the floor. "Saturday night is bath night." There was yet another door, this one to a small room that held a tank with a chain on it. "You shower after the bath. Then dry over there by that other door." He walked us back to the first room and I saw a long, tin box stuck on the wall. "This is the *pisser*. What you should have used last night," he added. Without another word, all three of us lined up and took what the boy called *whizzers* in the pisser. It was obvious we were ready to bust.

Finished, we left the lav and found Gladys waiting for us. We followed the hall around behind the stairs. The boy opened a door that led into a dark room. He turned a knob by the door and a light in the centre of the room above a table showed walls holding boxes of clothes. We stood inside the doorway silently, as the boy took pieces of clothing from several boxes around the room and stacked them on the table.

"These should fit the little guy. Put them on."

I helped Earl out of his clothes and gathered them up and placed them on the table in exchange.

Turning our backs to the boy, one by one, we changed. The clothes were all in two shades of blue: a lighter shirt and darker coveralls. Gladys took her clothes into a darkened corner and came back wearing a dress with straps over a blouse in the same colours. After changing, we left the room and went back upstairs.

"We all got the same as him," Earl said, as we climbed the stairs towards the large front door. His face was very red.

"My name's Gladys," Gladys offered to the boy as she hurried up the stairs beside him.

"I'm Peter," the boy replied, and without turning to her he continued up the stairs.

I counted sixteen steps in each stairway and there were three stairways. That made forty-eight and I told Earl that as he began to falter at the bottom of the third staircase.

"That's a lot," he wheezed and sniffled. "I've never seen so many."

I pulled him up each of the last few as he puffed, out of wind. Looking down at him finally, I urged him on only to discover he had turned pasty white, his breathing hard. I noticed a strange wetness was on his face and his hair had become matted. I pulled him up the last stair onto the hallway floor where he suddenly sat down on me. His red-rimmed eyes looked at me in bewilderment. I looked for Gladys or Bob only to see Bob's back as he left the hallway and disappeared into the room where the girls were setting the tables with the tin dishes.

I tried to pull Earl up by the arm. "Come, Earl. Let's go. There's food."

I looked to the doorway as I pulled him by the arm. "We're just hungry."

I looked at him as he wasn't getting up onto his feet but instead started to lie down. The look of bewilderment went into nothing. He just didn't seem to look at anything and silently fell over. His little chest was rising and falling so fast.

Scared, I left him and ran to the doorway. Inside the room annoyed faces from countless boys on one side and girls on the other side of the room glanced at me then to the lady who stood at a table obviously waiting for Earl and me. I looked back at Earl. He lay in a pool of light from a window by the stairs in the darkened hallway. I could see he hadn't moved.

"Gladys!" I screamed, and ran back to Earl. I got to him but he didn't look at me, instead his eyes looked straight at nothing. Gladys came out of the room, then the lady and then a bedlam of chair-scraping sounds and voices as the kids rushed into the hall.

****

Only Earl's hair could be distinguished as he slept. His face was as white as the large pillow he slept on. Gladys, Bob and I stood outside the room in the large hall and peered in. Inside, the Headmistress and a scowling doctor stood at the head of the bed and recovered Earl in his blanket. His body looked so small and fragile.

The white-haired, old man with the wooden leg appeared out of nowhere and stood nearby as Gladys's whisper hissed at me. "You were supposed to look after him." She seemed to tower over me. "You promised."

It was true. I couldn't think of anything to say that would help me. I had promised to look after Earl, as Bob had promised to look after me, and Gladys, being the oldest was to look after all her younger brothers. It didn't seem to be worth anything to bring that up because I knew a punch would be the only result from bringing up her share of the responsibility.

There didn't seem to be any way that I could get through the awful feelings that tumbled through my mind.

"It wouldna be too wise to take too much onto yerselves," the old man said, obviously overhearing Gladys's anger. "These things tend to happen rather suddenly."

"Well, he promised Momma," Gladys shot back at him angrily.

The old man held up his palm to her in a quieting motion. "Aye, that may well be, but to stop the wee specs and tiny mites that bring in illness is difficult even for an adult, let alone a wee lad, dinna ye think so lass?"

His heavily lined face seemed to soften as he looked at Gladys with his watery, blue eyes. "My name is Flanagan, James Flanagan," he offered without pausing, "and I know of yer terrible misfortune. But ye must stay together tight to it now. You're the family. Stay together," he repeated, and gently urged Gladys to step up to me by pushing on her shoulder. I felt her arms around me.

I tried not to cry because that meant a pounding from Bob. I had to pull out of her arms and sure enough met Bob's angry eyes. Only babies cry.

The doctor came out of the room followed by the woman. She turned and pulled the door closed. He was talking to her angry face in a low voice. I turned just in time to see the top of the old man's silver head disappear on the stairs below us.

"These are the rest?" the doctor asked, and without waiting for an answer, came forward. Taking me by the shoulder, he drew me over to the outside light shining from the hall window. He placed a hand on my face and looked into my mouth, then summoned Gladys and Bob and did the same thing. Apparently satisfied, he spoke to the lady.

"Well these three are well enough," he said turning back to her. He straightened and put a hand on Bob's back then turned to Gladys.

"You have a very sick little brother." He looked directly at Gladys. "You feel you can look after him little lady? He's going to need a lot of care and attention. Earl, that his name?"

The doctor turned to the lady, "Mrs. Haywood?" he asked.

She nodded and said, "I believe so." She looked at Gladys who nodded.

We all walked together down the stairs to the front door of the building

"You're going to have to stay with him and make sure he gets his medicine. Mrs. Haywood knows all about it and will explain it to you. She's far too busy and if we can't look after him here we must take him away to the hospital."

"I can look after him," Gladys assured him quickly.

"We're all family and got to stay together," I offered up the old man's words and suddenly felt comforted by them.

"Exactly," the doctor said, putting on the funny black hat he had been carrying with his bag. It looked like a potbelly. He opened the large door and a blast of cold air from a grey sky poured in, backing us away. "I'll be back tonight to look in on the child." The door closed.

A bell from somewhere upstairs sounded. We could hear doors opening followed by lots of footsteps in the hallway and some voices. Girls could be heard.

"No talking in the hallways!" Mrs. Haywood roared.

All three of us jumped out of our skins.

"Upstairs for lunch, quickly now, we're running behind schedule and we've already missed breakfast."

We hurried along to the room that became known to us as the cafeteria, where we all were to eat three times a day, with the exception of Earl. Gladys would be taking his food to him on a tray from the kitchen next to the cafeteria.

Later, we helped the old man roll the mattress that Earl had peed on the night before. He covered the other side with a sheet of rubber. Earl was very white, his red eyes now sunk into dark sockets, and his breath came hard and ragged. The fact that I had betrayed him, and broke my promise to Momma to look after him, seemed so long ago. But it was only yesterday that I promised her – a thought that was almost unbearable. The old man noticed, I guess, for after helping Earl back to the bed, he came to the door where I stood.

"It's pneumonia, laddie," he said to me. "There's nary a thing ye could do about it."

I looked up at him and saw something in his eyes, a softness that matched his voice, and even as I looked away, I knew I liked him. He opened the door and left just as Gladys entered the room. She looked at me with angry eyes then went to the chair and pulled it up to the bed. She dipped a rag into the bowl on the little table beside the bed and folding it, placed it over Earl's closed eyes. Then with a deep sigh, she ordered Bob and me to leave.

The hallways were empty. The only sign of life came from the kitchen through the open cafeteria doorway. We walked by but couldn't see who was behind the counter separating the two rooms. We ended up exploring the halls, reading the signs on the doors on each floor and even opening a few to peek in. One, across the hall from our room, had a little table attached to the wall. A long-handled hand bell rested on it beside a door that said, '*Office*'. The next door said, '*Headmistress*'. We passed them up.

There were five more on the top floor: one, a mop closet and a second, another room with a single bed in it, much the same as the room Earl was in. At the far end of the hall were two other doors without lettering on them, one each side of the staircase that went down to the main floor below. Just before the top of the stairs, we could hear Mrs. Haywood talking loudly about numbers through the door. This must be the classroom. Bob and I quietly slipped by it and then past the two at the end of the hall before going downstairs to the main floor.

A window, across the hallway at the back of the building, was covered with a battered wire mesh. Looking down, we could see a yard divided into two by a high, wire fence. At the centre, was a flagpole that stretched right up almost to the roof above us. It was taller than the one at Bob's school. The grounds themselves were hard packed from traffic and only a few small patches of grass seemed to have survived in the corners of the yard.

"The recess yard," Bob said.

I jumped at the sound of his voice; he spoke so little. As a matter of fact, those were the first words he had spoken since the constables had taken us from the train.

We moved on down the hall passing several more doors. We stopped and listened for any noises from inside them before trying to open them. They were all locked. We rounded the corner to the front door where the stairs went down to the bottom floor. Rather then go down the stairs, I wanted to see what was on the other side of the hallway. Bob followed until we came to an open door. Inside the large room were two rows of beds, and at the far end, a barred window. The beds were neatly made up. The walls were badly cracked and chipped and, in some places, strips of wood showed through holes. In the middle of the room was the old man with a mop and bucket. He had his back to us. He pulled the mop out of the bucket, twisted it and limped over to a bed, swishing it underneath. We slipped away.

Back at the stairs, we decided to go down and explore. Here as well, the walls were holed and cracked. The worn wooden steps with the signs that read boys and girls on each side led us down to a hard, cement floor past the, now familiar, lavatories with their *pissers*. At the end of the short hall between them was a door that led outside to the recess yard. We could see the flagpole sticking in the ground and stretching up, and out of sight. A second hallway led off in another direction and we followed it to the last door that had a sign on it – *boiler room*. It was locked.

The sound of a door closing on the main floor above us echoed in the halls. We left the door to the boiler room as light footsteps clattered down the stairs towards us. They stopped abruptly near the bottom of the steps and we came face to face with an older boy who we must have startled.

"What! Ya can't get out. The windows are barred and the doors are locked," he said, matter of factly. "Hey, I know, you two peed the bed didn't you?" He finished the stairs and walked over to us grinning. He was quite a bit taller than Bob: skinny, with a sharp chin and a bird's nose.

"That was Earl, he's sick. He couldn't help it."

"Yeah right. You're breaking the rules. No one in the halls after the bell. You know what you get for breaking the rules...this". He gave me a painful punch on the shoulder.

"We were looking for the boys' lav," I lied, hoping to get out of a second painful punch. Instead he turned and raised his fist to hit Bob's shoulder.

Now, that was a mistake. Bob was not me. I try to keep from getting a pounding. Bob was forever pounding on me mostly because I knew more answers to questions than he did. Gladys pounded on both of us. She was one of the toughest boy/girls in town and not even Bob could stay standing when she was hell bent on making misery. Bob could give her a handful when he lost his temper. His black eyes would flash wide and that was time for me to vamoose and no one, even close to my size, could catch me. I had a lot of practice keeping out of the way because I enjoyed showing off with answers. But, of course, the boy didn't know this. I watched Bob's eyes flash in anger as the boy raised his fist to hit him. Damned if I was going to warn him!

The boy bent down lower than Bob as the air came rushing out of his mouth from Bob's punch to his stomach.

"You little bastard," he hissed in trailing breath, arms closed about his middle. "I'm tellin'." He turned and started back up the stairs climbing awkwardly.

I watched the coolness come back into Bob's eyes as he stood there, his fist still clenched, watching the boy leave.

****

I leaned against the wall just outside the office door. I could hear Mrs. Haywood's angry voice inside, then a loud 'ow!' coming from Bob. A minute later he came out holding his ear. He had been in the office for quite a spell. He pointed me to the open door then, as I entered, leaned against the wall. The look on his face was what Momma called a *smirk*.

"Close the door," she said sharply. "Now stand in the square in front of the desk."

She left me standing in this empty room in the white square and disappeared into another room through a doorway. Inside I could see an open closet with dresses hanging, a bed with a large bowl and pitcher on a table beside it. The bottom of a large pot could be seen under the bed.

She came back to the desk with some papers in her hand and, pulling a stool up to the desk, laid the papers on top.

"You are Thomas." She seemed to be reading from the papers. I was confused whether she was asking or telling me. I opened my mouth but, before I could answer, she went on. "You're six years old and your sister says you're very bright."

"I'm five and a half," I corrected, trying to be helpful.

"You're six, and don't contradict me," she warned.

"Yes, ma'am." I always wanted to be older.

Her head snapped up from the papers and her eyes narrowed. "Are you being smart with me?"

I had a certain pride at being smart but something told me this wasn't the time. Being quiet seemed to be the smart thing. I said nothing but fidgeted under her stare.

"You know your numbers, according to your sister."

I said nothing.

"Well, do you?"

"Yes, ma'am."

"Count for me."

I waited.

"Well?"

"How high?"

"Can you count to ten?"

"I can count to a thousand, or more if you want," I offered brightly.

"Hmm, your sister said you were the one who likes to show off. Let's try a hundred."

"Yes, ma'am," I waited.

"Well?"

"By ones, twos, fives or tens?"

"Never mind," she was sharp with me again. "Do you know the alphabet?"

"Yes, ma'am."

"Okay…well?"

"Frontwards or backwards?"

"You know it backwards?"

"Yes, ma'am, and the times tables."

"Really?"

I recited the alphabet backwards and started on the times tables but she interrupted me.

"That's enough, Thomas. Did your sister teach you that?"

"And my momma," I said, disappointed at being stopped. I really like the twelve times table.

I read for her, first out of a little book about John, Mary and Spot their dog, then from the Bible. Gladys and I read passages to Momma every night by the lamp light when she was sick. Momma loved for me to read and recite to her. I was a '*true delight*', she would say as she hugged me with skinny arms, and kissed my forehead with dry lips.

"That's enough, Thomas. I'm going to start you off with a second grade speller and you can start arithmetic."

She picked up a cane from behind the desk and laid it across the desk in front of me. "Do you know what this is?"

"A cane," I answered enthusiastically.

"Exactly. Do you know what it is used for?"

"Ah, to help hurt people walk…old people. I remember seeing old people in our town use them to step with."

"Not this one. This one is to ply on the bottoms of little boys who are bad and break rules, and most of all, boys who fight."

Now she had my attention and I was unable to take my eyes off of it. I sure didn't like where this conversation was going.

She got up from behind the desk while pulling a ruler out from under the cane and came at me.

"Stand in that square – that's the penalty box," she said as she walked around me. "Eyes ahead."

It wasn't a big whack, but the edge of the ruler on the ear from behind made me yelp in pain. I heard someone – Bob, laughing out in the hallway.

"Obey the rules and no fighting. Next time you'll feel that." She pointed to the cane.

My ear hurt like heck, and worse if I touched it. "Yes, ma'am."

I was dismissed from the penalty box and the room.

Outside in the hall, Bob waited with a grin on his face. Across the hall from him, Peter waited with the same grin. Bob called it a *shit eaters grin* but I had had enough misery for this spell and wasn't going to create more for myself by telling them what I thought they looked like.

Peter pushed us down the hall towards the boys' dorm. Hope as I might, I had a sinking feeling Peter was going to see we got the cane in short order.

Peter opened the door to the boys' dorm. It was the same room we had seen the old man mopping earlier, only this time, there were a bunch of boys sitting on the beds and a few standing and laughing at the far end of the room. These were the bigger boys who included the boy that had hit me earlier and got the payback from Bob. All were dressed in the same uniform. The room went silent.

"This is your bed," Peter said, looking at me and pointing to the first bed inside the room. A small, brown bag sat on a towel on a little table that each bed had at its side. I sat on the end and looked at the faces, each bearing a grin.

"And Bob?" Peter glanced at Bob. "Yeah, it is Bob isn't it?" Without waiting for a reply he went on, "This is your bed." He pointed to a bed across and three down from mine.

Bob went to his bed and was about to sit on it when he stopped and lifted his hand off it.

"Oh, we thought you might like it better if someone had a whizzer in it first."

Bob straightened up and wiped his hand on his pants, his angry eyes wide and dark. Four bigger boys gathered around Peter in a group.

"Gordy, you want to get him?" Peter asked.

The boy that hit me and received Bob's punch moved to the front. "Let's all get him," he said – but didn't move.

Bob moved out to the end of his bed and squared up. It wasn't going to be a long fight, the five boys were all bigger and older, but Bob was ready. The smaller boys moved out of the way by going to their beds and sitting…watching.

Peter moved forward. The boy, Gordy, was right behind him his lip curled up.

Peter suddenly smiled at Bob. "I see you got to stand in the penalty box. His hand moved up to his ear. Bob touched his ear in response but kept a distance between them by backing up a step.

Peter laughed. "Look, we've all got the Witch's wand." The tone of his voice eased the tension a little and the boys started to laugh.

"You too," the boy on the next bed, who looked about my age, said to me, touching his ear. "The Witch's elves, see we all got one ear pointed from her wand."

Both Bob and I studied the faces around the room. It was true, all of them, us, had a pointed ear. Ours were still painful, but sure enough, each of us, including Peter, had a small, white lump on the top of our ears from our visit to the penalty box.

"What did you think of the Witch?" Peter asked Bob.

I spoke up as Bob shrugged, "I think she's nice." It was quickly apparent to me that I alone shared this view, as the boys looked back and forth at each other in disbelief.

"Oh, you do?" Peter answered with a smile, as he stepped around Bob to look at me. A few boys snickered. "Well I guess as you're the youngest here, you get the job of ringing the bell tomorrow morning for reveille."

"What's that?" I asked the boy sitting on the next bed as he grinned at me.

"It's wake up. You'll be the new crier."

"Yeah? That's neat, I've read about town criers in the Medieval times…"

"That's it exactly," Peter said. "Your job will be to wake up each morning, go upstairs and ring the bell outside the office."

"And you say, *Hear ye! Hear ye!*," I interrupted.

"Exactly," Peter beamed, "except you have to yell for everyone to *get your asses out of bed.*"

"Really?" I said, not recalling hearing any shouting this morning. Maybe we were just too busy with Earl's bed-wetting and our scrambling in the dark, to notice it.

"Really," Peter answered. "That's important, if you don't say it they will all roll over and go back to sleep."

"And you really have to yell it real loud 'cause it's your job to wake everybody up," the big boy named Gary, shouted from the far end of the room.

"And we have to be up at five o'clock in the morning," Peter finished.

Five o'clock was early, really early, I knew that, and presented an obvious problem. "How will I wake up to be able to ring it?"

"Oh I'll get you up," Peter said. "I have the alarm clock and I'll let you know until you get used to it and can get up yourself, and don't forget, you'll be really helping Mrs. Haywood. You'd like to help, wouldn't you?"

"Sure," I said.

"Let's turn your mattress," he said to Bob, walking over to the wet bed. "Gordy doesn't seem to want to punch you at the moment." Together with the other boys, except Gordy who went to his bed to sulk, they turned Bob's mattress over and Peter showed Bob how to make the bed so it would be acceptable.

Raymond Stein was the name of the boy next to me. He seemed to be quieter than the others and I liked him right away.

"Visit?" he asked. "Can I sit on your bed so we can talk?" he explained when I frowned at his question.

He went on to explain that each time you wanted to sit and talk you had to ask permission. Each bed was the boy's own sort of space. If you wanted to talk and sit on the other's bed you had to ask 'visit', because after, the bed had to be remade. The Witch, Mrs. Haywood, would inspect the room and Peter would have to go upstairs to the penalty box with the boy who broke a rule, or was messy. They would take their turns in the penalty box getting a whack or two from the cane, depending on how bad the mess was.

She kept a small book in her drawer of each boy and each violation, and depending on the violation, she would give you up to three whacks.

That's why, Raymond said, each time a boy broke a rule, he got a punch on the shoulder, and the older boys had a way of punching that really hurt. Wandering around the halls, even talking in the halls, was *taboo*, and that meant forbidden, according to Raymond.

Peter called Raymond to go up and ring the bell for supper.

As the bell sounded throughout the halls we lined up, oldest first and me last. We marched single file up the stairs to the cafeteria. After climbing the stairs we fell into line behind the girls. They always got to the cafeteria before us, so that made me the last person to eat.

When the bell rang after the meal I wasn't near finished. I was so hungry I took the big boys' portion of fried oatcakes. I had to leave them as Peter waited at the door until the rest of the boys had left and called me with a crooked finger. I was still hungry and the girls hadn't left yet so I was a little reluctant and slow. He pushed me out the door.

Raymond told me after that the girls stayed and cleaned up and did the dishes.

Before lights out, Bob and I, along with Peter, were allowed to visit Earl. Peter left us as we came to the room beside the cafeteria and slipped in.

Gladys was there sitting with Earl. Her pretty face was pinched. Earl's sweaty face was pale, his eyes kind of blinked but didn't really open. Ragged sounds of breathing came from his open mouth.

"If he doesn't get better soon, he'll have to go to the hospital – the doctor said this morning. He's so sick," Gladys whispered to Bob. She ignored me like I was invisible.

There was nothing else for us to do, so Gladys told us to leave and placed another damp rag on his forehead after rinsing it out in a bowl beside the bed.

Bob and I left. Peter wasn't around so remembering the empty hallways weren't the place to be, we headed straight back to the dorm. But first I checked and found the bell was where it was supposed to be for the morning reveille.

****

"Okay, it's time." Peter's voice came into my sleep out of the dark. I woke up instantly.

"Away you go, can't be late. Hurry, you can go in your pyjamas," he said.

The door opened allowing a little light from the hallway to guide me up the stairs. The bell was sitting high on the stand but I could reach its long handle on my tiptoes. It was heavy and gave a noisy clang as I seized it with both hands and removed it from the table.

I swung it up and down; the noise made me jump and echoed loudly through the darkened halls. I rang it only for a few seconds then called out, "Hear ye! Hear ye! Get your asses out of bed!" I was reaching up to put it back when a door opened behind me.

"What in God's name do you think you're doing?" Mrs. Haywood's loud voice startled me and the bell rolled off the table and onto the floor with another loud clang that was nothing compared to the yelp I gave as it bounced upon my foot. I felt myself very close to peeing my pants.

"I…I," I stammered.

"Thomas? Get into the office at once."

I was thoroughly confused. I went to the door but it was locked. I turned and picked up the bell just as the office door opened. Fearful, I presented the bell to Mrs. Haywood's large figure that loomed before me, sounding one last clang in the process. She seized the bell by the handle and clapper and, brushing past me, replaced it on the stand.

I entered the room with a shove from behind that spilled me onto the floor. I quickly rose and walked to the penalty box. That became obvious.

"Now what's this all about," she asked, as she stepped behind the desk in front of me and produced the cane out of the air like magic and laid it across the desk. "Do you have any idea what time it is?"

I knew it was ringing the bell time because I was told to do it, but the sight of the cane seized my throat so I could hardly breathe let alone talk. I tried to speak but nothing came out.

"Well, I don't know who put you up to this but here is what you get. Bend over and put your hands on the desk," she ordered. She picked up the cane and walked behind me as I did what she said.

"It's three o'clock."

On three the whack of the cane sounded in the room and for a split second I thought she had hit something else…for a split second!

She had made her point. I was too busy getting out of the way, in case another whack was on its way, to even yelp.

"Get back on that spot young man," she warned, pointing to it with the cane.

She was still between me and the door, so rubbing my butt and blinking back the tears, I reluctantly stepped back onto the white square, but I wasn't grabbing any desk.

"Since you don't want to tell me, I think I can guess who put you up to this," she said in a lower voice. My spirits began to rise at the thought that maybe the truth would save me. I still couldn't choke out one word, but I did venture a hand to rub the burn off my bum.

"You may go back to the dorm now." She walked around me and put the cane on the desk.

I had the door opened in one second when she stopped me.

"Thomas, will you tell Peter that he can remain ringing the early bell, and you can ring in recess, lunch and dinner."

"Yes, ma'am." My voice came back from the hallway as the door behind me banged shut.

Back inside the dorm it was very dark and I groped my way to my bed. Just as I lay down a match was struck down the row, revealing a bunch of grinning faces.

"You have the honour of the first caning for today." Peter grinned at me from above the glowing light.

"That wasn't fair, you…you…" I searched for a word that was bad as could be, "bitch!" was the only one that came to mind.

"Bitch?" the older boys guffawed. "Bitch! That's a female," one said.

I wasn't doing too well. I wanted them to see my anger. I didn't want for anything like this to happen again. But all I could do it seemed, was make them laugh. I sure didn't think it was funny.

"Now I got to ring the bell at recess, she said, and lunch time and at suppertime," I said woefully.

There was quiet.

"What?" Peter asked.

"She said you could do the morning bell, Peter."

"Did she really say that?"

Peter's concern stirred a revelation inside me when a second voice, from the returning darkness after the light went out, said, "Damn, Tom, you get to be first in line. Whoever rings the bell the rest of us have to line up behind. You get to be first!"

It sounded like a good deal but I realised I had taken the oldest boy's privilege and Peter was not going to be very happy with me. I was a little nervous when I heard some grumbling as feet began to shuffle back to their beds in the dark. I lay on the bed in the dark, rubbing my sore butt, and wondering why they had played this trick on me and gotten me into trouble. Why me? Well, it served Peter right, I thought, but I didn't like being the messenger to making Peter unhappy.

****

Three months had gone by along with Christmas. It was a sad Christmas even though we received some winter clothes, cake and cookies from the Benevolent Daughters. Earl was still very sick, he seemed to get better, and then he would get sick again. Mr. Flanagan was a very skinny Santa Claus with a terrible beard over his own, all knotted in lumps. He gave each boy and girl a small gift and when he was through he visited Earl. Bob and I hardly saw Earl because of rules and Gladys was with him all the time, so we hardly saw her. Christmas night he 'relapsed' – as the Witch, Mrs. Haywood, called it – and the doctor had to be called.

Then a man, a minister, came from the church and we stood at dinnertime and said a prayer for Jesus, and for Earl. The minister went and saw Earl for a short time and this really upset Gladys. I made up my mind, I didn't like this minister man and was quite relieved when Gladys, Bob and I didn't have to go to church but remained with Earl in his room.

It was later in the night when the fever broke again and Earl's ragged breathing quieted into a sleep. Gladys cried but I couldn't understand why. She looked old and tired. She told us to go to bed and then hurried us out of the room.

****

The same day Earl came to the dorm, Peter left the orphanage. He was almost fifteen now and working age. The orphanage didn't have any babies. They were adopted out without even coming into the building. From my age until Peter's, people didn't want you. The farmers came for the older ones and gave them a home for work. Sometimes, after working on the farm all season, they were brought back to the orphanage so they didn't have to be fed in the winter.

Peter said, if that happened, he wouldn't come back, he would go on his own if the people didn't want to keep him. I liked Peter. He didn't pick on the smaller boys like me. As a matter of fact he was the only one of the older boys who would talk to me. I didn't want to see him go. Not just because I would miss him, but many times he had stopped the older boys from bullying the younger ones.

Both Bob and I had a difficult time. Me; because I couldn't shut up in class and got to be called the *smart ass*, and because I loved school and had knocked off grade three fractions – showing up the older boys. They were real dummies. Bob had a difficult time because he didn't take on any friends. He liked to be alone and had a few scraps with Brian Boudreau and Gary Govier – two who were in the big five. Bob had gotten a good beating and the cane because Gary had told on him, and then Peter put a licking on Gary for 'stoolin'.

The other two boys who ran with the older boys were Russell Keep and Gordy McLeod. They were both a little easier on Bob and me. They never hit us.

The day after Earl was allowed to come and sleep in the dorm, I took him around the halls to show him where everything was and we met up with Gary. Even though I had permission from the Witch to show Earl around, Gary was not going to pass up giving me the shoulder punch. I had learned to kind of move my shoulder with the punch and take some of the pain out of it so it didn't bother me. But then, he grabbed Earl's skinny little arm.

"No, don't hit him, he's been sick and he's too little."

Earl had come out from his illness really thin and pale, and he had a terrible wheeze that really started up when he was excited or climbing stairs.

Before I could act, he hit Earl, knocking him down instantly. His cry spurred me into action. I butted Gary in the stomach and flailed at him. I was so busy trying to hit him that, in my anger, I was completely surprised to find myself on top of Earl, my ears ringing. He hit me hard and furiously but I managed to stay between him and Earl.

After he left, Earl's crying subsided and I helped him up. I could taste blood in my mouth from a cut lip. To top if off, I got the cane later that afternoon after Gary had said Earl and I had started a fight with him. At least the Witch didn't give Earl any more punishment than a warning.

We tried to tell her the truth but she didn't seem to want to hear us.

"Thomas," she said, "you're such a bright boy, but this fighting has got to stop one way or the other." She liked to hit us but she was scared to hit the older boys, I think.

After dinner, back in the dorm, Earl made the mistake of sitting on Mike McLeod's bed without permission. Mike was Gordy's younger brother; he was two years older than me. He was at the other end of the dorm talking to Gordy and Brian. I had a book and as I loved to read, was doing just that, when I heard Gary yell down the room for the little *sickie* to get off Mike's bed. He started down the aisle, between the beds, towards Earl. I was up instantly.

"You leave him alone!" I started towards Earl who was scrambling to get off the bed – his eyes wide with fright.

I grabbed Gary just as he got to Earl. Gary pushed me aside and swung Earl around by his arm. I regained my balance just in time to see Bob fling himself onto Gary's back and, with two fingers up Gary's nose, pull him over backwards. He released the squealing Earl and went down with Bob on top of him – momentarily I knew. As Gary clutched Bob's wrist to reclaim his nose, he turned over on top of him. I jumped on Gary's back and, reaching around, took up Bob's hold on his nose. Bob squirmed out from under Gary just as he bucked me off. I flew over backwards but didn't let go of his nose much to his discomfort. Bob jumped on top and started punching Gary in the face repeatedly.

"I give! I give!" Gary cried out, and Bob stopped, but I wanted just one good one on him and punched him as hard as I could right in the eye. I got a real pleasure out of hearing him yelp from my blow. Bob and I both got off Gary who began crying about 'two against one'.

Earl was by now on his own bed. His eyes still wide in terror as he tried desperately to get air.

Gary's nose was bleeding and the eye I had hit was swelling up.

"You ever touch him again," I warned, but Gary was out of the room and on his way, no doubt, to the Witch's office.

I got my second caning that day. Bob his first, for that day. Only I got three; two on my bum and the third on my back because I wouldn't bend over one more time. The third drove the wind from my chest and I realised suddenly how Earl felt gulping for air when he got anxious or tired.
I slept fitfully, that night, on my face. The fact that we, Bob and I, had given Gary a pounding had at least one – actually two – good sides to it. Gary wouldn't, or better not, pick on Earl, and the older boys didn't prize what he was saying,

which meant he would not be in the running for *King Shit of Turd Island*, as Bob put it; Peter's vacated position of *Straw Boss*, as the rest of us called it.

Brian and Gordy decided to share it and teamed up to bully the smaller kids. Russell Keep, who had been badly scarred from burns in a fire that killed his parents and his sister, kept mostly to himself. Sometimes, he did put a stop to the bullying when he refused to partake and advised them to leave the little guys alone.

Russell was the brightest out of a dumb lot of the oldest boys. He was eleven, almost twelve, and because he was bright, he would leave the orphanage classes and go to a regular public school next fall.

Like me, Russell loved reading, and he let me read some of his books. My favourite was a big book on The Rise and Fall of the Roman Empire. We sat and discussed it almost chapter by chapter.

Russell was the only one of the boys who didn't have a pointed right ear from the Witch's ruler. He never had to be punished. Well, actually, his ears had been almost burnt off, only twisted stubs remained. He got the cane more than once but the Witch had never split what was left of his ear.

In the classroom on the top floor next to the cafeteria, Russell and I sat together. The girls sat in twos nearest to the windows because they didn't look out as much as the boys did – so Mrs. Haywood said. The older boys sat at the back of the room. The smallest were to sit at the front.

When Russell asked to sit up front with me, though I was the youngest in class, he said it was because he couldn't see the slate board. He said later, when we were talking about a book, that he wanted to sit beside me because, whispering, he was tired of the big dummies.

So we sat up front. That meant we got all the 'assisting' jobs like cleaning the slate boards, brushes and things like that. Russell was kind of sneered at because he sat with me, but it never seemed to bother him and it never went any further than that. No one ever picked on Russell. It just seemed like all of us felt he had had enough pain for one lifetime.

Mike McLeod, Gordy's little brother, sat with Raymond Stein right behind Russell and myself. Mikey was always goofing around and kept us, particularly Dennis Becker who sat behind him, in a constant fit of laughter. He was the most 'caned' of us all. He just couldn't stop adding little things to everything Mrs. Haywood said and would do a take off on her that would put the whole class, girls included, into an uproar. His morning routine was to wait in the hall after fooling around and then go get his caning before lunch. This settled him for the afternoon, as he had to sit on the hard seat with a burnt butt.

Raymond was older than me by over a year, almost two. He was small and really unhappy. Terrified of the bigger boys, he wept for hours after receiving their beatings. Once, I felt sorry for him and tried talking to him but he just wouldn't say anything. For days he would just sit in the corner of the dorm, down behind my bed near the door. The older boys called him the Mouse.

David Walischuk sat with Bob at first; he was always shadowing Brian or Gordy since Peter left. While he didn't pick fights, he was always in the background urging the bigger boys on and sneaking in a punch or kick. He thought everything the bigger boys said was funny. They called him *yukey*. Bob called him *peckerhead*; a term he used frequently, even sometimes at the *Terrible Two*, as Brian and Gordy liked to call themselves.

Bob disliked David very much and David wisely asked to sit with Gary. The Witch decided to move Bob instead. For Bob, it was a move in the wrong direction, as he liked Gary even less.

The first time they sat together, Gary caught Bob off guard and sent him abruptly onto the floor with a push along the seat with his hip. Bob got up and promptly punched Gary in the nose, just as the Witch was turning from the slate board to see what the commotion was about. Much to Gary's delight, Bob got sent to the penalty box for a caning.

Gary was so much bigger than Bob that should he try and fight, he would kill Bob. But he didn't want to fight one-on-one, unless it was the smallest kid in class...meaning me. Eventually, Bob sat near the back of the room by himself.

Brian Boudreau and Gordy, Mikey's older brother, sat at the back of the room which was all right with everyone. Brian had green teeth and bad breath, and Gordy had just as foul a mouth but in another way, he was always cussing and swearing. He was caned so many times but never stopped with the dirty language.

Peter had said Gordy and Mike were found by skinners who had come to their family's farm looking for shelter from a storm. They found them the only ones still alive. The epidemic had killed both his ma and pa. The two boys had dragged their folks outside when they began to smell so bad and that's where the skinners found them, laid out on the porch.

The ground was too frozen to bury them so the skinners left the bodies in a shed and took the boys to the Mounties and reported the scene. The week they spent with the skinners did more to increase Gordy's words than all the time he spent in class so far.

We had to put up with girls in the class, too. Most of them weren't any better liked than I was 'cause they seemed brighter than the older boys. I think that's why the older boys made a point of never reading or doing their numbers, and badgering Russ and me to the point of giving me a pounding whenever Russ and Bob weren't around. It seems my biggest problem is the enjoyment of finding things out. I loved everything about school and not even Russ could answer all the questions I could.

There was one girl, besides Gladys, who knew almost everything I did. I always had my hand up first for answering, but if she put her hand up, I quickly dropped mine. She had long, gold coloured hair and sparkling blue eyes that almost closed when she smiled or laughed. She had a strange name, *Marlene*, but no one teased her about it and the older boys didn't badmouth her ever. She was so happy that the other girls seemed to always be around her.

One day, when we were playing tetherball in the recess yard, I noticed Marlene and some of her friends gathered around the doorway. The ground was still soft from the sun's warmth as the frost melted. When the whistle blew ending the recess period, some of the girls hung around until most of the boys had gone inside. I noticed the girls were looking at me then giggling. When I came to the door with Earl tagging along behind me, Marlene called out.

"Tom, wait."

I stopped and Earl bumped into me. Marlene broke from the circle of girls and walked up to me smiling. She sure was pretty, I thought. Marlene stopped and paused, then without a word, leaned forward and kissed me on the cheek. Some of the girls ogled while Iris, her best friend, seemed to egg her on. I stood there speechless, looking into those blue sparkling eyes, when she moved forward again and this time kissed me full on the mouth.

There was a volley of yips and yipes along with laughter as the girls ran past me into the building. Marlene moved past me and without taking her eyes off me walked into the doorway and disappeared. Earl walked around me and stared at my open mouth.

"She kissed you!"

I closed my mouth and looked at him.

"Tommy's got a girlfriend," he sang.

"You shut up, I'm warning, don't say anything, okay?"

He picked up the plea in my voice and just grinned back at me.

That night, and many more to come, I lay in my bed after lights out and thought of her. It was the strangest feeling I think I ever had. But, for the life of me, I couldn't understand what that kiss was doing to me. It was like a promise. Her eyes kind of said it, too. A promise of what, seemed to kind of haunt me.

****

With Earl feeling better, Gladys started coming to class. She was supposed to be using the intermediate library books for learning, but not only had she kept up with classes while looking after Earl, she had already gone on and finished nearly all of the senior books.

Gladys had only made one mistake, she had come to class in a blouse that was too small for her and she bumped out quite a bit in front – even more than June, the oldest of all the kids, who didn't go to school anymore but helped out in the kitchen with Mrs. Holmgren, the cook. Now, the boys made dirty sayings about Gladys. I was driven to the point of wanting to fight them, though Bob didn't seem to care, and there wasn't much I could do by myself. But I kept score.

One day Gary, who was one of the worst to say dirty things about Gladys, slipped on the stairs while going to the recess yard. He was struggling for his footing, about to fall, when I accidentally bumped him from behind. Old Mr. Flanagan, who was washing the walls, neatly lifted the bucket out of Gary's way so his plunge was completed to the bottom of the flight.

I moved quickly to the other side of the staircase so that when Gary looked back up the stairs he wrote off my assistance to his imagination. Mr. Flanagan, I'm sure, must have seen me, but apart from a sly grin playing at the corner of his mouth, never said a word. I liked Mr. Flanagan even more.

I had lost my job of ringing the bell before meals after my third caning in a week. I was no longer the first boy into the cafeteria. That didn't bother me. What did, was the first boy followed the last girl. That was Marlene. And while I was too shy to ever say more than 'hi' or 'bye', she was always talking to me in whispers. When she talked, her eyes would wrinkle and twinkle with her smile and I would find myself wondering why I liked those few moments talking with her more than I liked talking with anyone else. I decided it was her sparkling eyes that made me feel so strange inside.

Russ became the new crier with the bell for meals. Bob, after becoming the new champ for number of canings for fighting, had the wake-up and recess job. Even when the heat came on and you could hear it popping and creaking throughout the building, it was still icy cold. The window by Gary's bed got iced on the inside so badly, even a warm handprint couldn't melt it enough to see through it. Bob had to pull himself out of bed and make his way out into the hall and up the stairs to the bell. With teeth chattering, he would come back into the room and sneak under the covers. He did good, really good when you figure he hated getting up. That was part of his penalty and he would have to do it until someone got more canings than he did. I was probably the runner up and hoped the job was his or someone else's forever. Mike finally stopped his *antics*, as the Witch called them, and paid more attention in class, thus taking him out of the running.

Bob was very unhappy. While I loved classes, he didn't. He wouldn't do the lessons or even answer Mrs. Haywood when he was asked some question. The older boys began to nickname him 'Bob the Knob', but not to his face. It was usually said behind a hand with a sneaky, ducked-head snicker, just loud enough to bait him into a show of anger. Bob wasn't stupid in other things and I couldn't understand why he didn't like to read or write. In fact, he couldn't. At least not more than a few words. His numbers were okay but he got angry and just ignored the Witch when she singled him out.

It wasn't like Bob was alone. Like I said, I got pushed, punched and laughed at because I liked to learn and use the words in books as they are printed. Bob said *sonovabitch*; what he meant was, *son of a bitch*, the correct way to say it and the way I said it...at first. Then the hoots won out and my shoulders stopped being beaten upon every recess. They say *sonovabitch*! I say *sonovabitch*!

One day, after classes, we were in the dorm. Russ had just left to ring the bell for supper. I was laying on my bed reading a super book called *Moby Dick*. Bob was on his bed tumbling his pocketknife. Gordy had left Gary and Brian, and as he was going down the aisle, hit Bob on the shoulder as he passed by the bed, knocking Bob over. The knife clattered noisily to the floor but it didn't cover up Gordy's words as "Bob the Knob" could be clearly heard. That was stupid, but not nearly as stupid as turning his back to Bob as he continued on to the doorway to take his usual place as first in line.

Bob, as he flew through the air, landed two punches even before he settled on Gordy's back and sent Gordy staggering into the door frame just as the dinner bell sounded. Gordy straightened and shrugged Bob off his back but not before he had taken two more punches to the side of his head. Bob flew backwards onto Raymond's bed and sprang up immediately to his feet. The bed made him the same height as Gordy and Bob took full advantage and flung a punch at the older boy's sneering face.

I wasn't really experienced at what a good punch was, especially because I found it really hard to hit someone in the face unless I was really angry. Bob, on the other hand, showed shear concentration on getting in where the most damage could be done. He punched Gordy smack on the nose and I heard it break with a grisly crunch sound. Gordy straightened right up, his eyes flashed white then came back full of tears, a double stream of blood ran out of his nose.

"Yes!" I cried out to this thing of beauty. What a punch! But my joy at my older brother's success was short lived. Gordy came back with some angry punches himself, catching Bob with his hands low as he stopped to admire the effectiveness of his beautiful punch. Bob fell back on Raymond who was balled up in the corner, his face red with terror. Gordy was quickly on top, pummelling them both in a flurry of punches.

Raymond began squealing, actually more like a girl's scream, as punches fell around and on his head as well as Bob's. Gordy was cursing swear words at the top of his lungs.

Bob was still fighting back but Gordy was too big and I could see his punches really hurt. He hit Bob twice in the face while Bob held out his arms, fingers out, trying to stop the punches. I knew he was hurt and told Gordy to stop. Ignored, I flew off my bed and aimed a running punch at Gordy. Then suddenly I was smacked down in mid flight after a collision with the Witch's ample hip as she burst into the doorway and into my path. Without a word, the Witch pointed to the three of us and motioned us upstairs with her thumb.

I swear I didn't feel the pain. Nor was there any I could see in Bob's face. But when Gordy let out a muffled yelp after his second and last stroke of the cane, Bob and I looked at each other and, for the first time, I felt I understood him a little. And I was really glad he was my brother.

"You sure got him a good one," I said, as we made our way down the stairs, hiking our burning bums back to the dorm. "Did you see his eyes? I thought you had him."

Bob pulled me to a stop in the hallway. "I stopped!" he said angrily. "I stopped and I am *never* going to do that again," he promised himself.

"I guess you amazed yourself, huh? That was the Sullivan smacker of all smackers. Did you hear it? It crunched!" I added, as we got to the dorm's closed door.

Bob didn't say anything but gave me his biggest smile. I could see it plainly, pulling at the corners of his mouth.

****

I didn't have to get to the bottom of the steps to know the door was open to the recess yard; my breath was whipped away by an icy wind coming up the steps. I went and looked out into the wintry light just in time to see Mr. Flanagan slip and fall into the heavy snow lining the cleared pathway. He kind of thrashed about getting his peg leg back under him so he could stand.

I ran out into the snow and saw he was trying to carry a large pail that now lay in the pathway on its side where it had obviously been dropped.

"Are you alright, sir?"

"Watch yerself laddie, a slicker deck ye'll no see on any named plank," he said, finally standing on the small 'foot' attached to the end of his wooden leg. He began brushing the snow off his coat.

I reached the pail and, taking it by the handle, pulled it upright. The printing on the pail said *linseed oil – 5 gals.* It was heavy, but it slipped along the icy path very nicely to the doorway as I pushed it. Mr. Flanagan followed me, keeping his good foot on the path and the other on the side with the deep snow. I lifted the pail into the hallway and dragged it past the lavatories to the boiler room where I stopped. I heard Mr. Flanagan stamp his foot then whack his wooden leg off the wall before the outside door shut. I left the pail at the door and returned to the boys' lav meeting him as I turned the corner.

"I'll thank ye lad for the rescue. It's Thomas, is it not?" he asked, and nodded to his own question. He was about to say something more but my curiosity got the best of me.

"Did it come that way?" I asked, pointing at his wooden leg. "Or did you lose it?"

"Oh aye lad, born with it. Terrible burden on me mother," he began to chuckle.

"Ye finish up yer business and follow me below decks an' I'd ha ye help to stow the oil. Does the headmistress know yer sailing the hallways?" he asked, as an afterthought.

"Yes, sir, she does. I've finished my lessons," I added hopefully, "but she doesn't like us in the halls," I admitted reluctantly, for I really wanted to see *below decks*.

"Well hurry along and ye can give me a hand," he called over his shoulder, as he limped around the corner and disappeared.

The need to go for a whizzer all of a sudden wasn't so demanding and I let the door swing shut as I followed the old man. I rounded the corner as he was putting the key in the lock.

"That was fast." He opened the door.

I lifted the pail, it was all I could do, and swung it into the room and was immediately aware of the warmth.

"Good for ye. Push it behind the door." He pointed then began taking off his long wet coat.

Placing the oil where he wanted it, I turned and found we were on a railed landing even with the door. Below the landing I could see over a large room. Opposite the steps was a huge mound of sawdust enclosed by a wall almost as tall as me. A large furnace with a big contraption attached to the side of it seemed to take up the centre of the room. Beside the furnace was another one. It was called the boiler. Pipes with wheels on them went everywhere and glass dials were stuck on them, most of them near the boiler. A low whine of machinery came from somewhere in the room.

I followed Mr. Flanagan down ten steps to the concrete floor of the room and discovered his room, actually a bed and table and shelves made from wooden boxes and covered with sacking.

"Books!" There must have been a hundred of them stacked neatly in double rows.

"Do ye like books?'

I turned to find him watching me.

"Oh, yes, sir. I thought I read all the books there were but I don't think I've read one of these," I said, looking down the rows for one that was familiar.

"Here, lad." He knelt on his bed to reach for one, then presented it to me. "This is on the Boer War. It might be a bit much for ye." He began to set it back into the row.

"No, sir. I can read pretty good."

"You can read well?" he asked.

"That's right, sir." Hoping he would change his mind once again. "I read Charge of the Light Brigade."

He hesitated. "Tell ye what, lad, if ye promise to take care of them and return them just the moment ye finish, ye can read any of them, ah perhaps not this one." He pulled one of them out and I caught a glimpse of 'Lady Chatterly's...' something, as he laid it on top of the row of books. "Perhaps when yer a wee bit older. Aye, possibly quite a bit older," he coughed and handed me 'The Boer War'.

I took the book from him and sat on the edge of his bed and opened it.

"Ye kinna stay here and read it, lad. You'll have the Mistress spoilin' for a double caning, one fer ye if she catches ye below decks and the other fer me fer having ye. Ye take it and mind, look after it Thomas, or ye'll not get another."

I thanked him over and over again and scampered up the stairs and into the hall with my new found treasure and the promise within the cover of a new adventure.

"One more thing, lad," he called out, as I was about to close the door.

"Sir?"

"Use a bookmark, lad. Dinna fold the pages dog ear like!"

"Yes, sir!" and I left.

In class I found a piece of string and placed it inside the cover. I had my bookmark.

****

It didn't take long to lose my book. Two things hit me; panic in telling Mr. Flanagan and disappointment that I would lose any chance of being able to borrow any more books from him. Reading took me out of the orphanage to far away places. It took me to the lands of 'what if', and away from 'what is'. It would also bring an end to the only real friendship I had made.

Russell had stolen my book. Raymond quietly pointed to him when I was in my frenzy after discovering it missing from my table beside the bed. At the time, he was with a group of older boys at the far end of the dorm and didn't notice me slide over to his bedside table until I pulled the small drawer open.

Russell ran to me, but was too late to stop me from finding the book. Then he hit me when he saw what I had. The book flew out of my hands onto the floor. I dropped to my knees to gather it up and held it to my chest to protect it.

The first punch didn't hurt, except I thought he was my friend, and this meant he truly did take it and still wanted to hurt me even after doing so. There wasn't much time to think about it as his knee struck the side of my head – hard enough to bounce it off the corner of his bed frame and opening a long cut above my ear – spilling my blood all over my prized book.

I sat in the upstairs sickroom, the room where they had kept Earl when he was so sick, while the doctor put six stitches in my ear and head. The only good thing was the cut went through the little lump on my ear left by the Witch's wand. Gladys came in with a change of clothes. Everything I had, including the book, was bloody.

Russell got three strikes of the cane in the penalty box and took over Bob's early morning and recess bell ringing job. Mrs. Haywood had me back doing the meal bells *because I was good and didn't fight back*. But even that didn't take my sorrow away.

Mrs. Haywood allowed me to go to the boiler room to return the stained book. I approached the boiler room door with such regret that when Mr. Flanagan opened the door I could only hand him the book. To open my mouth was to weep. I couldn't even look at him and started to turn away. He took the book and placed a hand on my shoulder and guided me through the doorway into the room.

"Ooch, lad," he said softly, "come in."

"I'm sorry, Mr. Flanagan."

"How are ye, lad? They called me to clean up the mess."

He pinched my chin and turned my head to look at the wound.

"Ah, that's not too bad a thing," he said, looking through the bottom of his glasses. "Come and sit for a minute. Yer feelin' fine?"

I nodded and followed him down the stairs. He turned his head away and coughed for a moment while waving his hand towards the bed for me to sit. He cleared his throat.

"I got the call to the boys' dormitory to clean up the mess from yer little…ah, accident. The little fellow, ye know the timid one that sleeps next to yer bed, told me about what happened. Did ye not want the other lad to read it, Thomas?"

"I promised you…to look after it. Russell stoled it!" I blurted.

"Aye, that he did. And that was wrong. Do ye share things with Russell? The little one said you sat together in class…"

"Not anymore!" I vowed.

"Well now, maybe you're a wee bit hasty. Maybe he just dinna understand yer promise to me. You see, lad, I didn't understand ye had someone who shares yer love for books. If I had I wou' na' ha' made ye make such a promise. I'd a' never put something between a person and their finest mate."

"I've never seen him hurt anyone…until me. And look at your book, it's ruined!"

"Well laddie it does look like it's had finer days and I do understand yer concern, but ye know, yer defence of my wishes has made me trust ye. So in saying that ye see, there is better sailing weather between yerself and me. Now that's a good thing, do ye think…no?"

I nodded and wiped the tears tickling my cheeks.

"Do ye think maybe yer friend might have been hurt that ye dinna share with him something ye both loved?"

Again, I nodded. "We always shared our books."

"Well then, there ye are. Come over here and pick out two books."

It was like a huge weight had been lifted from my heart. I scanned the titles and picked the first two in the longest row. "These?"

"Fine. Now ye have my permission to share those books with yer mate. If ye so wish," he added, as a cloud of doubt passed through me which he obviously saw on my face.

"Did ye no have a value on his friendship?"

"Yes, sir."

"Well, lad, I'm going to make a suggestion to ye. Ye just leave one a' those on his bedside table and see what happens. Would ye do that for me?"

I thought about it for a moment. It would have to be for him because the thought of giving up one of these treasures to Russell wasn't going to be something that pressed me, that was for sure. "Okay," I said.

"Good lad. Off ye go."

"Thank you, Mr. Flanagan." I started for the steps.

"Ooch, lad," he called to me as I reached the top of them, "we'll be sailing mates ourselves therefore ye'll call me James, and I will be pleased if I can call my friend Tom."

"Yes, sir…James." I said.

"No, no, lad. Not, *Sir James*. The king never saw fit to knight me." He chuckled.

"Yes… James," I smiled down at him and left the boiler room.

I walked up the stairs trying to figure which book I should give to Russell. Entering the dorm I saw him standing at the window looking out into the street. The rest, other than Raymond who was in his corner, were out in the yard playing tetherball on the first warm day we had all winter. I walked to his bed and laid the book on his table then went back to my own bed to read.

Out of the corner of my eye I watched him leave the window and go to his bed where he discovered the book I had left. He picked it up and read the cover then looking over at me started to my bed. I pretended not to notice him but I felt myself tensing, as I wasn't sure if he was going to hit me or worse, drop the book on my bed and say something hurtful to me.

"I wish," he stopped and cleared his throat, "Tom…I wish I had never done that. I'm so sorry."

I closed my book and looked up at him. I found sadness on his face and all of a sudden I felt different and at that moment James's words came to me, and I knew Russell and I would be friends. Real friends.

"He must have a hundred books down there and he said we could read them all, well almost," I added remembering the one the old man had set aside.

Russell unfolded himself and extended his hand and we shook. In the corner, Raymond was watching and for the first time that I could ever remember, he smiled at me, and again James's words filled my ears. It was going to be okay

****

I left the classroom and headed for the lav. Part way, I found Bob, who seldom showed up for a day in school anymore. He was holding a ladder for James who was perched precariously, shaking his head as he tapped the plaster with a hammer. A great, dark stain ran from the top of the wall to a narrow shadow at Bob's feet near the floor.

"The ladies left a tap running in their sink and it overflowed onto the floor," Bob answered my questioning frown as I stood back from the falling plaster. "We're going to have to plaster this whole wall." He spoke with such authority that I knew he was repeating James. But the enthusiasm was his.

The ladies, that is The Benevolent Daughters, had the whole end of the building where they had their 'tea s', did their crafts and held meetings. These doors remained locked and were 'out of bounds' to us kids. The cane was waiting for any and all trespassers.

"Can I help?"

"Well I kin thank ye for the offer, laddie," James said, looking down from the top of the ladder, "but if I start having the whole class here, I'm afraid the …Witch," he continued softly, "would be up to caning me own fanny. Off ye go back to yer classes now. Me and my assistant will do just fine here."

I didn't share Bob's enthusiasm for this kind of work and since I had left my book opened on my desk without marking my place in it, I hurried on to my business. I knew Russell would close it as he cleared the desk for lunch, which was soon.

After classes, I got permission from the Witch to help James and Bob and together we loaded out all the broken plaster. The wall was just striped with narrow pieces of wood and would have to be re-coated with new plaster. James said we wouldn't have to do that. Other men, called contractors, would come and do it.

Bob and I put the tools away in the boiler room and left James to brew up his tea as he waited on his supper. It was June who usually brought his supper down to him each evening. He made his own porridge in the mornings and never ate lunch.

"Ooch, lads," he called to us as we reached the door on the landing above his head. We walked to the railing and looked down at him. "I'm thinkin' you two should have yerselves a real shower afore ye scamper back to yer bunks. Yer covered in plaster and look like a couple of pigeon roosts in Trafalgar Square," he chuckled.

"No thanks," I answered immediately, followed by Bob's same response.

Late Saturday afternoons were bath and shower time. The procedure meant stripping and lining up for a plunge into a stinking tub full of disinfectant, sitting in the middle of the floor of the boys' lav. Then a quick rinse off under a shower and a final inspection for 'wee, wild cooties', as James called them meaning head lice, and towelling down with wet towels. The towels were wet because there were only two of them and the older boys got to go first and almost always dropped them into the puddles they had left on the floor. At least James had them in and out of the tub before they could pee in the water.

"Noo, noo, laddies, I mean a real shower. Ye kinna go back looking like that!"

Bob and I hesitated.

"Look, I have some fine soap and ye dinna have to go into the dip. Just a long hot shower."

"No dip?" I asked warily.

"Now isn't that what I said," his voice had an edge to it. "Here," he tossed the soap up and I caught it. "Off with ye now, and I'll turn the valve on here."

"All the water you want!" James shouted after us as we left the boiler room.

We stood under the shower for a long time taking turns with the soap. It smelled different, not perfumed but kind of like new leather.

"Beats the hell out of navy showers," Bob said as he stood directly under the shower, the water beating on his upturned face.

"Navy shower?"

"James said when you're on a ship you're only allowed to wet down, shut the water off, lather up, and rinse off. You can't use any more water than that. And that's only when you go on shore leave."

"Was he ever in a war?"

"Never said, didn't ask."

We dried off and after shaking the white dust off our clothes, dressed and returned the soap to James.

"Now ye look a tad more respectable." James said as we stood on the landing and tossed the soap down to him. "How was it?" he added smiling as if he knew the answer before we spoke.

"We smell good."

"Great," Bob agreed.

"Off ye go now or you'll be late for mess." He hobbled back to his chair below us where his plate of half eaten supper lay

* * * *

Earl's red-rimmed eyes were full of tears. His tiny face seemed nestled in a sea of pink wool; a woman's old sweater that wrapped around him at least twice... "And your friend," he said, pointing from his bed to Russell who lay on his bed reading. "Didn't even help me." He sniffed between sobs.

Russell lowered his book and looking back at me held up his hands in a sense of helplessness.

"There is, you know." Earl went on between sobs and sniffs. "That asshole." He pointed this time down the dorm to where the older boys were gathered, smirking to themselves and each other. "Brian! He's the one that said it." "I seen him, Tom! I seen him when I was sick. They're all just stupid!" Earl threw his head back on the pillow. His skinny little chest rose and fell in spasms as he closed his eyes and struggled for breath. After a pause, he seemed to rest easier. "You know don't you?" he asked quietly.

"Yeah, I know." I reassured him, hoping he would settle back and go to sleep. I was surprised he remembered James's visit to him at Christmas dressed as Santa.

"Brian opened his mouth and told Earl there wasn't a Santa Clause," I said to Bob when I met him out in the hall coming back from the lav.

"There isn't," Bob said, as a matter of fact, "and he might as well learn that now."

"Yeah, I know that! Maybe you oughtta tell him 'cause it's for sure I ain't gonna."

Bob's eyes flashed anger as I said it with a challenge in my voice. I didn't give a damn, I knew what Earl's reaction was going to be, or a least I had a good idea.

Bob brushed past me and opened the door to the dorm and went straight to Earl's bed.

"What's the matter?"

Earl struggled to sit up in his pink cocoon and once settled, pointed down to where Brian was standing. "That asshole says there's no Santa." Earl's eyes started brimming with tears as he sniffled loudly.

"First, you stop swearing," he told Earl firmly, then spun on me. "You're supposed to be looking after him. If Momma was here she'd wash your mouth out with lye soap," he said, turning back to Earl.

Earl mushed into a swamp of tears; his shoulders shaking so hard the pink sweater began to unravel from his skinny body.

I reached over and began re-wrapping him. "Jesus Christ, Bob!" I said angrily, knowing by the time he finished up with the Santa problem, Earl would be really squashed. I glared at him not caring if he punched me or not…at least not until I saw the eyes flare coal black and he started around the bed after me.

Brian saved the day! He was walking up the aisle between the beds and met Bob as he stepped out into the aisle.

"That little peckerhead calls me an asshole again, I'm going to slap him silly!" He walked up to Bob and stood there with his hands on his hips.

I had moved up to the head of Earl's bed trying to put enough room between Bob and myself, hoping he would cool down enough not to hit me too hard. But Brian, I suppose, although twice the size of Bob, must have had a short memory. Anyway the shock was all his as Bob spun and in a blur, buried his fist into his belly.

A rush of wind blew out of Brian's mouth with a little "oh" trailing off as he doubled in two and fell on the floor. Man, could Bob punch!

"Wow!" Earl said, eyes bugging out of his head and finishing with a sniff.

Bob turned and without a word walked out of the dorm. Behind him no one moved until the door closed. The older boys came down and tried to help Brian up. He seemed to be quite occupied with laying on the floor and silently, looking like a fish out of water, trying to catch his breath.

"Your brother is going to get the beating of his life," Gary said, looking at me as he and Gordy helped Brian up, "you just wait and see!"

"Yeah?" Earl shot back. "It sure won't…"

"Shut up, Earl," I hissed at him, knowing we weren't too far from getting a pounding ourselves.

His red, rimmed eyes looked at me with something between anger and hurt. "There is so a Santa!" he said defiantly at the big boys as they half carried Brian away. He fell back on the bed, gave me a look then pretended I wasn't there.

Bob came back just before supper and walked to his bed and sat on it ignoring everyone in the room. The place was like a dog kennel with everyone walking stiffly up and down the aisle, the older boys bristling with angry looks at Bob. And Bob, looking almost through them as if they weren't there.

After supper, on the way back to the dorm, Bob pulled Earl and I away from the door just as we were to enter. "C'mon, James is waiting to see us."

"You got permission?" I asked, as I looked up and down the hall for the Witch. Bob nodded and led us down to the boiler room.

James seemed pleased to see us and had us sit on the edge of his bed. He pulled up a chair from his little table and sat facing us. The fresh smell of wet wood came from a new pile of sawdust heaped high in the bin. We just kind of talked about a few things as Earl and I looked around the room. It was real interesting. Pipes of all sizes popped through walls and ran around the room with steering wheels decorated with red, blue and white paint on them. Great square tubes ran out of the furnace and went through the ceiling. Finally, Bob gave a great sigh, got off the bed and grabbing a large pail, began to scoop sawdust from the pile. He climbed a small set of stairs next to the furnace and dumped the load into a large container.

"What's that?" Earl asked.

James turned to see what Bob was doing; his wooden leg stuck straight out and almost hit our knees as he did so. "That's a hopper," he answered still looking at Bob who had now dumped the last bucket, filling the contraption almost to overflow.

"Does it hop?" I asked, trying to be funny. The look from Bob told me to shut up.

James at least had a smile for me as he turned back to Earl and I. "Now let me see, where was I?"

"It's about Santa Clause," Bob huffed. His patience running out.

"Ooch, yes. Well…" the old man hesitated.

"Is there or isn't there?" Bob asked as he walked over to something behind me which I hadn't noticed. It was a sack of something hanging from underneath the landing on a rope. We all watched as Bob unfastened pieces of leather with strings on them and slipped them over his hands. He began to hit the bag and sawdust began falling almost as dust onto the floor.

"From the shoulder, lad. How many times must I tell ye? The weight from yer toes up through yer shoulders."

We watched Bob rock the sack with blows until it was swinging back and forth, almost out of control. Then he fell back and picked at it whenever it swung close to him.

"Hey, neat," Earl said, taking the words out of my mouth.

"Remember keep your elbows close to yer body." James turned from us to watch as Bob pounded the sack. We watched as Bob moved in and out picking at the sack now, then driving a punch that swung the sack in wild circles. Soon he was winded and let up on punishing the sack and just tapped at it with what James called 'jabs'. "Pound for pound, I never seen anyone hit so hard," he turned from Bob back to us.

"Well, let's see now?" he sighed. "Santa Claus, is it?" he asked, knowing full well it was. "Well, he is a mystery and that's for true."

"He's real?" Earl asked, almost insisting on a positive answer.

"Well, real enough," James answered, "least wise for children to believe in. Do ye believe in him?"

"I saw him! I saw him when I was sick. He came to see me!"

"And I can tell you were excited from listening to ye right now. My word ye do believe, don't ye?"

"Brian says he's a hoax. Not real," Earl said, in a defiant tone.

"Santa Claus is a spirit," James said, looking at Earl. "He's a spirit that comes at Christmas to bring happiness to little lads and lasses and further when mothers and fathers see their children happy they become happy."

"Then he isn't real?"

"Were ye happy to see him?" James shot back at Earl.

"Yes!"

"Then he's real to ye. That right?"

"Yeah," Earl answered in a deep breath, not at all convinced.

"It's kind of like God!" I said, trying to help.

James kind of rolled his eyes and for a minute I thought he was angry with me trying to help. "Well, you know Santa Claus is known in many other countries as St. Nicholas or St. Nick. So he is considered a Saint, so I suppose he does take a thing called *faith*: which means to believe without looking for proof."

Now I was confused. More about which God we were talking about. Momma took us to house meetings where God was full of vengeance and there was hellfire and brimstone and pain and agony and a place called *hell* where you would have your gizzard roasted out. This he would hand out to anyone, including children, who were bad.

Then there was the God we would talk about every Sunday here at the home when the weather was bad and we couldn't go to Sunday school. The lady, whose name was

Mrs. Simmons, told us about a God who loved us and was forgiving when we were bad. This God had my vote.

On Sundays, when the weather was good, we lined up and marched through the recess yard and down the lane to the church basement where we had a Sunday school. We made things for the celebration of things the church wanted to celebrate, mostly God things, but sometimes for an outing like spelling bee's or picnics. This God was the third choice: the one you made things for and who needed money to make His word more powerful.

Bob and I talked about which God we should have. "Shit," Bob had said, "we got a pa that would put him to shame if all Jesus wanted was to punish sinners." We both decided it had best be the one who continued to love you no matter what.

"Do ye know what I'm saying, lad?" James asked Earl, snapping me back to the conversation at hand.

"There's no Santa Claus," Earl whispered.

"It's the spirit of it, lad. If Santa is someone who makes ye happy then be happy. Let the unbelievers find whatever will make them happy. The secret to the whole thing is to be happy."

James looked hopefully at Earl but Earl only looked back at him still unsure.

"Ooch, give it some thought, lad. There now ye three, off ye go, I got things beggin' fer attention!"

We left James and went back to the dorm.

We sat till lights out trying to put together exactly what ol' James had said. The bottom line was Bob still thought there wasn't any *real* Santa while I wished I hadn't mentioned anything about God because He was no different than Santa in my eyes, and Bob's too, for that matter. The only thing that came out of it was that Earl now accepted the idea that perhaps Santa was kind of like a magician who had mystical powers at Christmas.

Poor Mouse, he sat in the corner next to Earl's bed and listened to our bullshit. All this religious stuff terrified him, but so did everything else, as he cowered in his corner every minute he was in the dorm. He would only answer to Earl or me; if anyone else asked a question he'd clam right up and stuff his head down between his shoulders and look for some place to run and hide.

The next Sunday meeting Bob and I pestered Mrs. Simmons with endless questions asking her to explain all the different Gods that we had known so far in our short lives. Surely there must be more. Maybe He had some Brothers – that would explain a lot.

"No, there is only one God! And He is full of love!" she screamed in frustration.

That ended that for us. Bob and I disrupted the Sunday School class so badly that we were told to stay in the dorm and not attend these meetings anymore.

****

Earl got sick once again in the late winter and was finally feeling better as the weather grew warm. He never managed to stop his sniffling and his nose and eyes were red and runny all the time.

Also in the spring, the war in France came to our attention. David Walischuk, Brian Boudreau, Gary Gavier and Gordy McLeod were told to pack their clothes and, in no time, left with farmers who needed new help on their farms for planting because so many men had gone to war.

The rest of us boys who were too young had a flaming great time. We sat and messed around on the older boy's vacant beds. Even Raymond got giddy and had come out of his hole to nervously horseplay.

That lasted two whole days 'til fat Gary was dumped on the sidewalk in front of the orphanage by a disgusted looking farmer. He then threw Gary's bundled clothes down from the wagon while we watched from the dorm window, driving off without a backward glance.

The summer days passed quickly with the older boys gone. Only Gary lurked around threateningly, and with Russell keeping to himself, it fell on Bob to keep Gary's nose out of the younger boys' fun. He seemed very much afraid to mix it up with Bob and he also knew that I wouldn't be far away should he try and single out Earl or Raymond to bully.

The canings now were almost non-existent with only Mikey and Bob having one each for swearing in the hallway. These were the first days I had known here in the home that everyone seemed happy. There were no new orphans all that summer and into the early fall.

In the fall, the police brought Gordy back. David and Brian lit out just as harvest ended.

It was after supper when I snuck down to James's room to exchange books. James was exchanging books himself to keep Russell and I supplied in reading material. Neither he nor Russell could keep up with me and over the next winter it was I who was the first to read and recommend the books. James would just shake his head in disbelief and soon called me *Gutenburg's disciple.*

James was out on his runs as usual after the evening meal. He left a key for me and I found several books just inside his door in a box. I put the returned book down, picked up the two I had found and started back when I heard voices murmuring from up the stairs. James had freshly oiled the stairs and it was possible to climb them noiselessly because the squeaks were gone.

Halfway up the steps I could see the silhouettes of two people very close to each other. I made out the man to be the constable that brought Gordy back – the same one that brought us to the orphanage over a year ago. The same one who came through the back gate in the recess yard at night to see the Witch, I bet.

They were in the front hall by the entrance, standing close to each other and speaking in soft voices. In the dim light I could see the constable's hand was inside the top of Mrs. Haywood's dress and moving over her body. Her hand was inside the front of his trousers and likewise moving in little punching motions. A door slammed from somewhere upstairs and they jumped apart and began straightening their clothes.

"As this is an official call," the constable said out loud, then whispered. "I'll be leaving by the front door."

"Thursday," she whispered, and reached out to squeeze the front of his trousers. I'll have Mr. Flanagan leave the outer gate open."

"'Til then." He backed away and her arm dropped, opened the large front door and left.

The Witch dropped her shoulder, pulled herself together and left the doorway buttoning up the front of her dress. I waited until I heard her door open and close, then quietly returned to the dorm.

That night, after the light was out, I laid in my bed and wondered at what I had seen. A strange feeling moved through me, and Marlene with her blonde curls and blue eyes entered my thoughts. I found my hand resting between my legs and squeezed. No, that wasn't it, I thought, as

Marlene's eyes closed off some unspoken promise and the confusion swished me off to sleep.

Russell left classes in the orphanage that fall for a public school. After three days of it he refused to go any further. He was smart but his scarred face made him the brunt of cruel jokes. He agonised because he knew he would never be adopted or find a home and family. They wouldn't even take him to work on the farms during the summer because he looked freaky. That night, I heard soft weeping coming from his bed and I felt so bad for him.

The following morning, two things happened that would change our dorm. One good: Russell was called to Mrs. Haywood's office when she found he hadn't left for school. He returned later and was flushed with excitement. They were going to see if his classes could be carried in our school and his tests would be sent to someplace where they would be marked. The second wasn't good: Gary had heard Russell in the night and now he had a new nickname for him, *the Freak*.

It was a name that had been murmured under the older boys' breath and coupled with dirty snickers and sly smiles. But now it had come out in the open, Gary, who by the way had teamed up with Gordy as the new Terrible Twosome, couldn't wait to show his stupidity in Russell's face.

Before the end of that snowy Saturday, Gary had given me a pounding for calling him an asshole when I came to Russell's defence – as Russell just sat there when Gary called him a freak. Bob came in after helping James shovel a pathway to the rear gate, and he and I pounded Gary, who at the end of it, went to the cafeteria and got Gordy and pounded Bob and I in return. It was a terrible fight that seemed to go on and on.

Moments of clarity emerged from the blanket of pain. The weightlessness of flying through the air as Gordy threw me into a table and the numbness of pain as glass from something bit deeply into my ass. Leaping on Gary's back to shake him loose as he held Bob while Gordy punched him, I put my arm around his neck and pulled for all I was worth until I felt him release Bob. Gordy hitting Bob and Bob hitting back – just as hard. Gordy screaming swear words at us as he punched. A bed collapsed and Bob went down with Gary. There was blood everywhere and I was conscious of my pants sticking to my legs as I kept slipping.

The Mouse was screaming and ran from the dorm. I hobbled through the open door after him, suddenly knowing I was hurt bad, when Gordy caught up to me screaming. "You fucking little know-it-all." He punched me down to the floor out in the hallway.

People and voices seemed to be coming from everywhere. I opened my eyes and was aware of the Witch's presence and then out of the fog, Marlene's face above me, her hand covering her mouth and tears running out of those blue eyes. I wanted to say something to her but couldn't think of what. Then a cloak of darkness seemed to close about me and I felt myself give up to the dimness.

There were men's voices. Weightlessness from being carried. The rattle and jostling of people moving quickly around me. A bell ringing, again and again, and people in funny hats with their mouths covered with white masks. I recall hours of pain and I was aware of the sickening smell of ether that wafted through the hallways and stunk up absolutely everything, and everybody, in the building. Then, I woke up for real and became aware of things around me. Like some great nightmare – it was over.

****

It was dark when James and Bob came for me. It had almost been four weeks since I had seen anyone from the home. I still had a little difficulty getting around and found the cab ride a little uncomfortable as it bounced my butt. James reached inside his coat and handed me a gift. I could tell right away it was a book and started to unwrap it.

"Now hear me, lad, I've no bin a religious man with all that I've witnessed in and out of the ports of the world, but I made a pact with Him that if it was in His mind to spare ye, I would be obliged to set a new heading and sail a straighter course. Now mind you both, I said *straighter*," he coughed. "Nevertheless, it was with…ah well, between Him and me."

It was a small bible. I opened it up and by the light of a passing lamp I could read the beautifully crafted script, 'To my gifted friend, Thomas. November 30, 1917', and signed simply, 'James Flanagan esq.'

"Thank you. It's…really nice." I knew about the bible but still wondered – was it about a loving God, or the one you were supposed to be afraid of?

Bob sat motionless in the shadows, a passing lamp reflected light off his face as he looked out the window. I hardly recognised him. His nose was crushed to his face making his black, shining eyes appear even larger than before. He glanced at me and the corners of his mouth pulled up into a soft smile, then he looked away.

"Yer brother has become my first mate," James said.

"I don't go to classes anymore." Bob's face broke into a real smile. "I help James now. Everyday!"

Bob went on to tell me about the events that happened since I left. Gary and Gordy had been taken to the police station and when it was learned I was going to be okay, they were paddled and Gary was returned to the home. Gordy was turned out as he was near the age to get work and they thought it would be better. Bob himself got one stroke of the cane from the Witch and since he wasn't doing well in classes anyway, he was forbidden to return to them. He laughed out loud at this. I declare, I had never seen him talk a blue streak.

"He's going to make a first class steam engineer," James said. "Already knows 'ow to make steam," he finished with a hand slapping Bob's knee.

They were obviously getting along really well and for a brief spell I was just a tinge jealous. Yet I couldn't remember Bob ever smiling more than a twitch let alone laughing and I found myself laughing back. After a moment, I looked from Bob to James and found James studying me.

"You're two fine sons," he looked to Bob and patted my knee, "and ye know," he hesitated a moment, "I never needed the help more."

The cab stopped in front of the home just as the snow began to fall. The two gas lamps in front were on and for a moment I watched the flakes dance and swirl around them.

I felt very happy to be back. Bob handed me the crutch sticks and ran up the front steps to open the door as James and I hobbled after him. Bob held the door open. It must have already been open, but I didn't give it a thought, and followed James through the door.

Once inside, he stepped aside quickly to reveal a large Christmas tree glowing with candles. A cry of SURPRISE came from everywhere. The Benevolent Daughters came forward, and shook my hand and patted my back. Mrs. Haywood shook my hand, though she didn't smile, and reminded me out of the corner of her mouth that I still deserved a caning.

After a party with cake and ice cream that was churned out in the kitchen, we went to the dorm and waited for the supper bell. I realised I hadn't seen Marlene. There were so many people moving around, perhaps she was in the kitchen, I thought. That's where she always was – helping out because she was a server.

"I didn't see that blonde girl, what's her name... oh yeah, I think it's Mar-lene? Or something like that," I asked Bob as casually as I could as he sat on the end of my bed with Earl.

"Oh, she got adopted, I think...left yesterday."

Earl stared at me.

"Oh." Was all I could say, but I knew Earl could read the devastation on my face, no matter how hard I tried to conceal it.

****

"Well at least we ain't sinking," James rasped, as Bob chased a rat back through one of the dozen or more holes. The beasts had chewed through the lumber nailed over previous holes.

"They must be sailing the great Atlantic from Europe. This country sends 'em our boys to be chewed up over there and the *frogs* must be replacing them when they get off the ships with a hold full of rats for the return trip."

He sniffed, hocked and spat into a rag feebly held in his hand, then laid back and closed his eyes. A moment later, a wheezing whistle, and a moment after that, a soft snore escaped from his open mouth as he fell into sleep.

Bob had moved out of the dorm when James's illness first hit as influenza and then went into his lungs as pneumonia. The old man's energy had left him, what was left of him that is, for he seemed to be growing smaller. To me, *growing* and *smaller* didn't seem right, but it must have been because James had said it himself. "I'm shrivelling up," he'd say. "Growin' smaller by the day. A great ship to a wee leaky dory." And he would shake his head unhappily.

At least the boiler made this room the warmest in the building, yet near the floor an icy draft seemed to hover almost knee high. The deep scar, between my butt and the back of my leg, ached with the cold.

"Mrs. Haywood wants me to bed down here until James is better," Bob said, as he neared me. He placed the large bucket used for hauling the sawdust from the bunker to the hopper back near the gate of the bin.

"Mrs. Haywood!?" I blurted. I had never heard him call her anything nicer than *the Witch*.

He shrugged, "Earl kind of went bonkers when they took you away. Jesus Christ, Tom, I was so Goddamn scared myself. Shit there was blood everywhere. We, well, nobody said it, but I saw that fat copper whisper to her when they took you out, and shake his head. They thought for sure you were going to die."

I grinned at him, "Hell, Bob, I wasn't going to die." It seemed funny that anybody would think that Tom Thompson was going to die. I chuckled at the thought, yet a twinge of fear remained at the back of my mind. Was that what it was like to die?

"They thought so for three days, Tom. Mrs. Haywood stayed in the sick room with Earl all that time, Tom. Gordy scrambled me up. He was a real madman."

"Hey you know what, I saw Gary's ass on Saturday bath night. Man, was it pretty pink an' purple. That paddle leaves a real dotted mess. He got three strokes, and Gordy, I heard got five. Could hear him screaming to Camrose, Gary said."

"I know who was screaming," I said. "Gary is the sissy."

"Yeah," Bob smiled, "Gary wouldn't be outdone there."

"So what do you think, Tom? You care if I come down and stay with James? I really think he needs me here."

"I wonder if I could, too?"

"You got classes."

"I know but I could still go to classes and…oh damn, there's Earl." I got up and unlocked the door.

"He's been kind of stickin' close since you've come back huh?" Bob remarked, as Earl followed me back and sat quietly down beside me.

"I could come down before and after classes and help," I offered, picking up the conversation where it left off. I wanted to be with them so badly.

"Ooch sure, and it would be a blessin' to have you, Thomas," James said in a weak voice. The snoring had stopped but his eyes remained closed.

Earl got up and left when he found James's need for sleep greater then his urge to talk. Bob and I had to tell him to keep his voice down. He left in a little snit but then thinking better of it, smiled down at us from the landing before closing the door.

After supper, the boys in the dorm helped carry Bob's bed and clothes down to the boiler room. There were now more empty beds than full ones. Six of us moved our stuff to the beds closest to the door. Only Gary remained at the far end of the room. He wouldn't even speak or look at me. That night, after returning from the boiler room where he'd been with the others moving Bob's stuff, I lay quietly in the dark and figured it really didn't matter.

I also figured that I was starting to collect some things in my life that couldn't be shared: dying, the copper and Mrs.

Haywood feeling each other up...and Marlene. These were things I didn't need to grow up into. They had arrived.

Earl became my shadow. In the beginning, when we had arrived at the house, he preferred Gladys to give him the things he needed. But now, Gladys was getting bumpy, screaming at him when he went to the girls' dorm and found her dressing. He told me later that the girls had curtains between their beds.

At night, I read to him then figured out it was time to teach him to read for himself. It wasn't easy, not that he was slow, but rather he developed the two word sniffle and two sniffle-long words. He never stopped sniffling, and when I told him to stop because it was driving me nuts, he would cry out that he couldn't help it. Gladys asked Mrs. Holmgren to get some hankies and gave Earl three for Christmas, but getting Earl to use them instead of sniffling was impossible. He'd sniff, look at you with those red-rimmed eyes, and then blot his nose with the hanky. Lucky for us both, he learned to read quickly, and soon was only coming to me for the big words and what some of the words meant. It was easy to explain words to him because he was into the primers now.

It was not as easy for me, however. I was having a hell of a time trying to find out what was being said and meant in this wonderful story I was reading. I tried asking James, but soon saw conversation was hard for him as his illness seemed to get worse.

The doctor, Dr. Roach, who I remembered from the hospital, came to him and had us lift his bed up onto blocks and out of the cold draft that clung to the concrete floor. He left him some pills, then looking around, shook his head.

"You, young man, can peel off your britches and let me see your derriere. Your *buttocks*, boy," he said, reading the frown on my face. "*Ass* is probably the trigger word around here," he said to my shocked look. "I want to see how your wound is healing while I'm here."

I did as he asked.

"Bend," and a moment later, "Okay, son, button up."

"Well, son," he said, as I pulled up my coveralls and fastened my strap. "You are a very lucky boy. The glass from that lamp broke and a piece stayed in there effectively blocking the blood loss rate from the severed artery. Otherwise, my boy, there wouldn't have been a drop of juice left in you by the time we got you on the table. You're healing just fine."

"No more crutches? Good," he went on without waiting for an answer, "I'm going to talk to Mrs. Haywood. I want you to climb all the stairs in this place for at least an hour everyday. You've got some muscle to rejuvenate to get rid of that limp."

He wiped his hands on a cloth after washing them with a little bottle from his bag.

"Christ, it's cold in this building. You got the heat up boy?" He turned to Bob who nodded.

"The Witch, er, Mrs. Haywood has been ringing the bell every two hours for the last two days. It's wide open and gulping down the sawdust," he explained.

"Well, it's been a long cold spell. Can't start automobile nor horse alike on days like this," the doctor responded.

Just then the bell that was kept mounted to the wall near the garbage chute rang and

Bob threw up his hands in frustration.

"Ain't nothin' I can do," he gestured "She can ring that bell for more heat but she's as hot as she gets without bustin' her open. That's what James says."

The doctor buttoned up his overcoat over his pudgy body and started for the stairs. He seemed lost in thought until he reached the top; there he turned back to us. "I'll be back tomorrow to see Mr. Flanagan. Can't say I'm delighted to see two children running the place," he added almost to himself. He popped his black bowler on his head, turned and left.

It was late spring on the calendar when winter finally unclenched the icy fist that gripped us with sickness in the home. Five kids, Earl, the Mouse and three girls came down with pneumonia, but while Earl was terribly sick again, it was the Mouse that almost died.

James improved but didn't really get better. A cough racked his body heavily at night. I helped Bob before and after classes and Mrs. Haywood let me have the run of the halls. I became the errand boy. When I finally finished the books and exercises to complete my fourth grade, I was free to spend the days with James as he slowly recovered

****

"We got to do something about it!" Bob said, as the two of us sat watching the rats rummaging through the garbage pile at the back of the boiler. "Man, there's got to be a dozen of them at least."

"Ooch, dinna ye think I've talked to her a dozen times at least?" James said from his bed.

"When you young lads came down here, I told her it was something that would have to be dealt with. But no! She tells me the *Daughters don't give it a priority*. It's not them that have rats to contend with! Maybe if they had rats running around their room they would change their minds,"

I looked at Bob and watched his eyes brighten.

The following night Bob and I left the dorm and opened the door to the 'Daughter's kitchen' with James's keys. The faint patter of little feet could be heard as we emptied the sack of its three small occupants. We closed the door and locked it, then returned the sack and keys to James in the boiler room.

"I hope ye young scallywags don't rue the day," he said, rolling his eyes at us, but there was a smile twitching at the corners of his mouth.

****

"They're going to get rid of the sawdust and bring in a coal furnace," I cried, as I leapt down the stairs to the cement floor of the boiler room. I threw myself up onto the foot of James's bed. "And," I continued, as Bob hung up the sawdust bucket by the bin door and sat on a box, "they will be extending the garbage chute to go outside." I finished with a shit-eatin' grin that matched Bob's. "Seems the rats are getting very aggressive and the ladies found droppings in their pantry."

"I just heard it when I was kinda walking past the *ladies* door. It was open. The Benevolent ladies were inside meeting with Mrs. Haywood. Some business or factory is going over to gas so they're donating their heating system to the orphanage. It's bigger and should give us more heat in the winter."

"Is that a fact now?" James, who had been resting on his bed, pulled his knee up to miss me as he swung his wooden leg around into a sitting position over the side of his bed. "Well," he sighed with wheezing breath before starting again. "Well, it's fair and ill both. We'll be a damn site warmer, but the sweet smell of wood in here'll be replaced with the damnation of air befouled with coal dust. They'll have to finish the walls of the bin right to the ceiling or move us out of here, I'll tell ye." He paused. "Nice about the garbage though!" He looked at us both and smiled.

James had told us stories of his adventures as a true sailor, becoming a stoker and then engineer when His Majesty's ships converted from sail to steam. He told us how he had seen seamen cough up their lungs with the miner's death after breathing in the dust from the ship's bunkers.

"Sure, and it's my fate to go down with the same," and a cough rattled in his throat that sent a chill of finality up and down my spine.

****

The warm air of summer blew through the hallways. It came from the opened windows at each end of the top two floors of the building. I loved the smell of the fresh air inside the building and since I lost my limp long ago, I could fly up and down the stairs. A deep dimpled scar was the only reminder on my butt. Bob said you really couldn't see it unless I was bent over. Once again, I was able to take two at a time going up the stairs, and bounce down a flight in two jumps.

I opened the boiler room door and found James and Bob putting their coats on over their Sunday best.

"B'jases, lad, we could hear ye coming from the very top of the buildin'. Stairs are to be walked down. One of these fine days, I swear we'll find this, this blob of unrecognisable matter, imagine now, with all ten toes stuffed up two nostrils at the foot of a flight of stairs."

Grinning, Bob took his arm and helped him up to the top of the stairs where I waited for them.

"Boom, boom, one flight: boom, boom, two flights." He mussed up my hair as he passed me and together, Bob and I helped him out of the building and into the waiting cab.

Once inside and settled, the cab lurched forward as it pulled away from the curb.

James coughed and cleared his throat. "How do ye feel, lad?"

"Fine," I answered. It had been over two months since Mrs. Haywood announced there was to be a city-wide spelling bee. I had won our class and the district spell-offs.

"Good, ye'v no reason to fret. Excited?"

I nodded. We had spent a lot of time getting ready for this, the city spelling bee. James had quizzed me until he was certain I knew how to spell *almost* any word he asked. *Almost*, meant I had spelled the word 'criteria' wrong because I thought it had a 'y' in it. That's because words I don't know the meaning of were harder to remember. So James would give me the word, then if I didn't know what it meant, he would explain it to me and give me the word in a sentence.

When I returned books, I would ask James about words, especially if the rest of the sentence or paragraph did not describe them to me, and together we would find the word and he would explain how and why it was used. It was like a missing piece in a puzzle, once it was discovered, the picture became clear and the adventure complete. He worked with me for hours at a time until I could see he was exhausted and needed to rest.

We travelled west through the centre of town. The road wound down to the park beside the river. There below us were so many people, automobiles, wagons, carriages and buckboards that it seemed the whole world must have gathered here.

In the centre of the park was an open air building with tall poles all around it. Flags and streamers flapped and shimmered in the warm breeze. Blankets, umbrellas and canvas chairs spread before the building on the grass, creating obstacles for kids to run around. Families and larger groups of people dotted the entire field. Closer, I saw a group of people in army uniforms setting up their instruments inside the 'bandshell', as James called it. The bleeps of horns and blats of tubas directed their sounds over the settling crowds. There was an excitement in the air that was truly contagious. I could feel it down to the soles of my feet.

The cab stopped in a line. People were climbing down off wagons, women and children lifted in the air and bounced onto the grass and then the vehicles moved away 'down wind', James explained, as he paid the driver then slipped a small flask to him from which the driver took a healthy pull. After wiping his mouth and the top of the flask with his coat sleeve, he handed it back to James, touched his hat, and with a smile, bid us a good afternoon.

We headed for the refreshment area where tables were set up to sell wares of all kinds. The Benevolent Daughters had two tables, one with pastries and the other lemonade. James struggled between Bob and I, his breath whistling, but his grip was firm on each of our shoulders. We stopped at the stand and he bought us a sweet pastry and large lemonade.

We moved to a grassy spot and sat. James took off his coat and folded it. Placing it behind his head, he lay back with a heavy sigh from the exertion.

"Here you are!"

We twisted around to see Mrs. Haywood approaching with a parcel in her arms. "Thomas, this is for you." She stood above me and handed the parcel to me. Somewhat bewildered, I took it from her.

"Stand in the presence of a lady," James demanded, and we obeyed. "Please excuse me whilst I catch me breath," and remained stretched out.

"Of course, James." She turned to me. "Open it, Thomas."

As I did, she said, "The spelling contest isn't until three so you have over an hour."

I opened the box and found a blue garment, unfolded a coat and held it up.

"Well," James said, raising himself up on his elbows to look, "a blazer!"

"Jesus," Bob muttered, a little too loud.

"Robert, hush up!" Mrs. Haywood whispered harshly.

I was speechless. Over the breast pocket was a patch showing two lions resting their paws on each side of a crown. The word 'Benevolent' arched over the top of the crown with 'Daughters' under it. With the help of Mrs. Haywood who held it for me, I slipped it on.

"A perfect fit," she said, obviously pleased. "You represent the home today, Thomas. As a matter of fact, the home has two children in the competition, but Russell will represent his public school."

Russell had become stoical about the remarks from the public school children regarding his scars, and though it hurt him deeply, he insisted on continuing with his schooling by attending his classes at the public school instead of at the orphanage. I think every day he became more distant with everyone and I felt the strain on our friendship. But I was bound and determined to be there for him even though, now a' days, we seldom spoke. I continued to leave new books beside his bed and received a quick, whispered 'thanks'. That was it!

She studied the stunned look on my face for a second, then bending, picked up the box.

"Good luck, Thomas, I'm sure you'll do us proud." And she walked back towards the Benevolent Daughters' tables leaving me to feel and smell my new blazer.

"It's new. Do you think I could keep it, like after?" I looked at James who lay back and smiled at my question.

"Have a tough time getting it back, especially when ye win," he smiled, his eyes closed against the sun.

"You look fine," Bob said.

"Thanks," I said, then remembered neither one of us had ever had a *new* anything, and for a moment felt a little sad. "Here," I said, slipping it off, "you try it on." I handed the blue blazer to him.

He looked at it, then to me. "Git," he said, "ain't new to me. You had it on, and...," he smiled at me, "'sides you're gettin' tall and skinny, probably wouldn't fit."

It was true, I was as tall as Bob but he was a lot bigger especially in the chest.

I laid the jacket on the ground. "It's too hot to wear it now," I pretended to explain, but had a terrible time taking my eyes off it.

"Hey," I said, "isn't it funny Russell never said a word about being in the contest? He's real smart." And for the first time I felt nervous about the spell-off.

"He ain't a' smart as you," Bob said, "and you're younger."

The army band played through until almost three, then a man got onto the front of the steps and announced through a big megaphone mounted on a metal stand that the spelling contestants were to come to the back of the bandshell.

Earl and Gladys, who had come by wagon with the rest of the kids from the home, joined James and Bob in wishing me luck as I slipped on my new blazer and left them. They all started to move closer to the front of the bandshell while I went around back.

There were eight of us competing, four boys and four girls. At first I couldn't find Russell, but then noticed him sitting on the corner of the steps, alone.

"Hi, Russell." I walked over to him.

"Tom," he said quietly, not looking up but instead continued digging the ground with a small stick. He was dressed in the home's coveralls.

"Didn't you get one of these?" I asked holding open the front of the blazer.

"No, I don't represent the home, I won my school competition".

I felt bad for him because his school didn't get him anything to represent it.

Russell jabbed the stick into the ground then pulling it out, threw it away.

"Good luck," I said awkwardly.

He stood up, sweat glistening on his disfigured and scarred face. "Don't you look the dandy," he smiled and shook my hand. "Good luck to you, Tom."

A man gathered us together and explained we would draw first for order, then in turn would draw a piece of paper from a bowl and then without looking at it, hand it to the judge. One of them would tell us the word and then we would spell it and use it correctly in a sentence. Much the same way we did it in class, except there was no bowl in the class, Mrs. Haywood just took the words from all our spelling tests.

We sat in order on the top step of the bandshell, the judges at a table in front. The bowl under the megaphone was cleared of the numbers after our order was drawn and filled with pieces of paper with the words we were to spell on them. We were introduced by name and school, and in turn, were each to stand. I was third and got a great amount of clapping and shouts as I stood at the introduction. I was so proud of my blazer, and it was easy to find my rooting section from the noise they created. It was the same for the others; each had their own noisy section in the crowd. When Russell's name was called, there was a lot of murmuring and only some polite clapping. The home kids clapped loud but it was different and ended quickly and awkwardly. He sat down on the step quickly and stared at his feet. The enthusiasm was re-established for the eighth and final girl.

For the first bowl of words, only one boy failed, but not for misspelling. On his second turn, he reached into the bowl, withdrew the paper and looked at it. He left the judges' table and sat in the crowd with his disappointed friends.

The second bowl of words was harder and a boy and a girl misspelled their words. The third bowl eliminated the three remaining girls. One girl cried because she spelled the word correctly, but misused it completely in a sentence.

Russell and I remained for the fourth bowl. Almost an hour had gone by. The crowd had made me the favourite and clapped and cheered. I knew I was going to win. Russell got a polite response and continued to look at his feet when he quietly sat down. But he was very good and I had to admit, spelled out the words and used them in a sentence faster than I could.

We knocked off words until it seemed endless – then the judges changed the rules: two points for correct spelling and one point for using it correctly in a sentence. They asked us to each draw out a final three pieces of paper from the bowl. I drew out the first three and handed them to the lady judge. Russell did the same. As he handed his to the judge, a voice from the crowd called out, "You sure is ugly!" Russell turned from the judge and crowd and I could see the pain on his face. There was a tittering of laughter and some ladies who muttered "shame".

Russell was asked to go first and got the three points for the first word. I followed doing the same. We were still tied after the second word, but on Russell's third word he ran into a problem. He spent several minutes sounding it out over and over before spelling it out correctly. It was his misuse of the word in the sentence that brought a mixed response from the crowd. He got only two of his three points and left it open for me. Dejected, Russell sat down and stared at his feet.

I stood and took my place in front of the megaphone. The lady judge read the paper, folded it, then looked up at me and spoke, "The word is *criteria*."

Of all the words! I couldn't believe it. I'm sure I must have smiled at James as I found him in the audience smiling at me. "Criteria," I repeated. I glanced sideways at Russell and paused.

"The word is *criteria*," the lady judge repeated. Some people started whispering.

Something was wrong. Wrong inside me. The excitement had left me as the bee went on and I felt different.

"Criteria" I repeated.

The judges waited.

"Criteria" I said again and the woman judge nodded to me.

"Criteria. 'c-r-y-t-e-r-i-a' I said and waited, looking down at my feet. There was a pause and some groans from the crowd.

"You have misspelled criteria," the woman judge said. "Russell Keep is the champion."

Her words seemed to echo in my ears. I looked at Russell's bewildered face and was quickly joined by the crowd in clapping for him. Somehow, as I left the stage to Russell and the judge, I knew James would forgive me.

* * * *

The conversion from sawdust to coal took nearly all of the fall. As the mornings grew chillier, James was moved to a hotel at the Benevolent Daughters' expense and Bob was moved back into the dorm. Sledge hammers pounded at concrete and soon a large hole had been opened into the back alley. The whole sawdust furnace was lifted through the hole and the larger coal furnace just squeezed through the opening without an inch to spare. The sawdust chute was removed and a wider coal chute with double steel doors replaced it, allowing the coal wagon to unload right from the alley. The garbage chute, that came down from the kitchen and emptied into a large bin behind the furnace, was extended outside through the wall and into the alley. This helped in controlling the rats that were attracted by the smell. The boards covering the holes were removed and cement was used to fill and seal them. A small water pipe was installed over the sawdust bin that was now a coal bin. It could be turned on and a little propeller, like the kind used on an aeroplane, misted the water and kept the dust down when the bin was being filled. At least it was supposed to.

While all this was being done, Russell left the home for an indenture as a bookkeeper with the electric light company. On the morning he left, after packing his sack, he brought the rest of James's books over to my bed where Earl, Bob and I sat playing mumbly peg on a board with Bob's pocketknife. He handed me the books.

"You know," he said, standing by my shoulder, "if I hadn't won the bee this never would have happened for me, Tom."

I got off the bed without answering. I felt awkward and couldn't speak of it now, we never had. He put his hand out and I shook it.

"You got a friend for life," he said looking me in the eyes. Then turned to Bob and shook his hand, then Earl, and without another word, swung his little sack over his shoulder and left.

"You knew it!" Earl cried.

I sat, picked up the knife on the bed and began to play. I felt Bob's eyes on me and met them with mine, a small smile pulled at his mouth.

"Pie," I said, taking the knife out of the board after my score. No win would ever replace that moment, as Earl and Bob just stared at me. I never knew really why I had done what I had done. There were moments, in the days after it was over, when I felt different about it, foolish even, but the look on my brothers' faces would carry me for a lifetime.

At the end of the spelling bee day Mrs. Haywood had come for the blue blazer. The Benevolent Daughters presented it to Russell during a special ceremony at the home the following day. It now lay over the foot of Russell's bed.

****

In the home, a brother and sister came as orphans. Their mother and father were hit by a drunken automobile driver. The boy was the same age as Earl, the girl was an infant and adopted out within a week. Three girls came in, their father was in the war and their mother ran away with a Raleigh salesman, leaving them with a neighbour overnight.

The rooms and halls were filled with the cries of the new ones for weeks. Then one by one it stopped and they would move about quietly with sad little faces. Soon, with the other children playing and their schooling, they would come to life, but the nights were still filled with muffled sobs and it would take a long time for that to stop.

This would be Gary's last year in the home. In the spring he would go into the fields and probably become a labourer. "Indentures," James had said, "don't come knocking for criminals or orphans."

June, the eldest girl in the orphanage simply refused to leave the home and go into a residence. She became a cook, and with the guidance of Mrs. Holmgren, a good one at that.

Gladys was soon to be taken out of class. *Girls*, it seemed, *did not need education*, according to the Witch. *They would only end up married anyhow.* She wanted desperately to be a nurse and studied very hard. Mrs. Haywood had her attending Dr. Roach on his visits. She always sat with the sick kids and cared for them. But she was in the orphanage, and while we weren't really orphans, it was going to be hard for her to get real training. She was hopeful on two counts: Pa was in the medical corps, they told us, and nursing was about the only thing girls could hope for. She also prayed Dr. Roach would have the Benevolent Daughters sponsor her training. It would be too much, she knew, to ask.

It was now a rare occasion when our little family would meet in the cafeteria. Bob would be running the boiler room for James now and even I could fill in and keep it running. We knew where to run to for any repairs, and could shut the boiler down and divert the steam and hot water from anywhere to any place on the schematic. The workers' boss man even had us paint the piping and valves in blue for cold and red for hot. 'Upstream and downstream', that's what they called it. With all the changes we would have to learn the new system, so Bob was down watching every move the pipefitters and boilermakers made. Truth was, he knew he would have to help James get acquainted.

Earl hadn't been sick for months although he still continued to sniffle the rest of us to distraction. His dark, red-rimmed eyes looked at us balefully each time his shoulders went back to draw a drip back up into his nose.

The Mouse and the new boy, Stephen, played together with Earl in the dorm and were quickly becoming inseparable. Dennis and Mikey chummed together and Gary just stayed to himself, much to the relief of everyone else. Bob and I pretty much had the run of the place. Mrs. Haywood became more tolerant as the fighting had stopped. No one had been caned for months although she did threaten a few times when one or two of the boys became a little rowdy.

James came back to us claiming to feel better but looking awfully sick. He was present for the first delivery of coal. The coal was dropped through the large open doors into the chute from the wagon bed. The mister failed to dampen all the dust, and before the floor of the bin was covered, we had to retreat with James to the cafeteria. Later when we returned, everything was covered in a gritty black dust and little white rivers ran to the drain from the water dripping off the bin walls.

James found some old bed sheets, and after we cleaned up, had Bob and I hang them from the pipes around the coal bin. The next load which would fill the bin came the next day. The spray from the mister hit the sheets and soon the water dripped from them around the bin and pretty much stopped the spread of the dust. The only thing we had to do was sweep and collect the remaining dust from the blackened rivulets that ran to the drain in the centre of the boiler room after it dried.

In a matter of hours, Bob had James *versed and trained*, as James put it, to operate the huge firebox. A lever was pulled to the floor and the large cast iron doors lifted like eyebrows over a surprised face, revealing the bed where the coal was consumed. Slowly, one after another, James had us *crack*, then open, the wheels attached to the water valves. Once going, the dampers and draft were set and we could leave it for eight or more hours. Even in the coldest days, which got to minus fifty, the boiler only had to be stoked every six hours to keep the building heated. A large metal box was placed over the furnace called a plenum. It stretched up to the ceiling and a big hole was cut in the floor of the main hall just inside the front door. A fancy metal grille let the heat out into the main hall. The building was warmer, and if anyone liked it the most, it was the boy whose turn it was to get up and ring the bell for reveille.

There was one other piece of construction that the worker boss took a great deal of pride in. The sawdust ashes cooled quickly and were carried by pail out the recess yard to a special steel bin placed against the building in the alley. But the coal ashes stayed so hot that you couldn't touch the pail handle without burning your hands. The heat sent the ashes everywhere as they rested in the pails.

The boss, seeing our fix, had his workers take the old sawdust hopper, and punching a hole in the outside wall up high near the ceiling, suspended it there with the bottom of the hopper leading outside to a new bin. He bolted a piece of track to the ceiling and put a car on it. The track ran down to the top of the hopper.

He was really excited about his work and looked down at me with a constant grin on his face as I watched this creation unfold. I thought it was best to smile back even though I didn't have a clue as to what he was up to. He put a pulley on the side of the car, then on the track near the ceiling, he put a 'brake'. Two days later, his contraption was complete. I arrived to join Bob as he stood in front of us ready for the *unveiling* of his contraption which now had three ropes suspended from it.

"Here jew boiss try diss." His heavy accent was unfamiliar to me.

He placed a big chunk of coal into the bucket that was at his feet and attached to one of the ropes. "Now jew pull first diss rope," he said, handing the rope to me. I looked up as the bucket left my feet and began to rise towards the ceiling as I hefted the rope. "Now hold," he instructed, "and pull this rope." He handed me the second rope. At first it was a little awkward but I managed to hold the first rope and pull the second. The little car became unlocked and almost pulled me off my feet as it shot the bucket and me towards the hopper. Only the wall saved me as the bucket hit it and tipped. The piece of coal fell out of the tipped bucket into the hopper that acted as a chute.

"Yass!" he shouted as the large chunk of coal now free from the bucket rested inside the hopper's chute.

"Now diss one." He handed me the third rope while he was still looking at the swinging bucket. "Pull it back to de lock." He grabbed the second rope from me and held it aside so I could manage resetting the car into the lock with ease. Once set, I let the bucket down.

"Slow!" he cautioned me. "Jew burn de hands, too fast."

There it was! Bob and I looked at each other with the realisation that our heaviest job in the whole boiler room had vanished with this contraption.

"No wonder you're the boss," I said to his beaming face.

He left us, and climbing the ladder, pulled the large piece of coal out of the chute and dropped it back into the bin. Once back down, he took the ropes from me and handed them to Bob.

"Jew do it."

* * * *

I finished my sixth year class before my ninth birthday, and while Mrs. Haywood went to the authorities to see what to do with me for enrolment into the seventh grade at a public school, I didn't have to attend classes. As much as I loved school, I liked being with James even more and when not helping Bob with the duties, James and I would sit and discuss literature for hours while Bob punched the old sawdust bag – completely bored with us.

James was finding it more and more difficult to get around so Mrs. Haywood found some money in some fund or other and had a plumber build a makeshift loo that featured some kind of seat affair with a removable commode under it. But best of all, James instructed the plumber to take runs from the hot water line and cold water line and drop them into the middle of the room over the drain. There, with a stopcock on each line, he merged them. We now had a neat bathing apparatus and could control the temperature of the water by turning the valves. I was the first to use it and found that you didn't want to be standing under the spigot while adjusting the temperature.

The final days of our third winter moved by so quickly – one proving to be a day of discovery for Bob. James and I were talking of people, just in general, when he asked me whether what I had done at the spelling bee was because of a fear I had for Russell after he hurt me. I tried to explain how

I felt and what I felt, but I wasn't able to put it exactly the way I wanted.

Bob, sitting on his bed, spoke. "I knew the second you misspelled it, something wasn't right."

"Ye mean when the judge spoke and told us Tom had misspelled it, do ye not?"

"No," Bob shook his head, "the minute he spelled it with a 'y' instead of an 'i' I knew it."

James lifted his head to look at Bob. "Kin ye spell it for me now lad?"

"Sure," Bob said, "c-r-i-t-e-r-i-a."

"Spell military for me," James asked, again referring back to another word from the contest.

"m-i-l-i-t-a-r-y," Bob answered.

"B'jases, lad, if ye can spell why in hell can ye not read, nor write for that matter?" he added.

Bob shrugged, "Just can't."

Three days later, Bob printed his name for the first time. He learned what the letters looked like as he spelled. That came to him fairly easy. Using his finger, he moved to each letter sounding them out. But reading was always very difficult for him. For Bob, knowing he could print and using his finger, read simple words, helped him to understand he was not stupid. The notion that, for some reason, words were just scrambled to him, lifted a terrible weight from his shoulders. James and I worked with him before supper everyday after all the duties were done. It still took a lot of concentration and Bob finally let us know, in his own way, that it was our excitement and his boredom we were dealing with. He soon found other things that needed doing instead of his lessons. We didn't push him. You couldn't!

These were the happiest days, as winter gradually gave way to spring, and the boiler would only need stoking once in the morning and again at night. James was feeling better so we opened the steel doors of the coal chute to the alley one evening just to feel the rush of cool, fresh, spring air. Bob and I climbed out and sat in the shadows of the chute doors. We were both aware that Mrs. Haywood's window gave view to the recess yard and alley behind where we were sitting – but her lights were out. Only the sounds of the occasional motor car or carriage came from the end of the alley.

We could hear the sounds of an approaching motor car that slowed, and with grinding gears, suddenly swung into the alley. The lamps on each side of the windscreen briefly lit up the alley then faded out. The driver's door opened and the huge silhouette of a man stepped from the motor car, then turned and dragged something from inside the car to the alley. The monster man lifted the object over his shoulder and turning, looked across the alley where Bob and I sat watching under the cover of darkness. He turned back and a piece attached to the burden was outlined by the lamp light at the end of the alley. It was an arm.

Bob nudged me. "Did you see that?" he whispered.

I had an uneasy feeling that we had seen something we shouldn't have and reassured myself that the chute doors were open and close enough, that if the man came back out the door and across the alley after us – we could skeedaddle. I got up, ready to go back inside, but Bob reached up and grabbed my hand. "Wait, let's see what happens."

Between Bob's assured voice and my curiosity, I crouched back down, but further back into the shadows. On the wall of the building next to the doorway the man had gone through, was a window painted over with whitewash. A light could barely be seen shining through the scratches in the wash. A few minutes later, a deep, gravely kind of voice could be heard. We couldn't make out the words but it was an angry voice, then came the scraping of a chair on the floor, a startled cry and a thump. Bob rose and started across the lane towards the window when the door started to open.

The deep voice came out the doorway clearly. "Give the welching sonovabitch the door on each wing."

Bob crouched and slipped back into the shadows beside me as the big man reappeared with his burden. He leaned back into the doorway after looking in our direction and a low conversation took place between him and whoever else was in the room. It lasted for a few moments, and then the big man shrugged and closed the door.

He walked around the front of the auto, and opening the door, sat the body upright in the front seat. Taking one of the body's limp arms, he brought it out of the vehicle and stuffed the hand into the heavy curtain behind the door. Standing back, he grabbed the door and flung it closed. There was the sound of a *crack* and the door bounced back open. A moan came from inside the auto. Then the big man swung the body around and did it to the other arm with the same result. He threw the disfigured arm back inside the automobile and slammed the door.

He started around the front of the auto then turned and walked quickly over to us, cutting off our retreat to the open chute doors. He was huge. If I stood on Bob's shoulders I doubt if I would have been as tall.

"You better come vit me, somebody vants to see you," the menacing figure said, in a soft but heavily accented, voice. "It's okay, nobody hurts you." He backed away. "Come…now," he demanded.

A whole mess of alternatives raced through my mind, but all I could do was run. He grabbed me by the scruff of my shirt and lifted me off the ground with my second step churning nothing but air.

"No, vit me, yes?" He set me back down on my feet. "You too, okay?" he said to Bob, as he guided me towards the doorway by the shoulder.

I opened the door and entered, followed by Bob and the giant. A small, bald-headed man sat behind a desk which held some papers and a lamp. The room was bare except for two telephones that hung side by side on the wall behind the desk.

The man sitting behind the desk had squinty eyes and looked up at me first, then Bob, and finally at the big man.

"Young," the bald-headed man said to the giant, who didn't reply.

He looked back to me then spent a long look at Bob. "You look like a tough little bastard." He looked back to me again, as I continued to glance around the room finding a second door leading to what must have been the front of the building. "He's the smart one," the little man said, looking back to the man behind us, but nodding towards me. "He's looking for a way out already," he grinned.

"How would you boys like to make some money?" He looked at each of us in turn.

I nodded.

"You see Igor, this one nods right away. You boys come from the home? Orphans?"

Again, I nodded.

He pushed himself back from the desk and in a chair that had large wheels on either side of it, and stopped in front of me. I could see his legs were skinny and bent so badly; I knew he couldn't walk

After a lot of questions, he asked Bob to run errands for him, and maybe in a while, I could, too. But right now, eight was a little too young for the job. He gave Bob three small packets, each with an address of a shop on it. When Bob said the shops would be closed, he told Bob to knock a code on the door and use his name, 'The Gimp', and it would be answered.

"Away you go now. I want to see you this time tomorrow." He looked to Bob then to me. "Be honest with me and do the job right, and you'll make some good money. That man out in the car," he said and nodded his head to the alley, "he couldn't be honest."

He turned in his chair just as one of the phones on the wall rang three short rings. "Away you go lads. Oh, keep all this under your hat, understand?" He looked menacingly at both of us.

"Yes, sir," we responded together.

Bob and I watched as the giant, Igor, backed out of the alley with the man beside him still slumped in the seat. A cloud of blue smoke remained in the lamp light at the end of the alley from the automobile as it disappeared around the corner.

Bob handed me the first packet. "Where do I go?"

He not only couldn't read, but neither of us knew the city very well. So we went together.

Our walk took us well over an hour, by the time we entered the coal chute and closed the doors over us, but the deliveries were all made without a hitch.

"B'jases, you scallywags, where were ye?"

Without giving our warning a second thought, we told James of our encounter.

"His customers call him 'The Gimp'," I finished enthusiastically.

"I dinna like it," he said finally. "Let's sleep on it though and talk of it in the mornin'."

I left Bob and James and slipped silently into the sleeping dorm. I was soon fast asleep myself.

James didn't raise the matter of Bob and me running errands for The Gimp. We left after supper, through the coal chute, and picked up the packets. Together, we ran through the neighbourhood handing them to those who were addressed and answered the code when we knocked.

After a week or so, The Gimp opened the storeroom door to Bob. The door that, I thought, led to the front of the building, actually led to a hallway, according to Bob. At the end of the hallway was a storage room with laundry baskets filled with dirty clothes. Under the clothes were bottles of *medicine*. Igor delivered the big orders of *laundry*, but Bob was to look after the small orders of one or two bottles. The Gimp liked to send a bottle every once in awhile to heavy losers in *appreciation of their business*, as he put it.

In good time, we discovered that there were about thirty or so drops we had to make, but not every night, and they were the same people most of the time. This all earned us almost three dollars a week.

In the beginning, we never concerned ourselves with the money. We simply stashed it in a tobacco can that James offered us after removing shaving soap that he hadn't used for months now. His beard had grown long, but even when he wasn't feeling well, he combed it, *to thin out the cooty population*, until it seemed to flow in silver waves down his chest. He was very clean and had driven Bob and I to distraction by insisting we showered every week under the plumber's nightmare in the middle of the room, and washed up before supper every night.

Dealing with the coal bin twice a day in the better weather created a problem in keeping our clothes clean. James had me take a note on this matter to Mrs. Haywood and Bob and I were issued a second pair of coveralls, boots and shirts. James made us change after every weekly shower.

This didn't make the girls in charge of laundry happy as the boiler room wash had to be done last and separately. On the line, drying in the back of the recess yard, it wasn't difficult to pick out the dirty 'guy clothes' that belonged to us. While I did enjoy the shower, it felt good to be dry and dressed. Neither Bob or I gave a damn, and only James's pestering made it so routine that we finally got into it.

The uniforms created another small problem. The Benevolent Daughters had embroidered 'BD' on the front bib of each and every pair. Unfortunately, it not only identified the uniform but also the wearers of the uniform.

Bob and I had been with The Gimp for one week. After dinner, we huddled in the doorway and out of the downpour, waiting for The Gimp and Igor to arrive in their…well, The Gimp's Maxwell. It was only a matter of minutes when we heard the, now familiar, sound of gears being crushed out on the street. Then it appeared under the lamplight turning into the alley. The car pulled up to the door, shook in an engine-killing stall, and was finally silent.

Igor opened the door and threw us the ring of keys. Bob caught them and while he opened the door to the building, Igor opened the back door of the automobile and disappeared halfway inside it for a moment, then backed out with The Gimp in his arms holding an umbrella. The Gimp quickly opened it and held it over his head to shield off the heavy rain. Bob opened the door and twisted on the light. I stepped out into the rain to let Igor and The Gimp go in.

"Good, you're both here," The Gimp said, as Igor slipped him into the wheeled chair then closed the door as I stepped inside. He always stood at the door.

"How many days you boys been working?" he asked, and then as an afterthought, added, "How many of you did I hire, by the way?"

He rolled his chair behind the desk. Just as he looked up, one of the phones on the wall rang four short rings. The Gimp pushed himself back from the desk, and picking the earpiece off the wall, turned and shouted "yeah" at the wall where the phone rested.

"Yeah," he said again, and fumbled for a small black book inside his coat. He withdrew it and began writing some figures down.

"Lansdown, yeah, last Friday? You trying to past post me you sonovabitch?" he yelled at the wall. "It went last Friday, what do you think…a fucking one-legged turtle could have brought the results here by now. No shit Clive, 'course I can't blame you for trying, it's Igor who can't forgive. You know what the fuck I'm sayin'? That's nice Clive," his voice softened as he began to write down more information. "I said that's nice, Jesus Christ, you going deaf?"

He kept writing, turning his head to yell at the wall when he had to. Finally, he pushed himself back to the wall and hung the telephone up then returned to the desk.

Looking up at Igor as he passed with a second basket of laundry he was loading into the Maxwell, he said, "You're gonna hafta visit Clive one of these days. He's a smartass. Tried twice now to past post me. Schmuck!"

He folded the book, and was about to put it in his pocket, when the telephone rang again. This went on for fifteen minutes, sometimes he had both lines open and gave a hold on, then shouted back what he had heard, all the while scribbling numbers and x's in the book. Finally the phones stopped ringing.

"Alright, I asked you how many of you I hired?"

"Me," Bob replied.

"Right. What the hell are you doing running with him?" His eyes squinted at me unfriendly like.

"I, I uh," I found myself stammering and fidgeting under his stare and didn't want to say anything. Bob came to my rescue.

"I have trouble with numbers. I can't read names and addresses so good." Bob shifted his weight onto the other foot a little awkwardly.

"I just got an earful on you two. Constable O'Malley paid me a visit here after lunch today. Seems like I hired the wrong brother. I hear you're the whiz kid and Bob is the muscle. That right?" A small smile appeared on his face as he gazed at me, but his squinty eyes looked as hard as ever.

"I could work for you too," I offered.

"Not too! Instead!" He shot back, meaning he wanted me and not Bob.

I hesitated, we hadn't been paid yet for everything we had done and I wasn't prepared to let seventy-five cents slip through our fingers by walking away. Maybe I should try to handle this The Gimp's way, doing business like I had heard him do it over the telephone.

"You could have us both for almost the price of one," I answered.

"What's almost?"

"Twenty cents for each run," I shot back.

"That's double!" The Gimp cried.

I nodded and shrugged. He could add as fast as I could.

"Thomas," he said, "it's Thomas, right?"

"Tommy," I answered friendly enough.

"Well, Tommy," he said, "you're the Goddamnedest, most ballsy, little eight-year-old I've ever met." He grinned up at Igor. "They make them like this in Russia, Igor?

"You smart? Look at me." His squinty eyes narrowed even further into slits as he looked back at me. I found I wasn't afraid of him. We did his business and hadn't *stiffed* him like everybody seemed to want to do. *Be honest* is what he had said.

"I like to read"

"He's already finished his sixth grade classes at the orphanage," Bob spoke up. "He should have won the city spelling bee too, but..." Bob shook his head leaving the explanation hanging on a string.

"You know," The Gimp said looking at Bob, "it isn't him. It's you that has to go."

"I'm muscle," Bob said.

"Oh, I'm sure. Nice to have you around especially when there are so Goddamn many ten-year-olds after me and Igor." He laughed out loud, a kind of whinny, his mouth displaying crooked, overlapping teeth. "Must be the elephant who's afraid of mice, like the fairy tale, eh?"

Igor laughed behind us. "Duh, huh huh."

Bob started for the door. I didn't move. I wanted our money, and short of The Gimp turning Igor onto us, I was going to stand here if it took all night to get it.

The Gimp seemed to study me for a minute. "You're the oldest eight-year-old I ever met. Yes, sir, you're going to do all right. If I don't want your brother, you're not stayin' right?"

I nodded.

"Figured so. All right, all right, here's what it is. The two of you run both ways for me. Bring me...you know what you're doing don't you?"

I nodded. "You're a bookmaker."

Bob's mouth dropped open. "I thought it was bootlegging?"

"We've been taking the winners their winnings," I said to Bob's puzzled face.

"Goddamn! Horse races," Bob said, catching on, and 'medicine' for the losers.

"Exactly," The Gimp confirmed. "The two of you can work together. Fifteen cents a run."

"Eighteen! I blurted…and a bottle for James" I added.

"Jesus Christ," The Gimp exploded, "the fucking kid is hustling me. You two are worse then the local constabulary."

"And you owe us seventy-five cents," I finished, not one bit distracted by his outburst.

"Alright, alright," he held up his hands then sat back in his chair. "I *was*…going to buy you two some clothes. You can't do my business in orphanage togs. O'Malley said the station got a visitor complaining that I was usin' poor little orphans, Christ, if he only knew. A little bandit! You two will have to buy your own clothes to do your runs in. I can't afford that now."

The Gimp fished the packets, which were already made up of the winnings, out of the desk and threw two shinplasters down. The phone rang again. He gestured to me to help myself. I did.

Igor left and returned with a shopping bag containing three bottles of medicine.

"One for James," he said, with a smile and wink.

As Bob and I were leaving, The Gimp covered the phone in his hand and said, "Clothes tomorrow!"

I nodded at him then walked past Igor on my way out into the rainy night.

We were soaked by the time we made our way back to the alley. We shot down the chute after closing the doors to the rain and landed heavily on our feet amidst the chunks of coal. The warmth of the room felt good. James lay propped up in his bed, a book in his hand, his reading spectacles perched precariously on the end of his nose.

"You two look like you could start flowing out to the ocean," he said, as we started shedding our dripping-wet clothes.

"You shoulda heard Tommy going at The Gimp a while ago," Bob said, as he pulled the last bottle of medicine out of the shopping bag and handed it to James.

"Ye didna get yerself into hot water, lad?" James asked. "That man is no to be fooled with," his voice was serious as he looked at me over the top of his spectacles before examining the label on the bottle. "Ooch, now isn't that lovely," he added. "Canadian Girl Gripe Water. Aye, ye have the best for these parts."

Bob went on leaving me to undress in silence. At the finish, James seemed to be chewing on something but decided not to comment. Then, looking up suddenly, he said, "O'Malley, that's the constable that Mrs. Haywood er, ah...entertains on a rather regular basis. Yes," he confirmed to himself, "O'Malley, I'm sure. He's the one we leave the gate unlocked for after supper. Always locked the next morning," he finished to himself.

The following day, I mentioned to James that Bob and I required clothes, other than the house uniforms, as they were getting us into trouble when we did our runs. Wheezing heavily from his efforts on the commode, he told me, between several breaths, to take the key I would find hanging behind the hallway door and see what I could find in the storeroom beside the boys' lav.

Bob and I left to scout.

Bins full of clothes and boxes stacked to the ceiling lined one whole wall of the large room. Some of the boxes were addressed to the Benevolent Daughters of the Homesteaders, others just Benevolent Daughters, and still others marked orphanage. Regardless of how they were addressed, they all bulged with clothes ranging from patched britches to frilly lace dresses.

An hour later, I returned with two coats and hung the key back up. Turning, I glanced down to discover James, white-faced, and hanging onto the shower spout, his chest blowing in and out heavily while his body swayed.

"James, hang on! I'm coming!" I yelled, and flew down the steps, in two leaps, reaching him as he let go and fell. I couldn't hold him, but managed to slip under his bony frame, cushioning his body with mine as we both went down.

I rolled him gently off me, stood, and lifting his arms, dragged him to his bed setting the top of his body on it, and swung his legs over. His eyes met mine and a little smile assured me he was with me. He gulped in air unable to speak. His skinny body was still wet so I grabbed his towel, and when I finished drying him, I covered him with his bedclothes.

I heard Bob come in from the hallway to the landing above me, and then the thud of the door closing. Backing away from James's bed, I looked up over the landing to see Bob set James's commode down then hold the two coats up for inspection. He launched the commode down to me and I caught it and slipped it under the chair, finding him with one of the coats on when I looked back up.

"Okay?" he asked, with his arms outstretched.

It was big on him. Almost touching the floor when he dropped his arms. He grinned, turned away, then instantly turned back, his grin disappearing. "What's up?"

"James fell," I responded, then quickly added, "He's okay."

Bob shrugged out of the coat and ran down the steps to James's bedside. James was a little more under control and raised his hand feebly as he smiled reassuredly into Bob's face.

"Should we get the doctor?" Bob asked James.

James shook his head. "No... fine."

In the following days, James slept a lot. Bob and I took turns washing and feeding him. In the evenings after supper, we both had to leave him, but as we got onto the routine, Bob took several familiar customers, and I the rest, so we could go our separate ways and finish faster. After our runs, I would read to James for long spells into the night until he fell into a light wheezy sleep.

The Gimp counted on us to start bringing the bets in as well. It was now twenty-five cents to handle money both ways, coming and going. This raise didn't come without watching the squinched up face, under the bald head, go beet red in anger. "You two make the Jesse James boys look heaven sent." We also told him that the *schmucks* would have to have the bets and money ready. We weren't waiting around while they made up their minds, changed them, then changed them back again.

"Jesus Christ," The Gimp cried, "another seven cents and the business still has to be run your way. Get out of my sight you schmuck," he responded to my shrug.

I didn't want to be away from James any longer than I had to be. In the summer evenings, after Bob and I returned, we would leave the doors to the coal chute open and allow the sweet, summer air to flood the boiler room, and the heat from the boiler to flow out into the alley. I usually returned before Bob, as I could run faster and forever, up and down the streets. Once back, I would settle down at the foot of

James's bed and read to him. He spoke in two or three word sentences between breaths and would point to select a book.

I spent some of my share of The Gimp's money buying at least two books every week. James was now into poetry and his breathing became easier when I read. Sometimes, when he drifted off, he would say a lady's name, 'Anna'. His lips moved, his eyelids seemed to jump and his face relaxed, and I knew he was thinking or dreaming. I liked to think he was drifting back, or maybe he was with his lady again. He never talked about being young, except when he was serving His Majesty at sea. Sometimes, when I read, he would ask what I thought the poem was saying. "Which means?" he would ask after I read a verse, or say, "What else?" and send me back to the lines, over and over again. Then, I would understand that poetry had meaning and the language was an artful way of saying it. Edgar Allen Poe's, *The Raven*, got James's interest. He was interested mostly in the Irish poets; Thomas Moore was his very favourite along with Byron. I began to really enjoy poetry and continued to read long after James had fallen asleep…until Bob told me to shut up and go to bed.

It was another humid summer night like so many others and I had just returned from my run and noticed James seemed very quiet, so we talked – well, I talked. I sat on the bed beside him. I began to reach for the new book I had snuck out to buy, and he held up his hand, rolling his head on the pillow.

"Good friend," he said, and giving my arm a slight squeeze closed his eyes, his arm dropped away and I looked up.

His mouth was open.

"Oh, God. Oh, God, James – don't, please don't, James!"

I sat on the bed beside him, tears burning my cheeks. I knew he was gone. It was the mouth; I had seen it before. My mother's mouth. Open. Her head bumping against the glass of the window on the train. This time I wasn't spared by innocence. The hollow pain came from the centre of me, and for a brief moment, I wasn't sure which one of us, or both, was no longer alive. His hand felt so hot in mine and I held it to my cheek. Finally, I laid it down, and leaving the bed, went to the corner of the room and sat against the wall. He looked like he was sleeping except for his open mouth.

I sat against the wall not knowing what to do but at the same time knowing there was nothing I could do. The pain turned to numbness then it parted like a curtain and I knew James wasn't dead. He would be with me. He would be with me in every book I would ever open. We would share the adventure. My eyes would be his, and I felt blessed for what he had given me. But I couldn't stop weeping for my loss. I closed my eyes and felt this comforting resolution surround the pain and fill the emptiness.

The coal chute door slammed and Bob came down the chute, bounded over the coal bin and onto the floor. He looked briefly around but missed seeing me in the corner. He walked to his bed, taking off his coat. Looking at James as he moved across the room, he moved past him, then froze, and turning, looked again. I stood as the coat slipped from Bob's hand and he stepped to James's bedside. Falling to his knees, as I crossed the floor behind him, he bowed his head and I could see his shoulders heave as he silently wept. I felt my own tears begin again, this time for my brother's pain. I knelt beside him and he turned to me and threw his arms around me. We held each other and wept, and after a long time, I told him what I had discovered at the very depth of my despair.

Together, without words, each of us placed James into our own lives, and together we pulled the blanket over his face as we had watched the conductor on the train do for our mother while we were being pulled from her, so long ago.

The seed of indignity was planted that early August morning, as a wagon pulled up in the alley, and James's body wrapped and tied in a grey blanket, was removed through the coal chute doors and laid in the open, in the back of the wagon.

In the meantime, we watched along with all that cared, at the window. Bob, Earl and I had spotted the wagon and took our place at the window suspecting he would be taken out through the recess yard. As it was, we were only able to see the horses until the cart pulled away and James's body became visible in the wagon bed bouncing and tossing as it carried on down the rough gravel in the back alley and then out of sight.

"Alright you children back to your rooms," the Witch said, as she huffed up the stairs. "Robert, I want you to stoke the fire for hot water, it's bath day. Come on now, get back to your rooms," she demanded, as we milled about. Some, including Earl, were still weeping and sniffing. "Get moving," she said angrily.

I moved with Bob down the stairs to return to the boiler room.

"Thomas."

I turned, but had no intention of returning to the boys' dorm. She must have seen this on my face along with my anger, because she looked at me, hesitated, then said, "very well," and turned and walked down the hall.

It was so apparent that this matter was nothing more than an inconvenience to her. Bob and I had both seen Constable O'Malley's uniform coat hanging on the back of a chair as the Witch stood in her doorway in a wrinkled up and stained nightshirt, and upon hearing our news of James's death, ordered us to the dorm. Bob said, in the dorm, that he had been told to unlock the gate.

I stood at the top of the stairs and watched her start up to the third floor, and her now empty room, before descending the stairs to catch up to Bob.

Standing on the landing inside the door of the boiler room, I was aware of the coolness. Bob and I had drawn the fire a few days after James had left. The coolness and emptiness were so strange that I hesitated before going down the stairs.

Our books, almost all of them, James's and mine had been removed by the Benevolent Daughters without a word to Bob nor I, and donated to the city library. I had rescued the ones under my bed and protested a week later to the Witch. I told her they were mine but she pooh-poohed me, asking where I would get the money to buy things. I was forced to back off. Telling her I earned three dollars a weeknight running for a bookie wasn't a wise move to substantiate my claim to the books.

****

The workmen had arrived, two days after Bob and I pulled the fire from the boiler, to inspect the furnace, boiler, pipes and chimney – or *stack*, as they called it. The company that had donated it had already done a refit so all that was really worked on was the stack.

Bob and I sat on James's bed and watched the workmen screw length after length of pipe together and push it through a trap door in the ceiling beside the chimney. It was funny, neither Bob nor I had noticed the trap door before. It was kind of hidden by the extension of the garbage chute. Only the bottom three steps on the ladder going up to the ceiling were visible on the chimney wall and you had to go behind the boiler to see them. They only came down part way and ended above our head so it took a ladder to reach the first rung.

Only after the workmen had gone up on the roof, did Bob and I wander over to have a look. We could see a small square of blue sky that gave enough light to see the ladder running all the way up. One of the workmen seemed to be watching the progress of the brush attached to the end of the poles as it came down one floor at a time. As he left each perch to follow it down, he removed a metal plate from the chimney. Bob and I moved aside to allow him to climb down from the boiler room ceiling to perform a final clean out at the floor bottom. Finished, he removed a pail of soot then closed the door and caught the end of the brush as it reappeared through the trap door. Then he began taking the lengths apart and laying them on the coal chute to the alley.

For the two days they were inspecting the building, we were without hot water. After they packed up, a steam engineer had Bob and me set the fire, check the gauges, and release the hot water back into the system. He obviously didn't think much of us running the boiler, and though he didn't say much to us, he must have said something to somebody because the authorities created quite a din about children looking after the boilers. The Witch got muscled, first from the authorities, then from the Benevolent Daughters.

The search was on for James's replacement. In the mean time, Bob and I both stayed in the boiler room. The coal chute doors leading to the alley were seldom closed, until the September rains and evening coolness finally came.

Our escape in the evenings to do The Gimps' running soured a little. Without saying a word to me, Bob had bought one of those wheeled chairs from The Gimp. It was an older, used one that looked so uncomfortable it reminded me of a picture I had seen of an electric chair – except for the belts of course. Bob had made a deal with The Gimp and before he would let Bob bring the chair to James, it had to be paid for. Of course, when James died before ever seeing it, Bob wanted to back out. "A deal is a deal," The Gimp had said, so Bob and I did the running for all of August to pay off the chair we didn't want, and left it with The Gimp.

The Gimp wasn't all bad, but he was all business. One evening before I left on my run, Igor, The Gimp and I were talking when Constable O'Malley's name came up. I mentioned the gate instructions on his visits, and finding the Constable in Mrs. Haywood's room. "We call her 'the Witch' because she enjoys dishing out punishment," I explained.

"Are you sure it's Constable O'Malley?" The Gimp asked, suddenly very serious.

"Yes, sir," I answered. "He was the one who brought us to the home first off. He's been coming and going ever since. James told me that."

The Gimp sat back thoughtfully, then looking at Igor, said, "Well, I guess you just earned yourself ten dollars for that little piece of information, Tommy," he grinned. "Seems Constable O'Malley screwed himself out of his weekly stipend, literally."

"Duh, huh huh," Igor guffawed, suddenly seeing The Gimp's reasoning. The Gimp reached inside his coat and brought out a packet of money held by a clip with a bright stone set on it. Without ever seeing one, I knew it must be a diamond. He peeled off an eastern bank note and flipped it onto the table.

I reached for the bill, still a little puzzled. "What are you going to do?" I asked.

"Nothing," The Gimp sat back, spread out his fingers and looked at them. "It's what I'm *not* going to do – pay off that stinking flat foot anymore. That sonovabitch has been holding me up for over two years. He's in here crying about Mrs. O'Malley and his poor children and gouging me. Well, Mrs. O'Malley sure wouldn't appreciate the constable dipping his wick into the widow Haywood, now would she? And come to think of it, the Benevolent Daughters wouldn't want the Merry Widow looking after all those poor orphans. You don't get paid for that one," he added quickly.

I put the money into my bib pocket while still trying to figure out what O'Malley and The Gimp had going. Then it came to me as I walked down the lane. Booking was against the law and O'Malley was on the take. Now, with my information, The Gimp had one on O'Malley. I was the stool pigeon. I didn't know it at the time, but it was all right with me, for Bob and I had our money back for the wheeled chair. And while I didn't have anything with O'Malley one way or the other, he was dishonest – I was sure. The Witch taught all the kids that the policeman was your friend. Whooee, I bet! Her friend! Not The Gimp's.

Two evenings later, I was running for my life. If I hadn't recognised O'Malley and two older boys following me, they would've had me for sure. I watched them shadow me from across the road as I hurried along after my final drop for the night. A carriage and a motor car were coming down the road one behind the other. The moment the motor car pulled around the carriage and got between O'Malley's friends and myself, I lit out. While they waited for the traffic to pass, I made a city block on them and found an alley to duck down, only to discover I had picked the wrong one. It was a dead end. Quickly, I headed back to the street but I could hear their running feet fast approaching. Near the exit to the alley was a drop fire escape that was several feet above my head. I ran and lunged for it, catching the bottom rung. I pulled myself up onto the balcony and flattened out.

"Down here," one of them said, short of breath. The footsteps turned the corner and seconds later came to a stop as they realised it was a blind alley. They began to kick over garbage cans then looked behind a mattress and some boxes, systematically searching every obstacle, making their way to the back of the alley. One of them turned in time to see me as I jumped to the ground and sprinted around the corner, headfirst into O'Malley's fat stomach. I heard the air rush out of him and felt his hands search my back for a quick grip, as he fell straight-legged back on his ass. He reached once more for me, rather awkwardly, as I flew over him.

The two older boys were now hot on my heels. They came around the corner but must have stopped to help O'Malley for I heard him shout, "Get that little bastard!"

By now, I had half a block on them and was headed back to our alley. I saw Bob standing on the corner by The Gimp's building and I was hoping Igor was around, but as I turned the corner the car was gone, and so was Bob.

"Stick around," I heard him say as I spotted him crouching in the shadows.

"They're too big," I whispered, as the two pair of running feet came upon us.

"Naw," Bob answered, as he swung a piece of pipe into the midsection of the first guy coming around the corner, doubling him over. The second couldn't stop fast enough and went diving over the first, landing on his hands and knees. Before he could move, Bob swung the pipe up between his legs, lifting the second boy clear off the ground.

The boy howled, and gripping himself between his legs, rolled over and over.

"Watch out for O'Malley, he's following."

Bob's eyes widened and he dropped the pipe and pushed me. "Go," he whispered.

We left the two older boys gathering their wits in the alley as Bob pushed me past the coal chute doors. "Keep going," he said.

We rounded the corner and went into the church cemetery. I stopped at the edge of the alley and looked back. The silhouette of big, fat O'Malley was visible as he leaned over to help one of the boys onto his feet.

I followed Bob through the cemetery and around two blocks until we were again in the alley, a block away from the home. Staying to the shadows, we crept up to where we could see O'Malley leaving the two boys and moving up the street. The two boys walked back to the alley then slipped out of sight into the shadows, but not before one of them picked up the length of pipe Bob had used and took it with him.

"They're waiting for us," Bob said.

We squatted down in the shadows across the road from them.

"Ain't no way in but the alley. Gonna have to wait 'til daylight."

"We can't," I said, "we have to be there for the stoking. It's still dark then, and what if they wait all night? What then?"

We sat in silence trying to think our way out of this problem.

"We should have went in when we had the chance," I said, referring to Bob pushing me past the coal chute doors. "As soon as we were inside we could lock the steel doors and that would have kept us safe."

"I didn't want them to know we're from the orphanage."

"It doesn't matter. They're with O'Malley and he knows where to find us anytime he wants."

"The Gimp's gonna be right pissed when he finds O'Malley trying to clip his runners," Bob said, as the pat of raindrops started hitting around us. "Shit, we're not staying out in this. Let's go back through the cemetery and see if we can sneak along the wall to the chute."

He stood just as the sound of an approaching motor car was heard.

Bob peered around the corner and looked up the street to where the car was approaching. "It's The Gimp," Bob said.

"You sure?" I tried to get closer but stopped short of getting the light from the lamp across the street on my face.

"I know that sound by now." He pulled back and stood against the wall.

Sure enough the Maxwell slowed and pulled into the alley. We were too far away to see the two older boys in the headlamps but we knew they were there. The automobile stopped and the door opened, the huge figure of Igor raised up out of the black body of the vehicle.

Bob lit out to the middle of the road with me behind him. "Igor, watch out!" we both yelled. "There's two of them waiting in the dark."

Bob stopped under the street lamp rather than running into the darkened alley.

Just then, there was a commotion coming from the driver's side of the motor car and a loud whack followed by a groan from Igor as the pipe was laid on him. Knowing where they were now and thinking Igor needed help, we ran into the alley just as the sound of a fist hitting meat could be heard. Then we heard it again and again. We got there and it was all over. Igor stood over the two boys who were crumpled at his feet.

"Igor, you okay?" The Gimp called from inside the auto.

I glanced in and saw The Gimp lying over on the seat, the lamplight was bright enough to see the glint of a shiny object in his hand. It was a six-shooter, sure enough.

"Broke my Goddamn arm," Igor said, holding it up for The Gimp to see.

"They were chasing us half the night," Bob said. "Damn near caught Tommy."

"They're O'Malley's boys," I added. "Seen him talking to them just before they started after me, and again when they missed us. They were waiting here keeping us from dropping your stuff and getting back to the home."

"That fucker, O'Malley. He was the one who called me saying the office was broken into. Said he saw you two looting it. It was a setup and now he's going to pay. You okay, Igor? Can you drive?"

"Arm's numb, but I can drive I think."

"Bob check the door to see if it's locked," The Gimp ordered, waving the gun towards the building.

Bob tried the handle. "It's been forced." The door swung open.

"You boys been in there?" The Gimp asked.

"Christ no," I answered, as the rain drummed against the roof of the car making us have to almost shout. "We were across the street," I pointed.

"That sonovabitch has turned on us, Igor. See if there's anything left in the laundry room."

All three of us entered through the broken door. Igor, instead of leading us down the hall, went over to the desk and seizing it, grimaced as he lifted up one end of it with his broken arm and then dropped it and wrapped his arm in a magazine he picked up off the floor. Bob and I watched as the pain on his face turned to satisfaction. He waved his bound up arm around. "Like new!"

"Hurry up!" The Gimp's voice carried into the room from the back seat of the car faintly.

"Coppers will be here any minute."

I ran down the hall and found about a half dozen baskets each containing six bottles which remained untouched. I ran past the others and out into the rain. "About a half dozen loads are here," I reported to The Gimp.

"That's what I thought. He didn't steal them because he wants to catch me with the goods."

"Igor!" The Gimp called, as Igor and Bob stepped into the alley. "Get me in there and those baskets into the car and make it quick!"

Igor brushed passed me, and reaching into the car, scooped The Gimp up with one arm and took him into the room where he slipped him into the wheeled chair. Bob and I raced down the hall and within a few minutes had the automobile filled with as many laundry baskets as it would hold. Desperately, we dumped the laundry out of the remaining baskets onto the floor and took all the remaining bottles inside one basket to the back seat. Finished, we closed the door in the back as Igor emerged from the building carrying The Gimp's gun. He threw it on the seat beside him. I raced to the front of the automobile as Igor cranked it.

Igor started down the alley only seconds before the black shape of a delivery truck turned and stopped outside The Gimp's door. Ignoring us, four constables burst from the back of the van and ran into the building.

"What's the meaning of this!" The Gimp cried out, his voice full of mock surprise.

Bob and I slipped into the shadows, and stepping over the two goons that Igor had clouted, started up the alley to the home. For some reason Igor had pulled the Maxwell over near the coal chute doors and leaving it, started back towards us in a hurry.

"What?" Bob asked as he came hurrying up to us. "Won't the police see the Maxwell parked there?"

"Can't leave him in there with those coppers," he answered.

"But they'll see it," I whispered aloud to his back as he went by us. I saw him shrug as he headed for the doorway. "Come with me." I grabbed Bob who was standing watching as Igor disappeared inside.

Running to the coal chute I quickly lifted the doors open. Bob was on to me without a question. I slid down the chute and was followed in a second by the first heavy basket of laundry. I caught it at the bottom of the chute and laid it onto the floor in the coal bin. Down came the baskets, only seconds between each one as Bob and I worked frantically to empty the automobile. I heard the automobile door close and looked up to see Bob at the top of the chute closing the doors.

"Did they see you?" I asked, as he slid to the floor.

"Don't think so, but I was too busy to look. They're taking The Gimp's place apart by the sounds of it."

We stood there looking at the stack of laundry baskets in the coal bin.

"What if they come looking in here?"

"Why would they?" Bob asked, taking off his wet coat.

"One reason would be not finding this," I pointed to the baskets, "and the other is the damn automobile parked outside our door," I answered, as I hung up my own coat.

"Well," Bob took a deep sigh, "let's cover them up." And with that he started laying chunks of coal over the laundry baskets.

A short time after we finished, a tapping on the coal chute doors sounded. Both Bob and I climbed up and carefully opened the doors.

Igor stood above us in the rain, his arm now in a sling. "You done good." He winked, then left our sight. We raised our heads and saw The Gimp in the backseat as the automobile pulled away. He gave a smile and little wave.

After, Bob walked over to his coat and took The Gimp's revolver out of the pocket.

He laid the gun on the bed and we looked at it.

"Guess we'll have to give it back," Bob said, and picking it up, he started pointing it around the room.

"Jesus, it's loaded, lets not piss with it Bob."

"Pow, pow!" Bob said, as he squeezed the trigger. The blast from the gun almost deafened us. The bullet exploded into the coal with shattered pieces flying everywhere. I was on the floor with Bob, and the gun, with a small curl of smoke coming out of its barrel, lay ten feet away.

"Enough?"

"Enough."

"It smells faintly of gunpowder, or something like it." The Chief Constable said, wrinkling up his nose as he leaned over the railing of the landing above us the following morning.

"Oh, really?" the Witch asked, and sniffed the boiler room air. "I can't seem to smell anything. Do you boys smell anything?"

"No, ma'am," we answered in unison, maybe a touch too fast.

The policeman studied us for a minute, took one final look around the room, and allowing the Witch to leave, followed her out of the room. We waited until the door closed behind them before we collapsed on our beds and let out a collective sigh of relief.

"God, I'm glad we hid that." Bob nodded towards the coal bin.

"That gun goes back to The Gimp tonight."

"Needless to say." Bob reached under his pillow to reassure himself it was still there.

That evening the boys were gone, only the pipe lay in a pool of water. We went to The Gimp's office and found the room had been straightened around. The Gimp sat back into his chair.

"Boys, I want to thank you. But first I want that gun back." Bob had it out of his pocket and on the desk in front of him before he finished.

The Gimp didn't touch it. "It's been fired," he looked at us, his eyes searching both Bob and I.

"It was an accident."

"Oh, really?"

"I did it." Bob fessed up.

"I would have put the odds on you that it was your doing. What did you shoot?"

"The coal," I answered quickly, trying to ease the glare The Gimp had fastened on Bob. "In the bin." I added.

"That's it?" He reached for the gun and grasping it, pressed something and the part carrying the bullets popped out. "One shot." He mused, and picked the used bullet casing out of the hole.

"You boys did a good job for me last night. Because you made me clean, there isn't a damn thing to worry about. That, I appreciate. Here's something for you both." He reached inside his pocket and pulled out a roll of money as big as his fist and pealed off five bank notes and placed them in front of us.

"Fifty dollars!" There wasn't that much money in the whole world. The Gimp put more than that back into his pocket. I knew then, that he was very rich. I picked up the bills and folded them into my pocket. "Thanks, uh…" Damn! I didn't want to call him *Gimp* "…Thanks again." I finished, somewhat lamely.

The Gimp wheeled around the desk and reached out for my hand, then after shaking it, went to Bob and did the same. "The visit from the Chief Constable to your building this morning caused me some concern. Igor went back last night to try and find the laundry and couldn't." He looked up at us and waited for a reply.

"It's in the coal bin under the coal. We slid it down the chute and covered it just in case…and," I went on, "the Chief Constable came into the boiler room this morning with the Witch but we were ready." I finished cockily.

He sat back in his chair and folded his arms across his skinny chest, a thoughtful look on his face. "Could you boys keep it there? Just for a while. Until this place cools down."

Bob and I glanced at each other. "It's in the coal bin and it's ok for now, but we'll get another load this week. It will be full." I explained.

"So, find another spot." He raised his eyebrows up expectantly. "Can you?" he finished, looking towards Bob then to me.

I looked to Bob and saw he was having the same problem. Where? "We can hide the boo…medicine," I corrected, "but there's no place for the laundry and the baskets."

"Burn em!" The Gimp said. "We won't need that cover." He grinned, his crooked teeth pouncing at us like some big rodent. "I like it. The boo...medicine..." He popped the teeth again, "being cached in an orphanage. What do you think, Igor?"

Bob and I both turned to see Igor's grinning response. I glanced down and saw his arm was in a cast with only the end of it showing out of his sleeve.

"How...where's the guys that chased us?" Bob asked, after following my eyes down Igor's arm.

"Seems when the law couldn't find anything here they decided to charge these boys with breakin' and enterin'. They'll be in jail just as soon as the hospital releases them. It appears Igor hits pretty hard when he's angry or hurt. And he was both last night. 'Course I don't expect they will ever come to trial."

"And you won't be bothered by O'Malley anymore." The Gimp said, as Bob and I left for our rounds.

The next day Bob and I slipped the bottles into boxes and slid them under our cots. We then burned the laundry after going through it for change, and finally, broke the baskets up and fired them into the oven before cleaning the place up.

We set up a system where we could see how many bottles of medicine we would need each night by looking from our coal chute over to The Gimp's window. His window was like a baseball diamond, where each corner represented a base. He would stick a piece of paper in the corner of the window and the base number was the number of bottles to bring.

****

As September moved us closer to winter, with chilly evenings and cold rains, it seemed that there was a sudden increase in children paraded into the home. Five, three girls and two boys, all arrived in one week. For Bob and me, it didn't make much difference. We now stayed in the boiler room day and night. Bob slept in James's bed and I in his. We ate in the cafeteria almost anytime after the regular mealtime.

Gary, staying true to course, had come back early from the harvest. He readily admitted to being *a lazy son of a bitch*, as the farmer who brought him back explained to Mrs. Haywood in the front hall. It was here that he dropped Gary's tuck bag, unceremoniously dumping its contents over the floor, then picked out the items Gary had stolen from him, and without another word, shook his head and left, carrying them in his hand.

Gary, unwilling to work and generally being disliked by all, became even more of a surly troublemaker. Earl on the other hand, found his way, and had the other boys his age and younger, following him around everywhere he went. This, I guess, singled him out and Gary began to bully him. Gary was a bully to start with but as both Bob and I weren't around much, he began to relish pushing Earl around. Earl never said anything and tried to stay away from Gary, but the more he back-pedalled, the harder Gary pushed.

Late in September, on a Sunday, Gary shoved Earl into a pole they were passing on their way to Sunday school. Earl fell hard and skinned up his face fearsome-like. Mrs. Haywood gave Gary a stroke of the cane, but on my return trip from the lav it was Mikey who stopped me and told me that Gary was picking on Earl. I found Earl in the dorm playing pie on the bed with a bunch of his friends. Gary lay in his bed at the far end of the dorm by the window.

"How'd you get that?" I asked. His forehead, nose, cheek and chin were freshly scabbed over. Earl shrugged while his friends to the last, turned and looked in Gary's direction. That was enough for me. I walked down the aisle between the beds towards Gary who watched and waited, then he swung himself into a sitting position on the bed facing me, watching me. I stuffed my clenched fists into my pockets and tried not to let him know just what I had in mind.

"Hi Gary, how's it goin'." I kept my voice friendly.

He said nothing, but watched me warily as I walked up to him. When he put both hands on the bed to get off his fat ass, I hit him flush on the nose. He yelped, and following the momentum of the punch, threw his legs around in an effort to get up on the other side of the bed. He was next to the window, facing away from me.

Gary was big; just sitting on the bed he was almost as tall as I was. I jumped on the bed, launched another punch and caught him in the ear. There was no doubt in my mind that if Gary wanted to, he could easily beat me to a pulp. He was a foot taller, almost twice my age, and three times my weight, but didn't have the stomach for a scrap.

I punished him until I was satisfied he looked worse than Earl did. I ignored his cries to stop, and carefully picked open, unprotected spots to batter him with my fists until I was winded. I turned, and saw Earl and his friends standing along the wall by the door – a few with tight little smiles. I left Gary and started down the dorm to the door.

"You're a fucking asshole, Tommy!"

I turned to see Gary standing and dabbing the blood off his lip. "Really? Wait 'til Bob finds out what you're doing to the smaller kids." I saw the sneer give way to fear. He turned to the window and I left.

Bob visited Gary that evening before lights out.

The following morning Earl came down to tell Bob and me that Mrs. Haywood wanted to see us in the office. "She's mad," he finished.

I fully expected that Gary would run and tell, and that a caning was in order. But right in the middle of the Witch's heated lecture Bob left the penalty square and went to the door.

"You get back here!" she demanded, pulling the cane into view.

"You want this place hot or cold?" Bob shot back from the doorway, and waited, then nodded his head for me to follow when she remained silent with the cane coming to rest on the desktop. We left.

"So, how do you like hustling out of your place?" The Gimp asked one night. Bob and I stood before his desk with three bottles as the white strip on the lower left corner of the window had advised.

Five minutes prior, Bob had slid back down the chute. "A triple," he sang out, and I slipped the three bottles out from under the bed and rested them on it, ready to go with us. We had almost finished the 'laundry' booze, when Igor slipped three wooden boxes down our chute in the middle of the night, each containing a dozen bottles of 'Canadian Girl Gripe Water'. Standing in front of The Gimp, we now had the first three bottles out of that shipment.

"The money could be better." I remained straight-faced and watched The Gimp's eyes snap an angry look into mine. It only took a second. I couldn't hold it any longer and felt my mouth twitch.

"You little bugger," he hissed, and shook his head. "You having any trouble with the boss lady of that place?"

"It's easier now that it's getting dark earlier. We don't have to keep tabs on her to make sure she's not around her window and will spot us when we're leaving," I answered.

The Gimp paid us up, a thing he had done regularly since the night of the raid. Bob and I then left to do our business.

It was the following morning, after we had received a load of coal, that Bob and I started our clean up. We moved our beds to sweep and left the boxes of 'medicine' uncovered. This was to be a mistake, for right in the middle of our cleanup…

"What's in those boxes?"

The sound of the Witch's voice made me jump out of my skin and Bob drop his broom.

"Medicine!" I blurted.

"Funny, it doesn't look like medicine," she said, almost to herself as she walked along the railing staring down into the open box with its three empty spaces from the night before.

Bob moved quickly to the bottom of the stairs as she came down. She was still studying the boxes and brushed right by him, over to them. I knew the jig was up.

"We found them in the alley this morning when we opened the door for the coal delivery. We thought maybe someone lost them in the alley and we …uh, thought we would look after them …uh, until we found out who owned them."

"Good for you," she said, under her breath while pulling a bottle of 'Canadian Girl' out of the box and reading the label. "Let's just take them up stairs to my room and we'll see if someone comes to claim them."

"Oh, they can stay here. It's probably better because we're closer to the place where we found them." Bob offered.

"Nonsense! Now take them up to my room and put them inside my door. I think I know who left them."

"Well, they're pretty heavy and it would be easier to leave them here."

"Are you arguing with me, Thomas?"

"No, ma'am."

"These don't belong to you, do they?" she asked, reaching into the case and extracting a second bottle of 'Canadian Girl'.

"No, ma'am!" Bob and I said at the same time.

"Good," she answered while studying the label once again, then placed it back into the box. Turning, she started up the stairs swinging the bottle by the neck. "Pick them up and follow me." She waited on the landing.

Bob and I looked at each other wordlessly as we bent to lift the cases. Five minutes later, all the boxes were stacked inside the door of the Witch's den.

As we were leaving she called to us from her room. "If you boys should somehow find the owners you will let me know?" She closed the door behind us.

"Christ," Bob said, as we went back to the boiler room empty-handed. "What are we going to tell The Gimp?"

"That's fifty bucks," The Gimp said, in a business-like manner, after he had settled back down from screaming at us. We stood in front of his desk after telling him what happened.

"Bullshit! Tommy and I couldn't help it."

"She recognised the label right away," I added.

"I'm not surprised. Thanks to O'Malley. He's been topping her up at my expense for a long time"

"She said she thought she knew who would have left it outside in the alley."

The Gimp let out a big sigh and sat back folding his arms across his stomach. "O'Malley was taking it to her on his...ah...visits. That sonovabitch gets to snicker, but I'm going to have the last laugh."

"Alright, I'll tell you what I'll do to be fair. You don't have to pay me."

I knew The Gimp would be fair.

"...Instead you can work it off. Let's see, about one month should do it. Away you go!"

At least the Witch didn't cane us for thumping Gary, I thought as we left.

The only thing that didn't happen was the fulfilment of her promise to get me the books for my seventh grade. It was felt that I was too young to attend public school in the grade that I had passed to. It wasn't a big deal. Igor, of all people, ended up getting me all the books. The Gimp had a teacher who loved the ponies and was only too happy to climb out of debt by snitching a few advanced school textbooks. He must have had some really bad luck because I received the seventh, eighth and ninth grade readers and exercise books. I poured over them for hours every day of the week. I also taught my reluctant brother, Bob, the third grade and found, after he learned his own system of reading, he could move through the material, but it was difficult for him. I had to admit, while it was easy for me to learn, I had to be really patient with Bob. Running out of patience with him earned me a very sore shoulder. Man, he could hit!

****

He came in with Mrs. Haywood one evening, early in October, while Bob and I were stoking the fires and setting the draft for the night. Neither Bob nor I heard them, but found them watching from the landing as we hung up our coal shovels. Neither of them said anything, just looked. Bob and I stood and looked back. While Mrs. Haywood fixed us with a somewhat unfriendly stare, the little man in the suit broke off his glance to look around the boiler room before they both left.

"James's replacement," I said to Bob.

"Ain't nobody gonna replace James," Bob shot back.

The next morning, Earl came down and told us that everyone was supposed to meet in the main hall. Bob and I left our chores and stood at the back of the hall with the younger boys and girls who were lined up at the foot of the stairs.

Gary, for some unknown reason, stood on the stairs. Looking up, he quieted the murmuring with a finger to his lips. Mrs. Haywood came down the steps alongside the man. He wasn't nearly as old as James, but more Mrs. Haywood's age I would guess. He seemed to look at each of the twenty children one by one, then his eyes came to rest on Bob, then me. They were unfriendly little slits that matched a lip-less mouth, under a long nose.

"Children, your attention!" Mrs. Haywood called to an already silent room. She waited anyhow, then finally said, "This is Mr. Warren Schlicter. He's come out from the east to both teach you and look after the home. The Benevolent Daughters have hired one man, who thankfully, can do two jobs." She began to clap her hands followed by Gary, who turned and faced him. The children started to clap as well, except for Bob and me. We were both more concerned with wondering what was going to happen to us.

Mr. Schlicter didn't fail to notice our hands were at our sides, and the little smile on his face disappeared as he looked at us in turn.

He held up his hand to silence the room, and waited. "You can expect things will go on as usual." He enunciated each word carefully, his voice so cold, it put a shiver down my back. "The rules will be obeyed," he paused. "You will find me fair, but I am not in the habit of teaching, or for that matter, entertaining any, and or all, undisciplined actions. Every rule has a purpose. Break the rules and you will be disciplined…thoroughly disciplined!" he added, looking again from face to face, and ending up staring at Bob, then me. I wondered if Mrs. Haywood had told him of our last problem.

"That's all," he suddenly finished.

Gary began to clap again and a few joined in as both of the adults headed back up the stairs.

Two hours later, just before lunch, Mr. Schlicter arrived in the boiler room. He was dressed in white, but well used coveralls with frayed cuffs and collar.

"Come here," he said to Bob and me, and pointed to a spot on the floor in front of him. I had watched him come down the stairs from the ladder. I was hanging the coal sacks for the delivery that came every Wednesday during the winter months. Bob was mopping the water from underneath the shower in the middle of the room. I started to tuck the last corner in, while Bob poured the dirty water down the shower drain.

"Come here, now! This Goddamn second!" he yelled.

I moved quickly down the ladder, and Bob left the bucket on its side still emptying. We moved to the place he pointed to.

"Stand at attention," he paused. "You two, it appears, are anti-social. You," he continued, poking Bob in the chest with his finger, "are the tough one, right?" He didn't wait for an answer. "The remarks I made this morning were made with you in mind. And you," he said to me, "are supposed to be bright, but I understand you think you're tough as well. I know all about the two of you. You will change your attitude and do as I say, when I say it! Or, you are not going to like your lives here. Trust me." He looked at both of us in turn.

"You will both keep your duties here until I say. I see you both have made yourselves comfortable enough." He walked over to our beds and wiped the dust off the frame. "Pig sty," he said, looking at his finger.

"Now, you listen carefully, I expect this room to shine and sparkle. This equipment will shine everyday, all day. I expect this whole building to shine, and don't you look at me like that Mr. Tough Guy, or I'll show you what tough is. I will not tolerate insubordination. You'll see." He smiled.

"Now you'll take your meals down here until I'm satisfied this place is clean. Pigs don't eat with the rest of us. I'll be here in the morning to check on you. This place had better be spotless." He turned and began to climb the stairs.

"That," he stopped and pointed to our shower, "will have to come down."

"It's our shower," I objected.

"Are you being insolent? I've forgotten your name."

"It's Tommy, and no, sir. The coal dust gets tracked everywhere. We clean ourselves here, and the rest of the place stays cleaner. We'll clean up," I paused, "sir," I added. I think the sir did it.

"Very well, we'll see." He turned and left.

"Oh man, is he for real?" Bob asked, still looking at the door.

"Hey, look at it this way, we stay here which means our jobs with The Gimp are safe, and nothing much changes. It could have been worse," I offered. "He could have sent us both back to the dorm, and it would have been tough to get out with a dozen pair of eyes watching us all night."

"The dorms are full," Bob said.

"Whatever, nothing has changed. We just have to say sir to the little asshole that's all. That ain't so bad, Bob, right?"

He shrugged, and we got to work cleaning everything in site.

"You know," Bob said a little later, as he polished the brass gauges on the water lines, "I got a feelin' we're gonna have some trouble here."

"You notice he's slick on the stairs. He's not going to be someone we really want to tangle with," I warned, thinking how the man had quickly and quietly slipped up them, two at a time.

"Well," Bob answered, "he's half the size of Gary and he's no problem."

"I think Gary's told him. You know, about our visit," I said.

"Shit, you think!? You know it! This peckerhead is stickin' on our ass right off. That's what I'm talking about. Gary is a mother runner, we both know that."

Bob and I cleaned the lavs and the boiler room like never before. We had just showered and were adding some coal to hold the fire until it was set for the night, when Earl came down with a pail containing our suppers.

"Right," I said, remembering that the man had said we would be having our meals down here and after I asked Earl what he was carrying.

Earl sat with us past the dinner bell. He was in a talkative mood and went on about the new rules. "He put Gary in charge of the dorm."

Upon hearing that, Bob and I looked at each other.

"Trouble," he said.

"Trouble," I confirmed. "Now listen, Earl. If he starts bullying you, you come straight to us, understand? No more letting him push you around."

"Four of us are now Indian brothers." He paused to sniff. "We cut our thumbs, see." Earl held up his thumb to Bob and me for inspection. "We're blood now. He picks on anyone of us, all four of us will bash his brains out," he sniffed.

"Good luck to that!" I said.

"I guess," Bob said, "that you're blood with us and now you're blood with them, then," he hesitated, "we all must be blood together, right?"

"Nope," Earl said, "ya gotta cut your thumb and press it to another guy's cut thumb. Then your blood mixes, and you're blood brothers. I'm the chief, mostly 'cause you're my brothers and keep that fuckhead Gary thinking about..."

"Hey, never mind the language. Don't swear okay?"

"What d' ya mean?" Earl huffed and sniffled. "You swear, I heard you lots."

"We're older," Bob explained. "You're just too little to say words like that."

"Oh right!" Earl said indignantly. "You've been swearing since you were my age, I can remember."

"Not me," Bob said.

"Not me," I said.

"Oh, oh, Jesus you guys lie!" Earl got up and gathered the plates Bob and I had just been eating off of, and put them back into the bucket. "See ya!"

He lifted the pail and got to the landing, then looked over the railing down at us. "You guys are just bullshitin', right?"

"Hey now, watch the language, I said!" I yelled back at him.

"You keep that up and I'm gonna wash your mouth out with lye soap, and then turpentine your butt," Bob said.

Earl studied us for a moment, then without another word, sniffled and left.

Bob and I chuckled.

****

"He's a German," Mikey said, buttoning up his fly as he backed away from the pisser. Bob and I stopped washing the floor.

"Bullshit," Bob offered. "He would be in jail, wouldn't he? Shit, it's the Germans we're fighting. He's the enemy."

"That says it all," I said.

Earl and his three friends got their first caning during the first week of the new command. The blood brothers had stuck together when Gary had torn Earl's bed apart because he said it wasn't made properly. Gary gave them a pounding.

"They're too small," Mikey said. "You know, if he wasn't so freaking gutless, he would be tough. Those kids were flying off him as fast as they could light on him. Gary wasn't satisfied at giving them a pounding, so he went to Mr. Schlicter and reported them. They got two each, and that sonovabitch cut their asses with the cane. Right through their pants. There's four tender little asses, I'll tell you. That guy hits hard!"

" 'We're launched into a sea of shit', as The Gimp would say," said Bob.

"Or, 'batten down the hatches and lash yourself to the mast, Neptune's headin' our way for a donnybrook', as James would say," I answered.

Either way, we had an idea of what was coming after we finished with Gary.

"Maybe we should just kill him," Bob said, with enough seriousness in his voice to make me study his face for a second.

"Jesus, let's forget about guns, okay?"

"I gotta go. Don't tell Gary I said anything okay? Otherwise, I'll be getting the next caning and that Heinie can hit."

The Germans were called *Heinies*. It seemed to be our favourite name for them. The word spread like wildfire through the dorm. Schlicter was a Heinie...the Enemy. Whatever the hell he was doing walking around in Canada, was a mystery. And the Benevolent Daughters hiring him to teach us, and look after our place, just showed that women should leave stuff like that to the menfolk.

It was two days later when Bob and I were letting ourselves out through the chute, when I happened to glance up at Mrs. Haywood's darkened window, and thought I saw the curtain move.

We continued across the alley and knocked on The Gimp's door. Igor greeted us at the door and gave us a gift. His arm was out of the cast and he was sort of celebrating. In appreciation for our warning the night he was attacked. The gift was a can of tobacco and the fixin's.

It was a night for us to celebrate, too. We had worked off The Gimps debt. He had, of course, found a different place to store his booze rather than 'in the fat gut of that thieving bitch.'

The Gimp wasn't impressed. He refused to let Igor smoke around him, which is why we had never seen him smoke. But he rolled us our first 'weed'. Bob and I left The Gimp's place with our night's deliveries in our pockets, and lit up on our way to the corner. It was awful, but in time we would get into it.

The Gimp was right. We never got a call again to open the gate for O'Malley's visits, nor did we ever see him again. We heard on the street that Constable O'Malley had left the city force and taken his family to Vancouver where he was hired onto the force there the very day he arrived. Now the gate at the back of the home was only unlocked on Sunday for the children to go to Sunday school. The Witch was getting lonely. Not even free booze could hide it. She was too cranky for company anyhow. She was caning kids for problems in the classroom, and had caned June and Gladys for practically nothing. Gladys told Bob about it when he was sweeping the hallways. The Witch had Gladys take her clothes off, and caned her until Gladys cried out for her to stop. June had told Gladys the same thing, only June was forced onto her hands and knees, while Gladys had taken the usual position of bending over and gripping the edge of the desk, like we had to. Of course, we never had to take our clothes off.

But in time, Mr. Schlicter did all the caning. Earl said he was very strict in the classroom, and told Earl he had to do better. Now Earl didn't like school anymore. "*School*," said Earl, "was a German word." Mr. Schlicter had told them that the English used all sorts of German words, and French, and Roman. I found this confusing, to make up a language using everyone else's because the English weren't very *intellectual*, was the word he had said.

"You have to remember," I said to Earl, "he is German, and they are the enemy to the English, you can expect that. Actually, many English words are derivatives of the romance languages of Europe," I added knowingly, having read that in the front of Webster's Dictionary.

Earl sniffed at me, rolled his eyes, then turned to Bob. "You have to put up with this sh... stuff all the time, huh!" He nodded in my direction.

Bob returned Earl's look and shook his head. "Worse."

****

Earl brought the breakfast pail down to us in the morning. The boilers had been stoked and operating full blast as the chill of late October started to creep into the building.

"Hey you guys, there's trouble," Earl said excitedly, and went on with a sniff, "Mr. Schlicter saw you both in the lane. He said he couldn't be sure, but thought it was you climbing out of the coal bin."

"Where did you hear this?" Bob asked, looking at me.

"I was waiting in the kitchen for Mrs. Holmgren to fix the pail with breakfast. There's a door at the back of the kitchen to Mr. Schlicter's room. It was open, and he was talking to Mrs. Haywood, she was in her nightie. The door to her room was open. You can walk right from the kitchen to Mrs. Haywood's room, through Mr. Schlicter's."

"Shit," I said, remembering the moving window curtain from the night before.

Earl sat on the edge of the bed while Bob and I ate our porridge in silence, each of us trying to think up a story to explain our being in the alley.

"Piss on him," Bob said finally. "We just say it wasn't us."

I wasn't so satisfied with that, as I wondered when I looked up at the window, if he saw enough to really know it was me, or if as Earl said, he really wasn't sure.

"Where's he now?" I asked Earl. "Do you know?"

"He'll be gettin' ready for class. It starts in a few minutes. Hurry up, Tommy. He really gets angry when I'm late, and I don't want another stroke from this guy."

I left my breakfast and gathered up a box full of dirty cleaning rags and papers, and climbing up the chute, opened the door with my shoulder just wide enough to drop them into the lane. Then, I gently lowered the door so it wouldn't bang and slid back down to the floor from the chute. "There, we were just putting garbage out if he says anything. We were going to put it in the garbage bin this morning because it was too dark last night."

"You're slick," Earl said, in complete admiration.

Bob finished his last mouthful and swallowing said, "That fixes last night – what about tonight?"

"What do you guys do?"

"Can't ask questions Earl, and not a word to anyone. Bob and I have a night job, that's all."

"Keen, really keen. What is it?" he sniffed.

"I said don't ask questions, and stop pouting," I added.

"How's your ass?" I asked him, referring to his caning, and changing the subject.

"He hits so hard, I had blood in my underwear. Jesus, I gotta get, there goes the bell." Without another word, only a sniffle, he grabbed the bucket and bolted up the stairs.

Bob and I picked up the mops and pails and started to the boys' and girls' lavs for their daily cleaning. Bob told me to do the girls' when I first started helping, and I thought it was because he was so quiet and really awkward around any girls.

You had to knock and yell 'cleaning' before you went in, in case the girls were in there, but I didn't mind. What I didn't realise is that the girls' lav was dirtier than the boys'. Damn, Bob still snickers when he goes into the boys' and leaves me knocking and yelling in the hallway.

"We gotta open another bag of sawdust. This is so dirty, I doubt it's picking anything up." I threw the last of it into the front hall. Bob followed with a push broom, sweeping it into a hall-wide line to be picked up and reused. "Better tell the Witch, we're down to two bags."

"That's still two weeks," Bob answered.

"You know what?" I moved closer to Bob to keep my voice down. The empty hallways could funnel normal talk like you were shouting, even from the top floor to the front door. "That Goddamn Gary has to be settled with."

"You looking for another caning, this time by the *male witch*?" Bob pushed the line of dirty sawdust into a pile in the middle of the floor.

"That's a warlock," I said, as I slipped the large metal dustpan opposite the pile to Bob's broom.

"What is?"

"A male witch is called a warlock. Warren the Warlock," I mused.

A door closed loudly on the top floor, and fast heavy footsteps started down the stairs. Feet, then legs, then Mr. Schlicter's body came into view.

"Just the lads I wanted to see." He marched up to us. Bob kept working with his head down, pushing the last of the sawdust into one final small pile in front of me. I met his eyes. They were clear, pale, ice blue, the same colour as mine. "I want to know why you two were outside after dark last night."

I saw Bob sweep the final sawdust into the dust catcher, and I raised it to return it to the bag when the man grabbed my arm, and squeezing it painfully, made me drop the full pan onto the floor.

"I am speaking to you," he snarled.

I tried to jerk my arm away, twisting it around, but he only increased the pressure and shook me. Bob dropped the broom and charged in with fists clenched and black eyes wide and blazing. As quick as a wink, Schlicter released me, spun on Bob, and had him back-pedalling until he was up against the wall, with Schlicter's hand around his throat.

"So, you want tough, eh? You little asshole," he hissed. Bob struggled, but failed to break away.

The damn handle on the dustpan whacked the floor, alerting him, after I let it go to launch myself at his back. He spun Bob around, still clutching him by the throat, and eyed me over his shoulder. "So this is how you two want to play?"

"We were putting out the garbage!" I shouted at him.

Bob's face was getting real red as his hands clutched at Schlicter's wrists, trying to get his fingers off his throat.

"That so! You were doing what?"

"Putting out the garbage from the boiler room. Go look." My voice echoed off the hallways loudly, and doors began to open.

"You were putting out the garbage…what?"

"Putting out the garbage." What the hell was he getting at? Then, I remembered… "Sir!"

"Better." He released Bob shoving him away. "If you lie to me I'm going to give you something you'll not forget."

"Go take a look…" *Moron*, was what I had in mind, "sir."

He marched us ahead of him, down the stairs and out through the gate in the recess yard, to the coal chute doors. I prayed that someone hadn't come along and for some reason picked it up. But it was there, all the garbage I had put out this morning. I strutted to the pile and for a fleeting second was so pleased with myself. I snickered at him.

I sat in the middle of the alley trying to cut through the buzzing noise and discover which end was up. I had been hit. My cheek burned to tell me where...but who hit me? Of course it had to be Warren the Warlock, the name for some strange reason sticking in my mind. I started to get up. I hadn't even seen him move, the blow seemed to have come out of nowhere.

There was scuffling behind me, as I slowly turned, trying to keep my balance. Two blows I heard, then focussed on Bob curled up against the wall, his arms holding his stomach. There was something I wanted to say or do, but I couldn't even raise my arms to protect myself when danger walked over to me, and grabbing my arm, pushed me through the gate into the recess yard. I held onto the gate, and suddenly began to vomit. I heard Bob shouting and cursing someone, and a struggle going on. Oh right, Warren the Warlock. I heard my voice saying the name out loud, then I needed very much to sit down, and go to sleep. I fell back against the fence and sat. I tried to focus my eyes but I couldn't seem to concentrate. Everything I heard seemed so loud and clear; kids' voices and blue blurs were coming out of a grey wall.

"Tommy!"

Earl's voice.

"You asshole!"

Earl's voice...and a struggle.

I felt like smiling, you have to give the little bugger credit. I felt the hard cold steel of the fence on my face, and that was all I was aware of. Then, nothing.

*＊＊＊

It was much better to keep my head flat, raising it sent my stomach into my throat. At one time, I heard Bob moving around, and the sounds of the shovel, the cleaning of the grates, and the bucket of ashes flying high above me, but they seemed disjointed and remote, trying to penetrate the thick fog that seemed to float in and around my head. I tried to focus my eyes, but the dizziness swirled again, and I felt my stomach jump. I closed them, and allowed myself to follow the waiting darkness.

A man appeared through misted glass. At first, he hadn't a face, then it became clear. "James?" The face smiled at me. It was James! His white hair was long and flowing like his beard. "Oh, James, I've missed you." The face smiled, and the arms gestured across his body in a sweep, then out. I looked down. Oh James! He had both his legs. His smile grew wider and he started dancing a few steps of a jig, then he stopped and sat at the end of the bed. His voice came to me, yet his lips didn't move.

"Do you remember me tellin' yer brother wee Thomas, that no matter how tough ye think ye are, that one will come along tougher, and it will always be a surprise?"

I felt myself nod, and was relieved my head had stopped aching. "Is it okay where you are? Like, are you okay, James?"

I knew the answer even before I asked. He had both his legs and his smile had never been wider or softer. "I'm really tired, James. Could I come with you? It's not very good here now you've left. Everyone seems to leave. James, have you seen my mother? I can't remember what she looks like except maybe her mouth would be open like yours…was," I added, not wanting to embarrass him.

"Laddie, if ye came with me now, all would keen for ye. The little wee brother ye promised to look after, and what about yer elder kin? It would be more than they could bare."

"I'm scared, James," I confessed.

"Aye, lad, we're born with it. Do ye no' remember when we talked of it. We are all scared. Fear leaves with good, and harbours in the bad."

"Are you afraid now, James?"

"No, laddie." He smiled softy. "You're not afraid here where I am. Nor is yer mother."

"Could I see her?"

"When the fears come upon ye, lad, close yer eyes and see me," he said ignoring my question. "See me, lad," he repeated, and got up from the bed. "Look, see me." He placed an arm behind his back and the other across his middle, and smiling, did his jig on his two good legs. "See me, lad," he laughed, and began to grow distant.

"James!" I called. "James!" And I awoke and sat up swinging my legs over the bed. My head didn't hurt anymore as I looked around the deserted room. My stomach fought the slight dizziness, and slowly settled.

A little later, a cold draft flooded into the room, seconds passed as Bob slipped down the coal chute. He pulled off his cap and coat and threw them at his bed.

"You okay?" He moved to the boiler and opened the draft, then held his hand to the escaping heat. "It's snowing like a bitch out there," he continued, without waiting for a reply. "I got all the runs done, but the last ones of yours weren't too happy about hanging around 'til eleven on a night like this."

"What time is it?"

"About 12:30. Christ, I'm frozen." He squatted by the draft drawer, then got up and jumped on the firebox lever, and swung the doors wide open. The fire sprang to life, as the air swept into the box and soon glowed a cherry red. "I hate to say this, but I think the Warlock saw me leave. I came back through the cemetery to scout the place out before I came in. Has he been down here?"

"I don't know. I slept, I guess." I wanted to tell Bob about James's visit but I figured it would sound crazy, and kept quiet. Yet, I thought of him doing the jig and grinning at me, and I knew regardless of what anyone would ever think or say, that comfort would never leave me.

I was more than a little shaky as I got up and moved to the furnace beside Bob. "Do you miss James?" I asked, as I stared into the red glow. I felt him look at me for a second, then back to the fire.

"More than Momma even," he whispered.

It snowed through the day and continued into the night, as Bob and I slipped out the chute doors. We both looked up at the window to see if there was anyone there, but the snow was so heavy that we could barely make out the dark shape of the building. The snow was now over our knees in depth, and we had to push our legs from the knees forward to make any progress. I looked back at the deep tracks and knew he wouldn't have to see us. It was all there for him to see, probably for the rest of the winter.

"Keep moving past The Gimp's, Bob," I called to him, as he was breaking trail.

"Why?" He stopped and looked back to me, puffing.

I thumbed over my back to the path we had made, without turning. "Go out onto the street, then we'll go around the block and it'll look like we came from a different direction. From our footprints."

He turned, and we pushed past The Gimp's car. By the looks of the snow piled high on it – it hadn't been moved today. Our try at the ruse didn't work. There was no traffic other than ours. The streets had been empty for most of the day. judging from a few ruts now smoothed over by inches of snow.

At the corner, Bob stopped. "Gimp's place is dark."

"Yeah, I saw, but he must be there. Where the hell is he going to go without the Maxwell?"

"Christ, Tom, you can't see five feet in front of you. This is ridiculous."

"Yeah, the tracks are there for the reading. Let's just hope the bastard wants to keep his own ass dry and warm more than he wants ours."

We turned and walked around the deserted streets and came back to the alley from the other direction and joined our earlier footprints at the coal chute doors. There was just a chance if the tracks weren't looked at carefully, it would look like they were passing by and not originating from the chute.

"Ain't gonna be any runs tonight anyhow, I'll bet."

I opened the doors, and Bob went down the chute. Resting the door on my back, I followed, quietly bringing the door to rest as I slipped down the chute. I caught a glimpse of the Warlock standing by our beds, as I landed and bumped into Bob at the foot of the chute.

"You young champions do alright for yourselves." He grinned, and held out his hand filled with money. Our money!

I glanced to my bed where the mattress lay halfway onto the floor.

"You put that back," I demanded. He grinned at me and folded the bills and put them into his pocket.

"Almost certainly," he laughed. "This money come from things you find in the alley?"

Bob stamped the snow off his boots, and moving toward the furnace, brushed his pants, never looking, or responding to the Warlock. Then, near the furnace, he casually picked up the grate key, and turning, he faced Warren the Warlock.

"Put the money back," he said, matter of factly, raising the pick end of the key, that was used for clearing clinkers from the grates, up head high.

The smile vanished from Schlicter's face. "Well, I was going to spare you two another lesson but..." He moved towards Bob and lowered himself into a half crouch.

Bob raised the heavy bar, gripping the grate nut on the bottom menacingly. "You ain't gonna hit us again." His black eyes were wide and wild.

Turning, I saw a piece of four inch lumber used to cap the doorway when the bin was full of coal, laying against the bin wall. I quickly picked it up and moved in. The Warlock's attention was totally on Bob and the bar he held over his head. He rocked forward and Bob swung the bar.

It moaned through the air and Schlicter sprang back. The bar missed him by a foot or more, clanging off the cement floor. Bob struggled to get control of it again when Schlicter moved in, then saw me out of the corner of his eye as I swung for his head. He threw himself back, and I missed his head by inches, but the board caught him on his foot. He yelped, and moved quickly to the bottom of the steps. Bob gained control of the bar, and raising it, moved towards him and swung. Again the bar moaned, the point arching through the air, fell with great force. Schlicter threw himself backwards, and landing on the lower steps, rolled barely out of the way, as the pick end hit the step an inch from him, taking out a large splinter of the wooden step. I moved in again, raising the board over my head. There was honest terror in his eyes as he flipped himself onto all fours and scrambled up the stairs

"You crazy little bastards!" he screamed, and feeling safe, turned halfway up the stairs. I stopped at the bottom, as he was out of the reach of my board, but Bob didn't. He leapt onto the lowest step and swung yet again, and again Schlicter was forced to throw himself backward onto the steps, as the pick split the handrail in a third near miss.

Schlicter scrambled on all fours again to the top of the stairs, then stood facing us. Bob almost casually, yet with great determination, climbed the stairs, the bar again raised over his head, then he stopped, as there wasn't enough room for me to help him regain control, and he would surely lose the bar to Schlicter if he swung it again.

"So this is how you want it," the Warlock hissed through clenched teeth. "I'm going to fix you little bastards good. You wait and see." His eyes narrowed.

"The money," Bob yelled back, breathing heavily. "You won't get any heat in this place until you give us back the money."

"That's right," I added, and moved up beside Bob, "we worked for that." I didn't feel that was entirely true; the running was so easy and I liked it, but I was so outraged by his theft that I was desperate.

"I mean it," Bob said, "I'll pull that fire and in two hours this place will be froze solid."

I could see the Warlock was thinking about it. It really would create a halibaloo.

"We'll tell them you stole our money," I added, trying to sound convincing.

"Well," he said finally, "maybe we should see how cold your little brother and your sister will get, or maybe Earl should get a couple of extra strokes added to the caning he's got coming, like a dozen?" He raised his eye brows and smiled at us.

"You touch him and I'll kill you," Bob warned.

"Oh my, my, such tough talk," Schlicter retorted, apparently unimpressed.

He didn't fool me, I saw the calculation in his eyes turn to terror when he was dodging the key Bob swung. Bob held back nothing in his intent to put that pick into him.

Bob slowly lowered the heavy key taking away the threat, but I rested the board on my shoulder and gripped it tightly, just in case.

Schlicter reached into his pocket, and gripping the wad of money, pulled it free and threw it over the railing, where it broke apart and fluttered to the floor.

"I'm a long way from being through with you two!" he said angrily, and turning, opened the door and left.

I lowered myself onto the steps and rested the board between my legs on the step. I felt flushed with victory. "God, for a few minutes there I thought you were going to kill him."

"For a few minutes there, so did I," Bob answered. Looking at me, he grinned, and the madness went out of his eyes.

"Do you think he'll come back after we're asleep?" I asked, as we slipped out of our wet clothes. "I don't think this is over."

Bob went and got the grate key and propped it next to his bed. "Just in case."

"That's not going to make me feel easier, Bob. We need to stop him from getting in here." I took the board I was using as a weapon and went up to the landing. I wedged it against the middle of the door and the railing post. It worked. "That should do it," I said, feeling better about sleeping.

We climbed into our beds after setting the fire for the night. A moment later, it dawned on me that he could get at us from the coal chute. It would mean he would have to go outside, and around to the coal chute – but would he? He could slip down the chute and be at our bedside before we could move. I knew all too well how fast Schlicter could move.

"The coal chute," I called to Bob, who was almost asleep. He was quiet.

"Yeah, he would," he answered.

We lay there for a few moments.

"Let's put some flatter pieces of coal at the top of the chute. He couldn't slide down without us hearing him. We'd have enough time to be able to fight him off," I said, then remembered my board holding the door was too far away.

Bob sighed and slipped out of bed and went up the chute in his stocking feet, scrambling all the way. I handed him some of the flat pieces of coal and he placed them to rest on the rim of the chute to stop them from sliding. "Three oughtta be enough," he said, and slid back down the chute before slapping the dust off his butt and feet.

I went over and found a section of pipe used for the brush when cleaning the chimney. It would make a lance for fighting. Different, but it would hold the Warlock at bay while Bob was struggling after a swing. There was no doubt that Bob would be intent on hitting him.

I placed a length of pipe by my bed, and with Bob equipped with the key, we hunkered down in our beds and slept, lightly – but we slept.

Earl didn't show up with our breakfast or lunch. Bob and I had cleaned the boiler room and had the mops and pails ready for the lavs. The kitchen and cafeteria had to have their weekly cleaning, which consisted of washing the floors, walls, chairs and tables. Going without meals, as part of the discipline was not uncommon, however, the Warlock's words about giving Earl a caning were a concern. Bob and I figured the lack of meals was part of the discipline.

Our bellies rumbled, but we packed our cleaning stuff up to the door, and I removed the board I had placed there. I went to open the door but it was locked! I wiggled the door handle and felt the catch turn, but the door wouldn't open. I tried with both hands and the door opened, pulling Gladys into the room.

"Oh," she gasped, as she regained her balance. "I tried to push and it wouldn't open, so I was trying to pull at the same time as you, I guess."

She pushed her hair back off her face. "How are you guys doing?" Her face was serious, as she looked at me, then Bob.

"Where's the Warlock?" I asked, looking nervously out into the doorway, expecting him to jump in any second.

"He's gone to the classroom last I saw." She turned and pulled out a small pail and brought it into the room. "I don't think you better go out there," she added, looking at the equipment gathered on the landing.

She then stepped in and closed the door. "Earl got disciplined this morning. That's why I'm here. He wouldn't let me come earlier. Look." She held out the pail. "It's bread and water. That's all he would allow Mrs. Holmgren to give you. He hit Earl so hard, he can't hold anything with his hands."

"What did he do?" Bob frowned.

"He used some kind of belt, or strap, and pounded his hands with it. Earl can't even open the door. His hands are all purple and swollen."

"That's it," Bob said, "this place can freeze!" He started down the steps. I stepped around the buckets and started after him.

"He said if you try anything, Earl will get a caning, and a strapping," she said hurriedly.

This brought us up short. Bob and I looked at each other.

"He said I would need to be punished too," she finished softly, as she carried the pail down the stairs behind us. "Bob, Tom…" She set the pail down and sat on the end of Bob's bed. "He scares me…" She looked around surveying the room, and then back to us. "He looks at me funny-like. He stares at me sometimes, and he stares at June, and sometimes he pushes up against us. Once he had her against a wall in the back of the kitchen when she was lighting the fire early in the morning, and he was rubbing her…" she paused, "well, top and bottom. June is afraid of him, too. He doesn't do anything when Mrs. Holmgren is around, but he waits until she's out of the kitchen, tells June he wants something, and then follows her. She turns on the kitchen light and he turns it off. I think he's doing things to her in the dark."

"She should go to Mrs. Haywood and tell her what's goin' on," Bob said.

I agreed with a nod.

"That's what I told June," Gladys answered. "But June says he's doing it to her as well, and therefore, she wouldn't do anything about it, and June would get into trouble. She's really afraid."

I remember Peter explaining one time, a long time ago, that men do *it* to women. He put a finger on one hand through a hole he made in the other, and pushed it quickly in and out. It was a silly thing and we all laughed. I couldn't imagine men and women putting their hands together and doing that *jiggin*, as Peter said, with their fingers. Now listening to Gladys, it must be true. But surely not fingers, but if not, what?

Bob looked at me and broke off any answers I may have pondered. "We shut down?" he asked.

"Uh, well," I stammered.

"You do and Earl will get it! I know he means it, and I will too," she added with obvious concern in her voice.

We sat for a few minutes trying to figure out what we could do. Gladys looked anxiously first at Bob, then me, but said nothing.

Finally, Bob reached down, and seizing the bread lying across the rim of the bucket, broke it in half and offered me a portion. "How long is this going to go on, did he say?"

Gladys shook her head. "I don't understand it, you two keep doing all the work and he really seems to enjoy picking on you."

"We had a pip of a tiff here last night. He tried to steal our…" I hesitated, the money was our secret, Bob's and mine, and I wasn't sure if he wanted anyone to know about it, "…stuff," I finished. "We caught him and kinda made him give it back, or else we were going to shut off the heat. We had the door blocked so he couldn't come back when we were asleep. That's why you couldn't get in."

Gladys frowned and opened her mouth to speak when there was a noise outside our door – voices, and hard things being dropped to the floor. Bob dropped the bread on the bed and bolted up the stairs. I ran and picked up the grate key and followed. At the top of the stairs, Bob grabbed the piece of lumber and slipped behind the door. I paused at the top of the stairs, the key raised. Below, Gladys had moved out into the middle of the floor and stared up at us, her eyes wide and mouth open.

Unfamiliar voices sounded outside the door. Then, metal objects being scratched onto the surface of the door.

"'E wants the bolts top 'n' bottom," one voice said, "then a bloody 'ole cut through and this 'ere box to it. Get crackin' mate. I'll get the welder movin' on the lane and it'll be secure before dark." The voice moved off and the silence was taken up with fresh sounds of a metal bit crunching into the door.

Bob relaxed and leaned against the wall. I lowered the key. Gladys came up the steps and stopped at the door.

She looked puzzled as she spoke to Bob. "Are you going to turn off the heat?"

Bob looked at me. I had no answer. My fear was for Earl, and for that matter, Gladys as well. I remember when she could whup Bob. Hands down. She was a toughie. But now, she was all soft and lumpy, the way girls get when they grow up. I felt regret for her. She didn't seem tough anymore, and there was no doubt that Bob could pound her easily. Maybe even I could. It was a shame to see her lose all that. I felt sorry for her. I shook my head to Bob. Warren the Warlock had beaten us, unfairly I felt.

"No, we won't, yet. You tell him if he does anything to you or Earl one more time, we will. And," I went on, "if he does, you and Earl have got to come down here. We'll be safe here together."

Gladys studied my face for a moment, then opened the door startling the worker who was on his knees working on the frame.

"Gave me a fright, miss. I's told there was no one in 'ere." He got up to let her pass.

Gladys glanced back briefly at me, a frown creased her forehead, then she stepped around the tools that were strewn in the hallway and left. Bob pushed the door shut before the worker could look back from watching Gladys walk away.

The workers weren't finished by dark, but by what would have been suppertime, they had us locked in. The final noise of their construction being the rattle of chain against the coal chute doors.

Bob and I both tried the door to the hallway first, then pressed mightily against the doors of the chute, but failed to budge either. The heat from the rivets melted the snow around the chute doors then quickly froze securing the doors from anyone getting in, as well as out. No need for the flat chunks of coal on the chute ledge any longer.

The bread and water Gladys brought us had a pleasant surprise. It wasn't water, but a clear chicken broth. We devoured it in a minute and not a drop was wasted. Bob and I agreed it was the most delicious meal we had ever eaten. However, around bedtime, hunger again was tapping us on the shoulders. We stoked and set the fire, then showered with all the hot water we wanted, before crawling into our beds.

I lay there for a few minutes thinking of The Gimp. He was gonna be annoyed when we didn't show up. It would be two nights in a row and I knew we'd lost our jobs. The Gimp was all business, and the streets were home to lots of kids who would gladly do the runs for less than Bob and me. Then a thought struck me, just because we couldn't get out, that didn't mean the Warlock couldn't get in.

I got up and went to the landing and propped the board against the door. It was now a standoff, I thought, before remembering we didn't have food, and he had Earl. The Warlock had won, but it was only round one.

The light burned out shortly after I had climbed back into bed. The only light came from the cracks around the furnace door and a soft glow from the lower clean-out door's partially closed vents.

I stared at the light.

"Bob? You asleep?"

"Just about, what?"

I could see the dark shape of his head move as he turned to face me. "How did you know about a bootlegger?"

"Jesus, Tommy, I remember Pa sayin' there's one in every barber shop and train depot across the country. He said it was the only thing that saved a lot of starve-outs. You mean you didn't know?" he asked, drenching me with sarcasm.

I ignored it because I had another question.

"What's *it*?"

"What?"

"*It*, what's *it*?"

"What are you talking about?"

He was awake now and there was a slight annoyance in his voice.

"Gladys said the Witch and the Warlock were doing *it*."

"When? Oh yeah. They were doing it."

"Yeah," I said, "what's *it*?"

Bob was quiet.

"Do they mean copulating when they say *it*?"

"Cop-u what?"

"I read a book where it said animals copulate to propagate."

"Jesus Christ, Tom, speak English."

"Is that what *it* means?"

"I don't know what the hell *that* means," he snorted.

I waited, then when Bob didn't say anything, I remembered what Peter had done with his fingers, and reminded Bob. "This," I showed him.

"I can't see, but I think I know what you're doing," he paused before continuing. "It's to do with a man and a woman. He lies on top of her and something happens. He gets it wooden, and they make a baby that way."

"Is he trying to do that to June, too?"

"Yeah, that's what Gladys is saying, I guess."

"Doesn't seem right," I pondered, "June is just a girl."

"June is sixteen," Bob said. "Girls get married and have babies sometimes a lot younger. But you're right, it doesn't seem right."

"Gladys is too young for him, right?"

"I dunno, Tom. Gladys is fourteen, soon to be fifteen, and she sure looks like a grown lady."

This wasn't helping. "If he hurts her, we'll get him, won't we?"

Bob lifted his head from his pillow. "I don't like him, Tom, but we're going to have one hell of a time fixing him good. He doesn't look tough, but he's so damn fast it scares me."

I remembered what James had said to me and now I repeated it to Bob. "No matter how tough you think you are, someone will come along who's tougher, and it will surprise you," I said. "James said that."

"I had a dream about James," Bob said.

"What!?"

"A little while back. I had this dream, and James was in it. He had his legs and was on a ship."

"Oh man, that's incredible, so did I but he wasn't on a ship, he was here, and he had his legs, both of them, and he was doing a jig. He was real happy."

We both sat up and looked at each other in amazement.

"You're kidding me, right?" Bob said.

"Not a bit," I answered firmly. "That's it Bob! I knew when he left he would never leave. That's it. We won't let him leave. Ever!"

"Jesus, Tom, you sound spooky."

"Don't you see it, Bob? People don't die if you remember them, they're just...kinda outta sight. James will never die for me," I finished.

Bob didn't answer me. He flopped his head down on his pillow, and in a short time I heard his breathing become even in his sleep.

I wasn't tired, what I really wanted was a way out of our predicament. I lay back down in my bed and watched the dim fire glow reflected on the ceiling. The Warlock had us locked in and I felt very trapped, and I hated it. I had a fear that coiled in my belly, and made me wish I was bigger. Much bigger!

We were up early the next morning and replaced the light first off, then stoked the fire and opened the draft to liven the fire up. In the corners of the room, the concrete sparkled with frost. It had to be very cold outside. We loaded the bucket with ashes and raised it to the roof, then tripped the car and let it run down the track and spill into the hopper. The next bucket seemed a lot heavier and I almost didn't make it. I was more than a little breathless as I settled the bucket back down on the floor.

"I'm out of energy already." I walked over to the bed and flopped down.

After a breakfast that never came, we heard sounds once again at our door. We quickly climbed up to the landing, Bob with the key in hand. We watched as a saw blade moved noisily back and forth through the lower part of the door.

After a while, a square was cut out and dropped onto the landing and a strange bearded face appeared through the hole.

"Well 'ello there, you been 'ere long?"

"We live here," I answered.

"Really?" His eyes looked around. "Cracky."

"I say." He looked up at the board wedged against the door from the railing post. "Would you be kind enough to pass me the piece that fell through?" he asked, referring to it with a nod of his head.

"Yes, sir." I turned the piece sideways and handed it through the hole to him.

The face reappeared. "I say, are you lads locked in?"

"Is the door locked?" I asked.

"Quite."

I nodded. "Then quite."

"I'm to put this box on the door. Do you know what it's for?"

I shook my head and shrugged.

"It's not much bigger than a mail box." It was half question and half statement. "I say, do you lads get out of here?"

I shrugged again. "I guess not, unless you open the door for us," I added.

"Well, bloody 'ell. You must be a pair of scallywags. Is that it?" the face grinned.

I shrugged for the third time. "I guess."

"Well look, lads, I want no trouble," he looked at Bob holding the key, "but I must come in to set some bolts for this 'ere contraption." He looked at the board. "Do you mind awfully?"

I lifted the board and rested it against the wall behind the door.

"Good chaps." The face disappeared and we heard a bolt slide on the other side of the door.

The door opened and a pudgy body belonging to the face entered, looking first at me, then Bob.

"I say, caught you working did I?" He eyed the key nervously.

Bob shook his head.

"Oh well, you won't run on me, or do anything rash, will you boys?"

"Maybe you should give us a key," Bob said.

"Oh, there's no key. No locks, just slide bolts top and bottom."

"Anyone can get in then?"

"Well, I suppose. There is a spot for locks on the clasp, but there aren't any ordered that I know of."

Just then, we heard someone coming down the stairs. Both Bob and I armed ourselves and backed away from the door to the head of the stairs. Then the sound of a sniffle as the feet approached along the hall. We relaxed and lowered our weapons.

"My word," the man said, raising his eyebrows, and quickly got down on his knees to work.

Earl stuck his head into the doorway and sniffed. "I got your bread and water." He looked at us, then at the man's legs, practically covered by the half open door.

"Hi," he said to the legs. The worker didn't answer but continued to set his tools up. Earl stepped through the door, and passing us, carried the pail down the stairs setting it on the floor. He reached under his shirt and brought out several fried porridge cakes. "Hide them," he whispered, "I think that Mr. Schlicter might be here soon."

I took the cakes and slipped them under my pillow.

"Mrs. Holmgren got caught putting soup into your pail. He grabbed me leaving the kitchen and looked, then he asked her if she liked working here. He made me dump it into the sink. Not even back into the pot. I get water now, too."

"Sonovabitch," Bob said out loud.

"You don't mean me, surely?"

All three of us jumped, and looked up to the landing where Schlicter stood, hands outstretched on the railing, looking down at us and smiling. He turned his head to the workman. "Knock off for a few moments."

The workman got up quickly with a 'yes, sir', and retreated out the door.

The Warlock watched him leave, then turned back to us.

"Show your brothers your hands, Earl."

Earl raised a pair of hands that were badly swollen and purple up past his wrists.

"That's what you are," Bob said angrily, "a son of a bitch!" He shouted it out.

Schlicter laughed, "Another week of bread and water."

"Now," he said angrily, his smile long disappeared, "you know how this is going to play out. You'll stay down here, locked in like animals, until you become civilised. Any more problems and I'll send Earl down to show you the results of your antics. Is that clearly understood?"

The three of us said nothing but looked down at the loaf and pail at our feet.

"I'm waiting?" he shouted angrily.

"If you lay a hand on Earl again you sonovabitch, I'll get you if it takes the rest of my life," Bob said, in an even, low voice.

I looked up at Bob and saw once again the madness come into his eyes.

"Bread and water for a month!" he screamed back. "Earl get up here."

"Remember what I said," Bob finished.

"Please you guys, *don't*," Earl pleaded in a whisper, then solemnly climbed the steps to the landing.

"By the way, Thomas, Mrs. Haywood put your name forward for a scholarship to the Benevolent Daughters. There's a new school started for gifted students, only a few blocks from here. Unfortunately, the new headmaster of this school here is not going to approve it. That's me!" He turned and pushed Earl out the door ahead of him. I heard Earl sniffle as the footsteps retreated.

Earl brought us the bread and water. And it was water. Every day the Warlock searched him before he left the kitchen. The loaf and small pail were left in the box in the door where we retrieved them each morning, and we would leave our crap bucket for Earl to empty and return every evening.

Bob started a frenzy of exercises each day. He did countless chin-ups on the shower pipe, which squeaked and groaned with each one all day. Then he got me shifting the chunks of coal with him, from the back of the bin to the front and then throwing them back again. Soon I was doing chin-ups as well. We loaded the ash bucket brim full and started raising it up and down to the ceiling with the pulley, but ran into problems when the live coals sputtered and snapped while the bucket was overhead, sending down showers of hot sparks around our ears. We got around this by filling it only three quarters full. This worked for weight, but we found the bucket began to rest on its side on the trip board rather than tipping over and emptying itself down the hopper to the bin outside in the alley. It became necessary to push it from the bottom with the grate key.

We began to compete with each other. At first, he left me far behind, but what my body lacked in power, I made up in stamina. Even on our restricted diet, I seemed to do better. Of course, his short compact body slimmed, while I became downright skinny. I could run up the wall far higher than he could, but couldn't touch him when it came to chin-ups.

On one occasion both of us were doing chin-ups when the clamps supporting the shower pipes broke free. Lucky for us they didn't break, but we had no way to reach the ceiling. The stepladder, used to reach the ladder on the wall going up alongside the chimney, was too short, and the broken clamps were too far from the chimney ladder to reach.

I stood on the floor trying to figure out how we might get from the ladder to the top of the plenum that sat above the furnace, when I was momentarily side-tracked. I looked for a long time at the chimney ladder used by the workmen who came once a year to clean the chimney. It went to the roof. It was four stories above, but it was outside!

While Bob lifted chunks of coal over his head and smashed them down on other pieces, I grabbed the stepladder and placed it under the ladder on the wall, and climbing it, reached the lower rung of the wall ladder. Behind me, the crunching of coal stopped before I reached the trap door in the ceiling.

"What the hell you doin'?"

I looked back down at him and had to laugh. All that was showing were the whites of his eyes, the rest of him was coal black, literally. "Let's see where this goes."

Turning around, I put my hand against the door and praying it wasn't locked, pushed. Pieces of dirt and dust came down around me as the door raised. It was heavier than I expected and I had to let it fall back. I climbed up to the second step from the top, and putting my shoulder to it, straightened up. The door raised then fell away on its hinges with a bang. A chilling rush of icy air pushed past me down into the room, then warm air started up into the hole.

The first thing I saw was a hurricane lamp and a covered box of tapers hanging on a big nail driven into the chimney. Above it, was a large coil of rope. I had seen the workers use it for pulling up the sections of pipe onto the roof. The chimney brush lay just beyond the chimney. In the dimness of light, I could see huge timbers cut at all sorts of angles and lined up as supports, disappearing into the blackness. A long, grey, concrete wall ran almost from the edge of the trap door and faded into the blackness. Heavily insulated pipes broke through the chipped concrete above my head and angled off into the concrete wall, and wires wrapped around little, white, glass spools travelled everywhere. The smell of musty mildew filled my nose so strong, it seemed I could taste it. But there was room to walk if I crouched over. Boards were laid between the white spools to walk on. Above me, on the chimney, the ladder continued on, and I could see another door.

It was like another world, a chill of excitement and cold made me shiver. Picking up the lamp, I slipped back down the ladder and closed the door. Another rain of dirt and dust showered over me, as I carefully made my way back down the ladder. We were going to need our coats on, that's for sure.

Bob took the lantern from me, giving me both hands to get back onto the stepladder.

"What did you see?" he asked, as I moved over to the stepladder that he held for me.

"Get your coat on, man. We're going exploring!" I answered excitedly. The ladder goes up to the top and we can get onto the roof."

"Yeah, I know that."

He didn't share my enthusiasm, that was clear.

"Man, it's neat!" I thought I would give it one more try.

He ignored me, instead shook the lamp. "Just about full."

"C'mon get your coat." My excitement refused to be dampened, so I got my coat off the nail driven into the support post for the landing. As I slipped into the sleeve, I glanced at a familiar sight, but one I had never paid much heed to. It was a door, I could see the rusty hinges. I've looked at it a thousand times. It was smaller than the trap door by the chimney, but it was a door. With one arm in the sleeve I dragged my coat over to it and squatted down. Letters were painted on it at one time but the moisture had almost peeled all the paint off, 'UTILITIES'. I had never seen it opened and judging by the rust on the hinges, it hadn't been open for a long time – years probably. Still squatting, I turned to Bob, "You ever seen this open?"

He looked up from tinkering with the lamp, first at me, then the door in front of me. Shaking his head he went back to the lamp. It would save for another day I figured, but the excitement of this second discovery had me bouncing off mountaintops. Screw you Mr. Warlock... *SIR*, I thought. We weren't locked in yet. My fear (I had to admit to myself it was a fear) of being locked in, now melted away.

It took a good ten minutes of talking to get Bob to even put on his coat. He just kept looking up at the door in the ceiling and made it clear he wasn't really interested in exploring. At first, I was disappointed, and found myself trying to almost sell him. Then I got miffed with him. "Do you want to get out of this Goddamn hole or not?"

To which he responded by looking around and shrugging. "Ain't that bad."

Finally, I got him into his coat and up through the trap door. He moved very slowly and cautiously, hanging onto the ladder, almost reluctant to move. It took me almost an hour from first opening the door, to getting him through it. I was about to pull myself through when I looked down into the room and suddenly realised that the board I used to wedge the door shut was not in place. If the Warlock came in…all hell would break loose. Again, I slipped back down the ladder carefully, then started up the stairs when Bob called me.

"Tom! Where the hell are you? Tom, Goddamnit!"

"Just a minute." It was strange, I didn't ever remember hearing Bob sound that way. Panic – that's what it sounded like. I put the board against the door as far away from the little opening as I could, so an arm couldn't reach through and knock it aside.

"Tom, Goddamn you…" came from the hole in the ceiling. I quickly climbed back up the ladder, and as I put my head through the hole, Bob grabbed the front of my coat and hauled me through. "You ever do that again," he stammered, while shaking the hell out of me, "and I'll give you the damnedest pounding you ever had."

"What? What the…what's wrong?" I asked, completely bewildered. I could feel my butt moving back through the hole. If he let go of me I'd end up on the floor of the boiler room. I grabbed his coat and held on.

"I don't like it up here," he hissed, "don't you screw off on me again."

"Okay, okay I promise. Calm down."

I brought my knees up and wedged myself against the side of the hole so I wouldn't fall, then let go of his coat. "I had to wedge the door in case the Warlock came down while we were up here."

Bob was panting and looking around wildly. He wasn't even listening to me.

"Oh, shit," he said almost to himself, looking back through the hole. "I ain't goin' no further."

He sat back on the plank then jumped, his arm flying above his head. "Shit, shit, shit, that's all. You gotta get me outta here!"

"What is it?" I looked around.

"The wires. They burn," he gasped. "Oh! Oh! Oh! Christ I can't get down!"

"Bob, it's okay, I'll help you"

"No, you can't, I'm gonna die up here."

"Bob, it's okay. We can go down." I had no idea what had happened, or what was happening now.

"Help me okay? *Okay*?"

"Yeah, easy," I said to him, slipping back onto the ladder and moving down so the top rung was clear. "C'mon." I watched his two feet come through the hole and he sat there. I grabbed his feet. "Roll over on your belly and I'll put your feet onto the rung."

"Oh shit, I can't, I'm gonna fall. Ouch! Ouch! Oh, these damn wires!"

I gripped his feet firmly, my arm wrapped around one rung, "Slowly, on your belly."

By the time we got back onto the stepladder and onto the floor, I feared for my life. There wasn't anything worse I could imagine than what he threatened to do to me when he got back onto the floor. I saw the lamp still sitting on the floor where he had left it. Best not to mention that, I thought.

"Oh," he groaned, and staggered to his bed where he collapsed. "You better go." He suddenly sounded completely in control once again.

I said nothing. I was just grateful that the Bob I knew was back. I was afraid I was going to be pulped by this time. He laid back and closed his eyes. His hands still trembled and the faint odour of urine came from him.

I climbed the ladder and closed the door, then put the lamp out of site under my bed.

Bob fell asleep with his coat still on. I laid on my bed trying to figure out what had happened to him, and then... where that dark space led to.

Late in the afternoon I was awakened by continuous knocking above my head. For the first moment I laid there trying to figure out where I was. I heard Bob stir, then his bed creaking as he got up. I swung my legs over the side of my bed. A cold layer of air just below the bed surrounded my feet. Bob picked up the key and went up the stairs.

"Who?" he asked, and a voice muffled to my ears, but young, I could tell, said something and Bob lifted the board.

"Okay, Earl."

The voice said something else, and Bob dropped to his knees and opened the inside door to the box.

I picked up the waste bucket and started up the stairs.

"The war's over!" Earl said excitedly. He had shouted it though the open door on the outside of the box.

"That's good, come on in," Bob added, as he got up from his crouch.

"I can't," Earl said, "the door is locked. There's a big lock on the bolt here. Where's Tom?"

"Here," I answered, setting the stinking pail down.

"The war's over, Tom. The Germans surrendered. We won!"

"That's great, Earl." I moved the bucket into the box. "Here's something for the Warlock."

"Phew." Earl pulled the bucket out the other side. "Pa will be coming home," he said excitedly. "It's all over."

The full meaning of what it meant to us hit Bob and me at the same time. Pa would be coming back and we would be out of here – away from the orphanage, the Witch and Warlock. I punched Bob on the shoulder and we laughed together. I crouched down to the hole in the door and saw Earl's smiling face...his *bruised* smiling face that sported a huge shiner. I stopped laughing.

"What the hell happened?"

"Gary beat me up," he answered.

"Didn't your friends help you?"

"They tried. Only Stephen was there and Gary beat him up, too."

"And the Warlock, where was he?"

"He won't do nothing. Gary's his ass kisser."

Bob and I looked at each other grimly.

"You okay now?"

Earl nodded. "The Warlock is *doin' it* to Mrs. Haywood and Gary says that's 'cause he's the headmaster of the orphanage. She doesn't teach anymore, mostly stays in bed or goes out shopping. How long are you guys going to be in there?"

"I don't know Earl, until that sonovabitch decides to let us out," Bob said with a scowl.

"He don't beat me anymore but Gary does, and he don't even get caned."

"I know Earl, but if we do anything, he'll come after you."

"Yeah, I know," he answered dejectedly. "I got to go, see you in the morning. Mrs. Holmgren feels awful about you two not eating good food," he added, then the outer door flipped and we heard him sniffle as he hauled the bucket away down the hall.

"How far is Europe away?" Bob asked, sitting on the edge of his bed.

"Thousands of miles," I replied.

"You think Pa will be long?"

I shrugged. By my reckoning another minute seemed long.

I had unscrewed the dead light bulb that had lasted only a few days, then partly opened the doors of the firebox to allow light and extra heat into the room. Earl had said that morning that the Warlock wanted all the heat we could give as the temperature outside had dropped to minus fifty degrees. Even then, the building creaked with the cold, and according to Earl, ice covered the inside of the windows. The walls in the boiler room began to whiten with frost, and walking near the corners, you could see your breath. Bob and I had pushed our beds closer to the furnace as the cold seeped through and rose higher and higher in the room.

"We're only gonna have enough coal for a week at this rate."

Bob looked at the bin and nodded. "We better tell Earl to tell Schlicter."

Bob sat on his bed and pulling up his knees, wrapped his arms around them and stared into the fire through the crack of the partially opened doors on the firebox. I watched him from my own bed as he rested his chin on his knees. Neither of us said anything, a slight roar could be heard from the draft through the firebox doors. The coal burned cherry red amidst the white ash but the gauges refused to rise.

"I'm afraid of heights," he said, still looking at the flames.

"No, *really*?" I answered, in mock disbelief. It was the wrong thing to say, or the wrong way to say it. He turned his head and I saw his eyebrows raise to about three-quarters madness. "I'm sorry Bob, I guess you scared me. I didn't know," I finished lamely, but the threat disappeared and he even smiled a little…I think.

"When I come in here, I never look over the railing, I always watch the step in front of me." He paused for a moment, then went on, "I dream of falling. I can feel it happening. Do you ever dream of falling?"

I thought about it. "Once," I answered. "In the dorm I actually did, and I fell out of bed."

"I'm at a real high place, and everything is far below me. Then I feel my balance sway me forward and I fight to get it back, but it's too late, and I fall and watch the ground come speeding towards me. Then I hit, and that's when I wake up. The whole thing goes through me when I get even a little ways up. Like yesterday, and I feel like I'm gonna lose my balance." he finished.

"Bob," I said, after waiting a while. He made a sound in response. "Do you think we should maybe make up with the Warlock. You know, say we're sorry?"

"You're gettin' fed up with this?"

"I'm not doing a very good job of looking after Earl, and I want to go to school. It may be too late this year but I really want to go."

"Those are good reasons," his voice broke, and he cleared his throat. A lower voice came out of his mouth. It sounded neat. "I'm afraid the Warlock would still…" his voice went back to normal, "screw us around." Bob turned and looked at me. "I think he likes bullying kids. Us. You and me. At least the Witch was fair, she made sure you got punished, but it happened to everybody. But you know, now that I think of it, she kinda enjoyed it, too. Do you think some people enjoy hurting other people?"

"God, I hope not, that would really be bad. The Warlock doesn't like us," I stopped to think about it, "because we fight? Maybe?"

"You know, Tom, if you look at it that way, you know, worried about Earl, look where you are. I guess I didn't do a good job either then. And how about Gladys, Momma wanted her to look after us. I don't think with us here locked in and everything, that she did a good job."

"It's not her fault," I leaped to her defence.

"Exactly!" Bob said. "It's too late to go to school like you said, so let's tough it out. Pa will be back soon and at least we're outta here."

"I wonder where we'll go. You think back to Viking?"

"I don't know." Bob raised and lowered his shoulders with a sigh.

"You don't like him do you – Pa I mean."

"He hits too many times. He even gave you a beating, do you remember it?"

"I think so."

"You let Foxy out and he got into the chicken yard. Killed three of 'em right off."

"Foxy, yeah I remember. He had a pointed nose."

"He kinda looked like a fox," Bob said.

"Pa couldn't catch him and threw a boulder at him, missed, and it went through the kitchen window. That riled Momma. He hit you so many times you went into convulsions. You bit your tongue. Momma thought he'd killed you. You were twitchin' all over the floor. Gladys picked you up and took off outta the house. She fell, and you went into the snow and then stopped twitchin'."

"Didn't remember any of that."

"He's got a terrible temper. His eyes widen up real crazy-like and you know you gotta get out. Hell, I lit out when I saw that, even if he screamed for me to stop and threatened me with every cuss word in the book. Don't go near him if he looks wild."

I couldn't help but smile at Bob. It was obvious whom he took after.

"What are you grinning at?" He flew off his bed and jumped onto mine. I laughed out loud, and we wrestled until he sat on my chest and I couldn't move.

"Hey you're getting hair all over your face."

Bob rubbed his face, "So?"

I laughed, and bucked him off, over my head, but he spun and grabbed me again from behind before I could move away from him. He put his face against me and rubbed his hairy cheek against mine. I reached around and got a hold of his coveralls behind his head, and ducking forward, pulled him over me. He somersaulted off the bed and onto his ass on the floor. I wrapped my arms around his head and held on for life's own sweet sake, but it wasn't long before I was back on the bed and pinned down again. We were both out of breath as he rolled off onto his back, and we laughed. This time, his voice broke again, and he sounded like a little girl. We laughed at that even harder.

Earl kept up the bucket brigade as the days rolled into weeks of being captive. Earl and his friends were given the cleaning of the lavs and cafeteria, with Gary as their overseer.

****

"The three of us are going to kick his ass good," Earl whispered through the box.

"And Warren the Warlock is going to do the same to your asses," I finished angrily. The frustration of being locked in, and as a result losing our jobs, was starting to tell on me, along with not going to school.

"We ain't gonna take any more of this shit!" Earl hissed back at me.

"Bob and I have been doing chores for over a year."

"Not with this asshole picking on you," Earl countered right back, and sniffed.

I took a deep sigh and pulled the pail out of the box.

"Here," Earl fished in his shirt and produced two large muffins and threw them right through the box where they landed at my feet.

I picked them up and looked back into the box but the outside door was down. "Thanks!" I loudly whispered to his departing footsteps.

Bob and I wrestled now just about every day. It started out as fun as long as I got licked, but I was learning fast where I could get an advantage – by not trying to match his strength, but by using it. The sessions took longer and longer. I never won, but the smile left his face, and his eyes sometimes got mad in frustration as I turned his attacks away time after time. I kidded him about his voice. It bounced from high to the occasional low at first, then low with the occasional high as time went on. That got him.

I guess it was just a matter of time before the inevitable happened. In his anger, he swung and missed as I rocked back and countered with a left over his right that found the target. Actually, his lunge carried him into my left. I saw his eyes roll for a brief moment and he went down on his knees in front of me. Before I could do anything he shot straight up with a head butt into my stomach that drove the wind out of me. Helpless, as I searched for air, he grabbed me by the front of the coveralls and I had a first class view of his fist coming towards me. Just when it filled my eye socket it mercifully stopped. I caught the anger subsiding as his eyes cooled and I struggled for air.

"That was a hellava good shot." A drop of blood sat on the corner of his grinning mouth.

I could only nod.

We continued to wrestle everyday and we never lost our temper with each other again; instead, we learned from each other.

Our routine of stoking the fire, setting the flow of hot water to the building, and hauling and dumping ashes, became monotonous. I read and reread my study books for the mid-grades and knew them to the punctuation marks. Only the coal deliveries, and any news that Earl would bring us, stopped me from going crazy. Bob pounded the sawdust sack until his knuckles became bumped with calluses and the sacking began to wear thin enough to leak the stuffing onto the floor. Another sack would be added over the last, and he would start again.

I'm not sure why, but Bob's fear and lack of interest had left further exploration of what lay beyond the trap door in the ceiling, and the one marked 'utilities', by the wayside.

It was a Sunday. The weather was good enough that the entire orphanage had gone to church. We heard them chattering away and the back gate to the recess yard clanged shut several times.

"I'm going up," I said to Bob, pointing at the ladder. I just had to do something.

Bob gave me a little girl's wave, "bye."

He held the stepladder while I took the lit lamp in one hand and pushed the trap door open with my shoulder.

Again, the cold air rushed past me as I climbed into the space and shone the lamp around.

"Close that door."

I looked down at him and felt the warm air coming up. I nodded and closed the door.

The reflector inside the lamp gave more than enough light to see the back walls of the room. The floor was about four feet below me. Large timbers rested in what must be the back alley wall and travelled over me to the long grey concrete wall. I shone the light around. Cobwebs hung from the top of the ceiling but there wasn't much dust. The light caught something in the far corner of the space. I could make out the door from here. It must have gone to the alley. Careful not to touch the white spools and the wires running between them, I quickly covered the space to the door.

It really was a door. I swung myself down off the boardwalk onto the rough concrete floor. It was an old plank door crudely built and unfinished. I pulled the large metal ring fastened to it but it wouldn't open, although it did move. I set the lantern down and pulled with both hands and the door scraped open...to a wooden planked wall. Disappointed, I kicked at the wall in frustration. It was solid. There had to be something worthwhile up here, I was sure of it. I picked up the lamp and shone it around again. Apart from the door, I was surrounded by solid concrete.

I climbed back onto the boardwalk and retraced my steps. There was no way but up the ladder by the chimney. I pushed the second trap door open and found a similar crawl space but it was only about two feet high. The insulated pipes that pushed through the concrete below appeared at my feet and travelled a short distance in two different, yet alike, groups, then disappeared through the floor which must have been the boys' and girls' lavatories.

Everything looked so different but that must be it. I crawled over and looked down through the holes chipped out of the concrete where the pipes disappeared, and recognised a small part of the shower room. The other set of pipes must be for the girls' room. A set of planks ran over to it. Carefully, I crawled over, looked down and recognised it immediately. God knows, I had cleaned these rooms often enough. Down inside the room, smaller pipes travelled out of sight. To the chamber water closets over the toilets, I had bet. I crept back along the planks, and looking off into the darkness of the crawlspace, I noticed a source of light. I headed for what was a vent overlooking the stairs. I had to be between the main floor and ceiling to the lavs. I looked down behind me and sure enough, there were the doors. I looked back through the crawl space and began to identify things in this new world of mine.

I crawled around to every corner of this space but only found a small crack near the stairs. I couldn't quite see all the stairs and retreated back to the chimney. Man, this storage area was dark.

I climbed the ladder, and in a few feet, found myself in a narrow confining space next to the chimney. Runs of wires ran in pairs under the ladder. Near the top, I found a nail hole and put my eye to it. The main hall was below me. I could see the door to the girls' dorm and the steps going up to the next floor at the end of the hall. Above me, yet another trapdoor. I left my peek hole and climbed up to it. Through it, I followed six pairs of wire that travelled at the side of the boardwalk, then left in pairs to travel through a wall at intervals about a room's distance apart.

I discovered another crack and found myself over the centre of the main hall. Something was wrong. I was against a wall that didn't allow me to travel any further towards the front of the building, but obviously I was only half way there. In the back of my mind I was hoping to get around the kitchen area. Unless I found a way around this wall or through it, that wasn't going to be possible. I crawled on the boards until the final set of wires left and the pathway stopped, then I crawled to the end wall of the space and found nothing further. Returning to the chimney, I went up through another confined space on the ladder, and following the last four sets of wires through the next trapdoor, I discovered, what must have been, the attic. It was cold, but not as cold as the first level above the boiler room. The roof was barn-like and I could stand as it was twice my height, with walls of rough planks. In the lamplight I could see small piles of sawdust that had leaked out from between them. I could smell the familiar odour of pack rats, but holding the lamp high and turning myself in a circle, couldn't see any return glow of beady eyes. I didn't hear any scurrying, nor the warning chatter they give when alarmed.

What was to be the last trapdoor, I was sure, sat at the top of a half dozen rungs of the ladder. I put the lamp down and climbed to the top. Putting my shoulder to it, I strained and managed to crack it. Swirling snow blew around my head and into my eyes. I quickly relaxed allowing the door to reseat itself, and climbed back down. I squatted down between the wires and looked around.

The wall that ran down the centre of the building continued to plague me. The empty classroom was to my right. I was sure I must be over the hall or at least half of it. I looked over that way and saw a large area lit up from light below.

I left the boardwalk that followed the little white spools, which continued to be evident, trailing off down the attic like railway tracks, and stepping carefully on the edges of the planks, made my way over to the lit area.

The plaster had fallen in the corner of the room leaving the wood slats underneath uncovered. It was easy to make out the corner of the white square of the penalty box on the floor of the empty classroom from the top of the crack. Lowering my head, I could see part of the desk and the open door to the Witch's den at the far end.

Moving back to the walk, I followed and found another crack over the doorway to the empty classroom, plus a vent high on the wall between it and the Witch's room. I searched over the rest of the floor which was actually the ceiling of the Witch's den, but found no other cracks.

Below, I heard the sounds of many footsteps and muffled voices. They were back from church. I quietly made my way back to the chimney and down to the boiler room, careful to close the trapdoors gently behind me all the way down.

The warmth of the boiler room actually felt hot as I closed the last trapdoor. Bob sat on the edge of the bed and watched me climb down the ladder and transfer myself over to the stepladder. It wobbled precariously, but remained upright until I was safely on the floor.

"Well?"

I explained to him about getting up to the roof and the various views from the cracks in the plaster, not to mention my disappointment in not being able to get to the front part of the building where the kitchen was.

"You could see into the girls' lav?"

"Crappers and showers," I confirmed, "wanna see?" I turned and grinned at him knowing the answer before I asked the question.

I brushed the dust off my clothes and hung my coat on the nail. "Christ, did you die when I was gone?" A terrible odour from the bucket pervaded my nostrils.

"Three day's worth of bread."

I knew what he meant. The diet didn't really lend itself to a daily smeller. I had the same problem.

"Christ, I'm hungry! I don't ever remember being so damn hungry! You think Earl could smuggle us something extra?"

"Damn, that would be good, I'm starving, too." I sat on my bed.

"I got no energy, I'm farting like crazy and my head aches," he complained.

"Let's start a club," I answered. When I sat still long enough the very same problems caught up to me.

"Earl gets checked out before he leaves the kitchen. The Warlock is watching him pretty close. Christ, I would hate to see him get caught."

A rap on the door above us stopped our conversation and we left our beds to climb the stairs. I heard a faint sniffle from the other side of the door.

"Get your bucket." I turned to Bob as he started up the stairs behind me.

"My bucket? Bullshit, get it yourself."

"Bob, that's yours and I'm not carrying it. Let's get it the hell out of here."

"It's you that doesn't like the smell...oh alright, I'll get it," he sighed, and started back down the stairs listlessly.

I bent over and lifted the flap. Earl's bemused face looked back at me.

"You hungry?" he asked.

"Who us? Hell no, we just learned how to digest coal," I replied in strong sarcasm.

"Look!" Earl said, and turning put a pot of cream soup into the box, then buttered bread with a thick layer of red jam spread on. I quickly counted them, six slices.

"Christ!" I grabbed the pot and smelled the soup. Chicken! My mouth started watering and my stomach snarled with impatience. I set them down and watched as Earl finished off with a stack of cookies.

"Oatmeal."

I snatched them up and bit into one as I heard Bob come up behind me. He set the bucket down and fell on his knees beside me. "Oh, God, a feast," he whispered, and began stuffing his mouth with bread and jam.

I shoved the rest of the cookie into my mouth and holding my breath, grabbed the bucket and set it into the box. "Fair exchange," I managed around the cookie.

"Oh, God. Did somebody die?" he wrinkled up his nose.

"I asked him the very same thing."

Bob had by now grabbed the bread and soup pot and headed downstairs.

"You ain't suppose to have this bucket emptied until I come back with the other one later on."

"Please, Earl," I held up my hand in front of the box.

"Okay, but the Warlock is betting you're gonna get sick. You might want another bucket."

I heard Bob below me slurping the soup.

"Thanks, Earl. Gotta go or there won't be anything left if I don't."

I dropped the flap in front of his laughing face and got up. I heard him sniff then cuss something. The bucket I suppose.

Later, I lay back on the bed, slowly losing the fight with the Warlock's prophecy as my stomach churned, threatening to unload. In the meantime, our butts were battling in a whoofing contest.

After a while, the sweats that came with the stomach problems left us both at pretty much the same time.

Bob got up to stoke the fire so I swept up the dust. The sweeping had to be done slowly as the broom simply lifted the dust back into the air, and within moments of finishing, it would resettle over everything.

We had just settled back to our cots when the snapping sound of the bolts on the door sounded from above. Bob flew to the key while I bounded up the stairs, and removing the board wedged into the door, moved behind it at the ready.

The door opened a crack. "You boys enjoy your meal?"

It was the Warlock's voice. Neither Bob nor myself answered. The door opened a little more. Bob rested the key on the stair railing, remaining alert. I backed as far away from the door as I could, feeling the railing of the landing across my back. It gave me enough room for one good swing if he attacked me, and I could run up behind him if he went for Bob. He didn't come any further and while I couldn't see him, I knew from Bob's eyes, raised in anger and wariness, that they were facing each other.

"Good food?" He sounded almost cheerful with the question.

Bob studied him for a long moment, then did something I didn't catch for a second. He leaned over the railing and looked down at our empty cots. "He wants to know if you liked the food?" he repeated the Warlock's question, then hesitated for a second.

"He nodded," Bob said to the Warlock.

The Warlock opened the door as if to come into the room. Bob raised the key preparing to swing it and the door closed back again.

"Now look boys, I was hoping you would come to your senses. You know, I could keep you locked in here and on that prisoner's diet forever if I want. Look," he said, I have a real good proposition for you."

Bob said nothing but held the key ready.

"You boys need your money making enterprise? I could let you out and we could split. Fifty-fifty. What do you say?"

Suddenly the door opened further, and I could see the end of something that looked like a baseball bat protruding from the other side.

"You boys…" Schlicter said, but was cut off when Bob swung.

The bat disappeared and the door swung shut in a flash, and just in time as the key clanged off it. I rushed forward, the board raised over my head, but the door never reopened.

We could hear a commotion and the bat falling on the hall floor, then the snap of the bolts being rammed home.

"Okay, you little bastards! Starve!"

I quickly wedged the board back into the door.

"Don't got but two days of coal left!" Bob shouted back.

We went back to our cots.

"Do you think he would starve us?" I asked Bob, as I reassured myself of our safety by standing in the middle of the floor, making sure the board was still wedged and the door secure.

"Don't care," Bob said, "he was carrying a bat."

"You think you fooled him by looking over here and making believe I was here instead of behind the door?" I asked, sitting on the edge of my bed.

"He was coming to see, I'm sure," Bob answered. "When he brought the bat out from behind his back I got skittered."

"That's when you swung?"

"That's when I swung. We ain't never goin' to do business with that asshole and he ain't never gonna get the chance to give us another beating." He looked at me and his voice was filled with resolution. "Pa should be home soon," he went on, "and it may not get better but at least we'll be able to move out."

I knew what Bob meant. I couldn't remember what Pa looked like, but it was the first time I heard Bob say he was looking to get out of here. It felt good to finally share that with him.

"Do you think now that we're old enough, Pa won't beat us anymore?" I asked Bob.

"Yeah, maybe," Bob answered, after a moment's thought.

"He had a real fearsome temper I remember. Do you remember him breaking the window when he threw a rock at our dog? I had him tied up in the field behind that old hay rake so Pa wouldn't find him."

"He did," Bob blurted.

"What?"

"Least ways he found the rope." Bob shrugged, looking into the fire through the crack in the firebox doors, squinting with one eye closed.

I sat for a minute trying to understand what he was saying. "You think...?"

"I dunno." He cut me off, then looking at me, shrugged. "Really, Tommy, I didn't want to know. I was gonna look for a grave but," he hesitated, "maybe he gave him away," he offered.

"Yeah, that must be it," I answered. I didn't want to know either.

It seemed later than usual when we heard a knocking on the door. It was like an alarm. Bob and I both jumped like there was a fire. It was the familiar sniffling that allowed my heart to stop pounding. I bent over and pushed the flap open and found Earl's face on the other side.

"Here's your bucket." He swung the bucket from behind his body and pushed it into the box. His eyes were darting to one side of the box. "Ain't no food." He sniffed as the door flopped closed, and then I heard him complain to be let go of as two pairs of boots retreated away.

I pulled the bucket out of the box and carried it back down to the corner and slipped it under James's commode. I turned to Bob and saw he was still staring into the firebox.

"I think there was someone with Earl at the door. Probably the Warlock," I surmised, going back to my own cot. "No supper!" I finished.

"I ain't surprised," Bob answered. "Why'd he come with a baseball bat but to get a reason to keep us hungry."

I wasn't so sure about that. I sure wouldn't come near Bob without something to fend him off with. When Bob swung that heavy metal key, the look on his face showed he was intent on hitting what he was aiming at. I wasn't about to argue with Bob's reasoning regarding the baseball bat, but continued to wonder if the Warlock might have been sincere. No, I thought, Bob was right. It would be a pact with the devil. We would end up working for the Warlock, not The Gimp. I dismissed the thought.

"Do you think Pa will get him for keeping us this way?"

Bob snorted and rubbed his face. "Unless Pa has changed a hellava lot, I would guess he would either say nothing, or add his own beating on us."

He got off the cot and walked over to the commode and took a whizzer into it. "God," he said as he turned away, "I can't remember being so damn hungry."

My stomach rolled loudly in total agreement. I lay back on the bed then rolled over onto my stomach to try and ease the hunger. It was best to lay on your stomach I found, particularly when it was full of gas as it was now from yesterday's feast. Bob did the same thing and we started a whoofing contest, allowing certain points for length and loudness of the farts. We ended up in fits of laughter.

"Hey, Tommy, do you think farts would burn?"

"I read it was a gas. Methane they call it. Like swamp gas." I noticed his eyes start to roll like they did when I gave too much information, "...but I don't know." I actually did, but I knew when people started rolling their eyes, it was best to shut up.

Bob reached under the bed where we kept the tapers for the lamp. "Let's see." He got up and lit it through the crack in the firebox doors.

"You're not holding that under my ass," I said emphatically, as he walked toward me with the burning taper.

"Oh, okay." He sounded disappointed, "you take it."

He handed me the taper as he unhooked his coveralls and lay down on his cot before rolling on his stomach. "C'mon," he urged, as I stood there wondering if he was really serious.

I stood by his cot with the burning taper in my hand. "You're serious?"

"Okay!" he cried, as he arched his back.

I lowered the taper as close to his ass as I dared, and the sound of gas chattered his cheeks, but nothing happened.

"Christ, this is crazy," I said, moving away from the smell.

I was about to blow out the taper when Bob suddenly put his hands under his hips, and raising his legs, spread them, and braced his feet against the wall. "I'm gonna burn your balls off," I laughed, as I put the taper just above them.

"Wait…now!" he cried.

To my amazement, there was an instant puff of blue flame that was gone in a split-second. I was about to shout out our success, but instead, found myself on my back, on the floor, as Bob shot off his cot towards the shower, gripping his crotch and knocking me over.

"Jesus!" he screamed, trying to hold himself and turn the tap on at the same time. "Oh Jesus," he cried, slapping water between his legs.

I held the dying taper in my hand, ignoring it until it burnt my fingers, forcing me to drop it. I struggled for breath between my gales of laughter. Even as he shut the water off and stomped towards me, with annoyance in his wild black eyes, I still couldn't stop myself. He stood over me, and between my outbursts, I could smell singed hair. All I could do was shake my head helplessly, completely out of breath.

He left me in disgust and went to his cot and took the sheet off to dry himself with. I sat up trying for control, but when he dabbed himself with the sheet tenderly between his legs, I lost it again, and fell back. It was minutes later when I struggled to my feet and made my way with bleary eyes to my cot, and fell onto it. A moment after that, I heard Bob's laughter, and I started all over again.

Later, we began a night of fitful sleep for the both of us. It was the first hunger all over again. After awhile you seemed to get used to it, but the first hunger after our feast brought back the knowing pain.

****

The tunnel on the other side of the small utilities door, with its creaking rusty hinges, was pitch black. The hurricane lamp that I held showed several long pipes that had been punched through a cement wall leading into the alley. The broken concrete around the pipes showed the scars of hammer marks, and left a large area around the pipes for rats to use the tunnel as a run. The scurrying noise was everywhere and pairs of glowing eyes showed from either end. Above our heads, other pipes, some abandoned stubs, had their wraps hanging in tatters, chewed up no doubt, by the rats. Above the pipes ran electrical wires that could be tracked easily by the white glass spools that reflected the light as they went down the tunnel. A stale, sour smell hung in the cold, damp passageway.

"You seen enough?" Bob whispered. "Or should I close this door to keep our furry cousins from joining us for some warmth?"

I had to admit to myself that the tunnel that carried on towards the front of the building didn't look like it would get us to where I had in mind. "Let's take a look," I answered, as I held the lamp back up towards the front of the building. "Close the door, but not tight," I added. I didn't want to be locked out.

There was enough room to walk beside the large pipes with their discoloured wrapping – caused by the rat droppings, I supposed. Our voices seemed huge in the tunnel, so I quieted mine to a whisper. "Close it, but don't push it too hard."

"I heard you the first time."

We moved slowly down the tunnel and came to a second door. The inside of the utilities door showed well-chewed edges from the tunnel side, but the second door, which was metal and rusty, but in good repair, had been installed much more recently. Maybe even James had done the work before Bob had come down. The second door surprised me. After we had laboured an hour to finally get the first wooden door open from the boiler room, I thought this second door would be difficult, but it swung open easily, revealing the continuing black hole of the tunnel that lay beyond it. Bob pushed it closed just enough behind us so that the rats couldn't pry at it.

Together, we moved down the tunnel. Suddenly, we both stopped and held our breaths. Listening, we could hear a murmuring coming from far off in the distance of the tunnel. We looked at each other, but just as quickly, the sounds stopped. We started advancing as quietly as possible. Even the sound of our boots on the wet cement floor seemed loud.

The pipes we were walking beside turned abruptly into the wall and I noticed the electrical wires above our heads also turned into the wall. We could no longer follow the pipes and wires because the space was far too narrow. We were forced to belly over them.

"That's gotta be the wall I kept running up against," I whispered to Bob, as I shone the lamp towards where the pipes and wires entered it. The opening was only about a foot wide, and the pipes and wiring disappeared into its depths. I turned the lamp back to the tunnel that was now empty, except for the beady pairs of eyes that shone briefly before the rats took refuge in the dark depths of the tunnel. Obviously, they were getting around the metal door from somewhere.

Again, from somewhere down the tunnel came a sudden rattle and bang.

"I will Mrs. Holmgren," said a familiar voice, followed by the fainter sounds of dishes rattling and another bang. A rumble, accompanied by a squeaking noise, carried on for a few seconds, then stopped.

"That was Gladys!" Bob said, then covered his mouth as his voice echoed back loudly.

"It's the kitchen," I whispered excitedly, "the lift."

Holding the lamp high to show the way, we continued. The end of the tunnel became clear and our hearts fell. We continued towards the end and as we approached, we could see that it turned sharply to our left. Maybe, just maybe…

We turned and were forced to stop. A wire screen separated us from the lift, and we had three rats trapped standing against the screen on their hind legs, chattering a warning to us. We both put our backs to one wall and slowly moved forward. The rats, seeing an opening, scrambled past us against the opposite wall, back into the darkness of the tunnel behind us.

We moved to the screen. On the other side of it, three milk cans rested on the lift platform. There was a door on the front wall of the building. Actually, it was half a door, as I remember helping Mrs. Holmgren unload the lift more than once. It was used for the dairy deliveries. This meant it had to be the door on the ground level beside the steps to the main entrance of the building. I hadn't noticed it, but we had to have been walking up hill, for the boiler room was below ground level.

Shining the lamp up, we could see only one level up the shaft. The screen held us back too far into the tunnel to see any further. But, it did show boards nailed between the runners of the lift which acted as a ladder.

The screen was secured tightly to the roof, floor, and both walls of the tunnel with large bolts. Bob and I both tried together to move it, but it remained solid in its steel frame. Faint noises of murmuring voices and movement came down the shaft from somewhere above us. Wordlessly, we began to retrace our steps back down the tunnel. Ahead of us, several rats scampered. We began to herd them with small steps in front of us. One stood in front of Bob in defiance, and in a second, its warning chatter turned into a squeal of pain as Bob kicked its ass out of sight back down the tunnel. In seconds, the scurrying noises stopped and the tunnel was empty. We got up on the pipes and pulled off layers of hanging pipe wrap, stuffing it into the holes of the concrete at the alley end of the tunnel, hoping to close out the rats.

As we left the tunnel, I noticed one set of beady eyes looking back at us from inside.. My wonder at where they came from dissolved when I remembered the openings where the pipes and electrical wiring went into the wall back in the tunnel. There didn't seem to be any place they couldn't travel if you didn't make a real effort to keep them out.

We had no sooner gotten back on our cots after closing the small door, when we heard the door of the box open above our heads, and the scrape of the pail being placed in it.

I rose from the bed and climbed the stairs in time to hear footsteps fading back down the hallway. I opened the door and saw a half loaf of bread beside the pail of water. The

Warlock was taking his threat into the second day. But where was Earl? It wasn't like him to just drop off the food without saying something. We always got some news about what was going on. I pulled the pail out with the bread, and turning, looked down to Bob, who stood in the middle of the floor with a scowl on his face.

"It wasn't Earl. There was only one set of footsteps that I heard."

I went down the steps and we sat to eat.

"We must get through that screen," I said, after clearing my mouth of dry bread with a gulp of water. My stomach kicked back a belch of joy as the food hit it. The pangs that centred themselves in our middles most of each day, finally subsided. After our meal, drowsiness would come upon us and we would sleep for several hours before waking up with the hunger pangs all over again.

"We could pry it loose with the grate key," Bob answered.

"Do you think we could do it quietly? It seemed pretty tight to me."

"Yeah, It's got to be quiet," Bob said.

We both thought it over as we finished our food.

"Do you think we will ever be full again?" I asked, as I got up from Bob's cot and went to my own. The drowsiness was creeping up on me.

"I've forgotten what it is to be full. I think I got sick before I got full that last time," Bob answered.

I rolled on the bed to lay on my stomach. "How's your butt?" I asked Bob, and began to chuckle at the memory of the thing.

"Screw you," Bob shot back good-naturedly.

Bob had spent a lot of time bent over and spreading the cheeks of his butt to let the water from the cold shower run over the singed area. The vision would never leave, I'm sure.

"Tomorrow will be the test," I warned. On this diet it took about three days to build up a crap.

"Should be okay, I think," Bob said. "The farts have stopped burning it."

Knowing Bob's limited sense of humour, I figured I better not push it any further. I could envision Bob chuckling at me as I tried to drink water through painfully split lips.

"We have to do it on Sunday," I said, referring back to the screen, "or maybe at night. No…" I followed up, "not at night, everything is too quiet. We'd wake the place up. I know!" I added quickly, "the noisiest time in the building is when the tables are set and cleared. It's got to be then." I paused, waiting for a response. "Right?"

Bob's soft snore was my only answer.

****

It was difficult to tell time. With no light coming through the cracks in the coal bin doors, our only idea of time came from Earl's – or his new substitute over the last three days – routine pickups and drop-offs.

Even this routine wasn't exacting. Sometimes we were fed before the regular meals in the cafeteria and sometimes after. Earl said it was when Schlicter decided to do it. Everything was so isolated in the boiler room from the rest of the building. In the good weather, we could hear the kids in the recess yard, but not in winter, with the temperatures seldom above zero, the recess yard was seldom used. The only way we were going to be able to get that screen out of the way was to get into the tunnel and sit and wait until there was enough noise. At least that's how I figured it.

I awoke to the sounds of the shovel scraping on the cement floor. The large pieces of coal were gone some time ago. This meant the feeding of the fire had to be at shorter intervals. The coal had dwindled down to a smaller and smaller pile. Bob was closing the draft and keeping a smaller fire as long as possible. This of course, meant less heat for the building. Bob told the Warlock we only had enough coal for two days and that had to be longer than two days ago. It seemed a strange way to punish us as the boiler room was still the warmest room in the building, and we were quite comfortable moving our cots closer to the boiler.

I rolled out of bed and put my boots on before my feet touched the freezing floor. Bob had tripped the double doors to the firebox closed. It meant we weren't going to get any extra heat for ourselves because the open doors created a draft, which gave a greater appetite to the fire for more coal and we were near empty.

The hunger made us both shiver. I was forced to climb the stairs and check the box in the door. Only the empty waste bucket awaited me, so I retrieved it and went back downstairs. Bob stood by the fire with raised, questioning eyebrows, but seeing my face, walked to his cot and slumped down on it.

"Get the key," I said, as I put the bucket in the commode. "Let's see if we can get into the kitchen."

Minutes after entering the tunnel we heard a loud banging coming from the boiler room. Bob and I looked at each other in panic, and I blew out the lamp and followed Bob back through the door into the boiler room. Closing the door quickly, I moved an old wooden box in front of it in an attempt to hide it.

I turned to follow Bob's attention to the coal chute doors where continued scraping and banging sent a flurry of ice and dust down into the bin. The familiar rattle of the chain being drawn through the handles of the bin doors sounded, and then the door's hinges screeched in protest as they were raised.

Sunlight streamed down along with a blast of bitter cold air that sent us both running for our coats. Looking up, it seemed like it was a long, white tunnel and at the far end, Earl's small face grinning and waving.

"We got coal, on a sleigh!" he shouted down to us. Then his face disappeared and the Warlock's replaced it, dour and unfriendly.

"Not too soon," he said to someone, as he studied the small mound at the bottom of the bin. "We're going to need two more loads at least."

His face was replaced by a coal monger's who took the sack off his shoulder and tumbled it in mid-air, landing it on the chute with the opening spilling out the coal, as he grasped the bottom, and jerked it upwards. The coal rattled down the chute and skidded on the bare floor, bouncing off the bin walls, and raising a black dust, impossible to contain. Bob walked over to the damper valve to turn on the water so to spray the hanging sacks and catch the dust.

"Don't turn it on, it will freeze."

Bob hesitated, studied the sprinkler over the coal chute, nodded, and left. He walked to the doors of the firebox and opened the draft wide, then lowered the double doors into a split. The smoldering fire leapt to a fiery new life as it sucked in the chilled air.

"Hey, Tommy!" Earl called down, his head reappearing on the side of the white tunnel. Bob and I walked as close as we dared. The black coal dust was suffocating.

"What?" I called back.

"We had to dig this whole Goddamn alley from Jasper Avenue to here."

"Lotta snow?"

"Lot? It's Goddamn three times over my head, almost ten feet. Been snowing for five days straight," he sniffed. "They had over twenty men with shovels. Horses couldn't even move. Snow let up last night and even us kids helped. Got two more sleigh loads on Jasper that's been there for a week. People been pinching it earlier, but then nobody could move. You okay?"

"Hungry," I admitted. "What time is it?"

"It's almost three, I think. Starting to get dark. I got you some food..." Earl's voice trailed off sharply as his head was jerked out of sight.

"The hell you will." Gary's face appeared. "You shoulda been up here to work, you lazy bastards. You don't deserve anything to eat. Maybe tomorrow or the next day." His face disappeared, and the rumblings of the next sack of coal coming down the chute covered Earl's protestations.

The bin was over half full when the chute doors were closed. As much as we wanted to keep the boiler going full blast, the temperature gauges had climbed close to the boiling point and we were forced to close the drafts. The black dust had settled everywhere and Bob and I began our cleaning routine as our stomachs growled in constant protest. In the end, we couldn't finish. Neither of us had the energy and we took to our cots.

After we rested it was too late, I was sure, to go back into the tunnel. The building would be settled down now. We would have to wait until morning for the breakfast noises to cover our break out to the lift. Sometime, in what I suppose was still the night, I went and checked the box once again. It remained empty. As I came back down the stairs Bob swung his legs over the side of his cot.

"Christ, this is no good," he said, holding his stomach, "can't sleep."

I walked straight over to the key. "Let's go," I said. "I don't give a shit if we get caught."

Bob eased himself into his boots. "Let me stoke first."

I moved the box that I had placed in front of the door earlier and started into the tunnel. I lit the lamp while I waited for Bob to catch up with the grate key. We encountered only a few rats on our way to the screen. Once there, Bob slipped the hook of the key between the frame of the screen and the cement wall. We waited…only our breathing and our grumbling stomachs broke the silence.

I held the lamp so that it shone on the screen to give Bob some light on our task. Bob eased the bar back, and without a sound, the screen moved away from the wall. The bolts had rusted through! I rushed to stop the screen from falling over on us and then, resting the key and the lamp on the floor, we manoeuvred the screen over to the side of the tunnel. We were through!

I shone the lamp at the boards nailed across the large posts that ran up the side of the shaft making a ladder. "C'mon," I whispered, urging Bob as I climbed on. I held the lamp up again to see that the boards disappeared from view. The bottom of the lift appeared to be hanging about two levels above.

I started up and then looked back to Bob who had not followed. I saw his eyes glance up briefly, then back to mine, shaking his head. "It's okay," I whispered, "just don't look down."

He squatted down by the wall and waved goodbye. I couldn't imagine any fear being stronger than my hunger was at this moment. Remembering the previous encounters with his fear, I didn't push him any further, instead I began my climb.

A few rungs up I came head high to a small opening that had wooden slats across it. Below, came the chattering of a rat, and I shone the lamp back down as Bob winged it with a stone and sent it complaining off into the darkness.

I started up past the opening when I heard what could only be snoring, then a boy's voice in a sleepy murmur. I realised it had to be the boys' dorm on the other side of these slats. I climbed on to the next opening and raised the lamp to look in, I could make out the line of beds, barely visible in the darkness below me.

I pulled on one of the slats, and found by lifting, it came out of the notches cut on each side of the opening. I wrapped my arm around the step and held the lamp up to see in. I was indeed looking down into the boys' dorm. I quickly lowered the light and waited to see if I had been discovered. The room remained quiet. Quickly, I replaced the slat and started up the next step only to bump my head against the bottom of the lift. Something hard bit painfully into my head, and I immediately felt the warm wetness of blood run over my ear and down my neck. I held on to the ladder and silently cursed my way through the initial pain.

A noise came through the vent that was now about stomach level. Instinctively, I turned the lamp away from the vent. I heard someone yawn, then muffled footsteps. The door opened, and the footsteps faded away. A moment later the bell clanged, and the home started to rouse itself.

I lowered myself back to the ground. The lower vent suddenly lit up a portion of the shaft and the bottom of the lift, as the light from the boys' dorm was switched on.

Bob got up. A look of plain boredom changed to concern as he noticed I was bleeding. "You okay?" He grabbed my chin and turned my head to examine the wound. "Christ, Tommy, that's a good cut."

I shushed him with a finger, but it really wasn't necessary. The building was alive with voices and slamming doors. Sounds seemed so loud coming into the shaft that I thought we could probably scream and not be heard.

Bob started down the tunnel but I wanted to wait to see when the lift came down.

"Christ, Tommy, that could be all day!" he answered, after coming back to see why I wasn't behind him.

As there was only one lamp and I had it, we both waited, but it wasn't long before we could hear the lift door being opened and milk cans being placed on it. The lift door was closed with a loud bang, followed by the groan of the brake being released, and then the squeak of the pulley as the platform trundled down the shaft.

We moved out of the shaft and into the tunnel. The platform appeared with three milk cans on it. On one, was an attached piece of paper. I lifted it off and read it. It was a list of stuff Mrs. Holmgren was ordering from the dairyman. The list made my head light and my stomach churn. There was no doubt in my mind, we were going to have to wait back inside the tunnel until the stuff was delivered, and then we were going to snitch it.

The dairyman would have to come inside the delivery door to put the heavy milk cans on the lift, as well as the cheese, butter and other things, including ice cream! When I read that I couldn't believe my eyes. Once, maybe twice in my life, could I ever remember having ice cream.

It wasn't Christmas yet, I was sure. I wondered who was getting ice cream and why? Of course, it came to me. The

Witch and Warlock probably ate it. Gobs of it, I'd bet. Bob agreed with me, as we discussed it while waiting.

Something metal rattled against the outside half door and in a second, it swung open. Bob and I flattened against the wall as even colder air from outside rushed in and we saw someone's steaming breath even before we could see their face.

"The screen!" I hissed. We hadn't replaced it. It would surely be noticed missing.

Bob hurried over to it, and seizing it, swung it into place. Before he could let go, the hunched figure of the dairyman, in a big, fur hat, entered through the door and grabbed the empty milk cans, not three feet from Bob. Bob froze. Clouds of breath came from the dairyman's mouth and nose as he grunted going about his chores on his knees. Bob's own breath rolled from him and added to the fog, as the icy air rolled into the shaft and tunnel.

Above, I heard a door slide open and the sounds of plates and pots being rattled, voices mingled with the rattle of cutlery.

"Okay!" the dairyman shouted, looking briefly up the shaft, then stepping out to gather the milk cans on the outside of the open door and closing the door behind him. The squeak of the pulley seemed barely audible above the pounding of my heart, which currently filled my ears.

The good news was we weren't discovered. But man it was tough trying to feed that to my stomach. I slipped past Bob who was laying the screen aside, and stood watching the bottom of the lift disappearing in the shaft above.

Bob squatted beside me looking up as well. I heard him whispering curses under his breath. The squeaking stopped and was followed by the thud of the locking brake. I could hear the door being slid open again and voices in the kitchen.

There was some grunting from up above as the milk cans were slid off the platform and into the kitchen. I was sure it was Gladys, and that only added to the frustration I felt. To call out to her would be foolish. The noise would alert everyone in the boys' dorm and God knows who else.

I turned my attention to the service door and pushed it. It moved slightly then halted abruptly. Ice cold air whistled in through the crack, but a heavy hook was holding it. I could see the shaft as I leaned against the door. The cold air rushed in as the crack widened under pressure, but the pressure against the door only held the hook more tightly in the ring.

Gladys's voice sounded from above us. "There's cold air coming up the shaft again Mrs. Holmgren. The door's been left open again," she complained. Her voice could have had her standing next to us – it was so clear.

"Oh, dear."

Mrs. Holmgren must have come up beside her. Her voice was equally clear.

"Would you run down and close it. It'll freeze out the building." Her voice was cut off as the door slid closed. "Mind dear, put on a coat," we heard her calling to Gladys faintly, and a distant mumbled reply.

"Gladys is coming, we can get out of here," Bob hissed.

"If we can get her to drop the lift," I answered, "maybe she could put something to eat on it."

We waited, both of us grinning at each other, and then we waited some more.

"The door is closed."

Bob and I both turned our heads to the sound of her voice above. "I guess it's just really cold out.

"Did you check it, dear?" Mrs. Holmgren called back to her from somewhere in the kitchen.

"I could see from over the railing that it was closed," she answered. The sound of the door cut off their voices as it slid shut.

We couldn't stay any longer. We were both frozen to the bone. Dejected, we slid the screen back into place and made our way back through the tunnel to the boiler room.

James said, "Every cloud has a silver lining." We had no sooner stoked the fire and began to thaw when we heard the box on the door squeak open and a brief knock that sent the inside flap to the box clattering in response.

Reluctant to leave the heat, we glanced at each other, then the prospect of food sent us clambering up the stairs.

I heard the sniffling before I even opened the flap.

"Where the hell have you been?" I feigned anger, but it was good to see his red-rimmed eyes peering back at me from the other side of the box.

"Don't get pissy!" he shot back.

"Pissy?" Where'd he get this stuff? I grinned. "How's it goin'?"

"That sonovabitch caned me again," he answered matter of factly. "Just started walkin' today."

Bob and I looked at each other.

"What happened?" Bob asked.

"Four of us tried to do a dance on Gary's head. He started pickin' on little Stephen. This new kid, Frenchy, tried to stop him and he got it, so Dennis and I saw Gary gettin' tired and figured we could take him. We woulda got him good too, but he ran and stooled. You can figure it out from there."

"Little Stephen's in the corner, has been ever since. Crazy, can't go near him. We haven't said a word, but man he's stinkin' up the dorm. Goes in his pants. We pick up his meals and move from table to table to cover for him. He's really scared. Warlock's done a job on him…" he faded into silence.

"What about you, Earl?"

"Me? I hate him. He likes it. He really likes beatin' on kids. He grins when he finishes, and says something like, '*Guess you boys have to learn the hard way, ya?*'"

"It all started when we had to dig the alley out. Gary was the *man*. Too cold for the Warlock to even come outside. Little Stephen was sick but Gary picked and picked on him. Anyway," Earl said with a closing sigh, "I ain't so bad. You two ain't got the best of it, but 'least you don't have that asshole in your face all day."

I contemplated what he said for a moment. Earl was right about that. The Warlock seemed to grow more and more distant from our lives every day.

"Earl, is Gladys working in the kitchen?"

"Yeah, look, she snuck some oatmeal cakes to me right under the Warlock's nose." He pulled two crumbling oatmeal cakes from under his shirt. Gathering the crumbs that had been caught at his waistline, he pressed them into the cakes and handed them through the door. Bob took them and immediately stuffed one into his mouth.

"Earl Thompson!" the voice of the Warlock sounded from somewhere up in the halls above.

"Shit!" Earl said, and quickly placed the bucket into the box. "He'd love to get me again. Gotta go."

"Earl!" I called him before he let go of the door, and his head reappeared. "Tell Gladys to send the lift down at night."

He frowned at me in question.

"Earl Thompson!" The Warlock's voice called again.

"Just tell her," I said desperately, "…please."

"Okay." His face disappeared from behind the bucket and the door fell back closed.

The cakes, bread, and water lasted what seemed like seconds. It had been days since we last ate. We just unfolded on our cots and within minutes, fell into a deep sleep that hunger had denied us all this time.

I awoke feeling a chill. I looked over and found Bob outstretched and still asleep, fully clothed. He was in a heavy sleep, dragging air in through his nose and making little puffs between his lips when he let it out. I got up and found the fire was too low for a mid- winter night. I went to the bin and found the scuttle empty. I heard Bob awakening as the shovel scraped the floor, slipping under the coal.

"What time is it?"

I knew he meant day or night. Looking up at the cracks in the steel doors at the top of the chute, I couldn't see light. I wasn't sure if it was day or night because it had probably snowed again since the coal was tossed in. Judging from the low fire and Earl's visit, I felt it must be somewhere in the middle of the night.

Bob sat on the edge of his cot mulling over my guess as I stoked the fire. I opened the draft to over half, giving the coals in the fire a chance to heat the fresh fuel before the box cooled off even further. The gauge on the boiler stayed steady, as almost always, on fifty-five degrees. It was always cool at night.

Glancing around, I could see millions of little specks of light dancing in the reflection of the fire. The sparkling frost crept down the walls, and out of the corners of the floor, in a never-ending icy attack on the furnace.

With the fire set, I tossed the pair of scuttles over the wall of the bin and went to my cot. I put on my coat and moved the box away from the utilities door. "You coming?"

I saw Bob shake off a sleepy trance and look at me in question.

"The lift might be down, remember?"

"I ain't goin' up in that thing," he answered.

"I didn't ask you to. I was just a little annoyed that my growing excitement wasn't contagious."

"You go!" he said, a trace of anger in his voice. He threw himself back on the bed and crossed his arms and legs.

The lift was at the top of the shaft. I sighed with disappointment and climbed up to the first floor level vent in the boys' dorm. Lifting out the wooden slats, the vent itself was perhaps big enough for me to squeeze through. A pair of shoes at the end of each bed told me that the dorm was full. A dozen boys in one room is never quiet. Even in their sleep, there was snoring, mumbling, whispering, and the odd one crying out.

I gave a brief thought of sneaking through the dorm, into the hall, and up the stairs into the cafeteria. Not knowing what time it was, and the fear of getting caught up there if it was close to the morning bell, put the kibosh on it. Besides, I had heard the kitchen was locked from the inside at night.

I quietly replaced the wooden slats and made my way back to the boiler room wondering why the lift wasn't down, or for that matter, if it ever would be.

Earl came to our door four times the next day, but each time there was someone, either the Warlock, or Gary, with him. On the third occasion, I met him on the other side of the box. He said nothing, but gave a little smile and a wink then pushed the bread and water forward, and disappeared. I heard him sniff and the parting footsteps of two people.

That night, I found the lift on the floor of the tunnel. Three empty milk cans rested on it and a note giving the order.

I shone the lamp up the shaft. There, somewhere above me, was the sliding door to the kitchen. On the other side of the shaft, from where I suspected that door to be, I could see a third vent. That must go to the larder next to the cafeteria.

There was a constant humdrum coming from the vents in the boys' dorm which told me lights out was still a time away.

At first, I was prepared to hunker down and wait until the place was settled for the night, but the urge to sneak up the ladder and spy was irresistible.

I stopped at the first vent at floor level. The light in the dorm showed me the vent was situated in the wall under someone's bed. I peeked in cautiously with one eye, only to discover pairs of feet hanging off cots, jumping, and walking all about the room. I recognised Earl's laughter followed by a sniff from somewhere nearby.

I climbed up the ladder until I came to the top vent. I was extra careful before I ventured a peek because the slats sloped downwards from the top of the room. There wasn't much in front of my face when I looked down, nor when they looked up. Even though I was in the dark, I thought I probably wouldn't be too hard to see.

Below me, two rows of beds stretched out on either side of the room to the hall door at the far end. At first, they all looked like strangers in pyjamas. A group of them were on one bed. There was a fat man with a blond moustache standing near the far door watching the group. I didn't believe it at first, but then I was sure, it was Gary. Man, I'd been away so long I didn't recognise anybody! I picked out Earl. He was sitting cross-legged at the head of the bed. It looked like he was holding court as he was surrounded by five other boys listening and laughing at his antics.

I looked back to Gary as he watched Earl and I knew Earl was in trouble. The look of contempt etched itself deeply into the lines on his face. It wasn't new to me, I had seen the same look, in fact, I had seen Bob wipe it off his face with a couple of punches.

I had a sudden feeling of loneliness in seeing the life in the dorm go on without me, then it was quickly gone, replaced by frustration in not being in there with them…and Earl. My hunger for school, and the memory of how I loved it, invaded me even greater than my hunger for food. I realised then, I was waiting for my dad, whoever he was, to come home from the war and rescue me. Us!

"Time!" Gary said loudly, and pointed to a red-headed boy on Earl's bed that I'd never seen before. The boy got off the bed, and as Gary opened the door for him, left the room. A moment later the bell rang and the group broke up as the boys went to their beds. The red-headed boy entered the room and went to his corner bed and waited until Gary sauntered down the aisle between the beds to his own at the window directly below and slightly past me, just out of site. The boy turned off the light and got into bed.

I reached for the lamp I had hung on the rung of the ladder below me, when someone farted, and there was a chorus of giggles and a few crude remarks that came out of the darkness.

Somewhere in the darkness, far away, I heard music playing. It came from above me. Keeping the lamp dim, and making sure the light didn't shine into the vents, I quietly moved up the ladder and came upon the third vent.

A pair of lady's high-button shoes was visible on the floor, not far from the vent. A dim light came from up inside the room. The slats pointed down to the floor – just as they did on the others. I couldn't see or hear anyone, but I was sure someone was there, very close. Without another thought, I started back down the ladder. It would be impossible to slide open the door to the kitchen without being heard. Avoiding the milk cans on the lift when I reached the bottom of the shaft, I replaced the screen and made my way back to the boiler room.

I brushed my pants ridding myself of the stinking mess of rat droppings, and God knows what else, that clung to my knees as I wiggled through the doorway. Closing the door, I pushed the wooden crate back into place in front of it.

Bob sat on the edge of his cot. "Anything?" he asked, his brows raised in question. His eyes were dull as he recognised the answer to his question by glancing at my empty hands.

Stretching out on the cot, I closed my eyes. "It's too early to try. There's someone in the larder. It's a woman, I saw her shoes."

"Have you ever been in that room?"

Bob didn't answer my pause.

"They were old lady's shoes with the high hooks on them."

I heard him sigh. His cot creaked as he shifted his weight and lay back down; I presumed, without answering.

I awoke abruptly out of a deep sleep. I wasn't sure if I slept for a minute, or an hour, or the night away. My stomach hurt from hunger, and I knew I was going to have to do something about it.

Minutes later, I was climbing the ladder in the lift shaft. Passing the vents to the boys' dorm I heard the normal mumbles and the soft cries from one coming out of the dark.

I carefully kept the light away from the vents and climbed up to the level of the larder vent. It was dark, and only a soft dragging sound alerted me that someone was sleeping on the other side.

Jesus, did I try to raise the sliding door to the kitchen on my right, or leave it for the night; lest I wake up whomever it was sleeping in the larder?

A blast of music filled the darkness and was quickly subdued, but remained playing. I damn near jumped off the ladder from that initial blast. It came from somewhere in a distant room. It was exactly what I needed. On the other side of the vent I heard the sleeper grumble something and the bed squeak under shifting weight.

I hung the lamp from the end of a rung on the ladder facing the wall. There was enough light reflection to see the door, but I could only free up one hand to try and lift it. The door rose soundlessly revealing the darkened kitchen as I slowly lifted it into place, but I couldn't hold it, and set the pin to make it fast. I poked my head in and let the door go. It gave me a smart thump on the back of my neck, but I could push it back up by raising my body, leaving my hand free to set the pin.

A light came from under the door at the far end of the kitchen, silhouetting the long counter that sat in the middle of the room. My nostrils were assailed by the smells of baking and cooking that hung endlessly in the air of this room. My empty gut gave me all the prodding I needed. I snaked out onto the floor from the shaft on my belly, then spun around to lower the wick on the suspended lamp. All the light I needed came from under the door, which I suspected, must be the one that Earl had described as the Warlock's room.

Quietly, I crawled around the room, opening cupboard doors and pulling out contents into the dim light to see what they were. One side of the long counter, leading up to the doorway of the cafeteria, was filled with baking supplies: bins of flour, seeds of some sort, and a barrel containing molasses. This, I found, by sticking my finger up into the tapped bung.

My stomach let out a grown of joy as the molasses reached it. I opened the tap onto my hand and then shoved my fist into my mouth. It was bloody well all I could do not to eat my fingers clean off my hand. Knowing I was going to be sick if I continued, I stopped after the second mouthful. I licked my fingers clean and searched for something to carry some back to Bob.

The music continued to play from under the door. Once I heard laughter and recognised the Witch's voice. I crawled around the end of the counter past the Warlock's door. The drawers on the far side offered only cleaning stuff. I crossed the room and began to work my way back along the far outside wall. The last cupboard in that row, right next to the Warlock's door, ended my search. Loaves of bread, buns, and cinnamon rolls lined the shelves, all neatly stacked, row upon row. There were pans of Christmas cake, jars of dark brown gingerbread cookies, light short breads, some cookies with raisins, and others with oatmeal.

My first thought was how in hell could I carry all this back to the boiler room? It would take boxes and boxes, and all night. It was only after I had removed a square of cinnamon rolls, and stuffed them between my shirt and coverall bib, that I looked back and saw the vacant hole it left in the neat stacks remaining. It was going to be discovered – that was for sure – but they would never know who. I pulled a jar of cookies out and set them gently on the floor. Next, I took a Christmas cake. I held the pan under my nose, I could see the lumpy top filled with baked fruit, and my stomach screamed in disappointment at the empty saliva which was drowning it. I surveyed the cupboards then discovered, if I turned the cinnamon rolls sideways, the hole was neatly filled. Then I moved the jars of cookies forward so the hole from the one I pinched was at the back. It was the best I could do, I figured, as I rested the door back into the closed position.

With the cake in one hand, the jar of cookies in the other, and the rolls stuffed down the front of my bib, I suddenly became terrified of being caught. I was tempted to sit right down and stuff everything into my mouth, sure that once I swallowed, I wouldn't really give a damn. I crept past the Warlock's door, determined to get out of the kitchen as fast as I could, but some intriguing noises coming from the room caught my attention. It didn't sound like singing – he wasn't even close to keeping time with the music.

****

"Bullshit!"

"I'm not kidding, so help me, cross my heart and hope to die." I did the criss-cross on my chest.

"She was buttin' him in the belly?" he asked again, this time half believing me.

"It was hard to tell because there was only a candle lit by the bed." I described the scene again from the keyhole in the Warlock's door. "He had his drawers down around his knees and a dark shirt on. All you could see was his white bum as he was standing facing her. She was sitting on the edge of the bed. I couldn't see anything except the side of her because his back was blocking my view."

I giggled as the scene got on in my mind. "He had his hand gripping her head like he was trying to stop her from butting him in the belly." I started to laugh, "Christ, Bob, you should have seen it." I shook my head to his puzzled face. "He finally gets her," I went on between giggles, "pushed her back onto the bed and flops on her. And there it was," I laughed aloud, "this little tiny white capital H of his ass between this big massive capital M of her legs just wiggling away to beat sixty. They were doing it, Bob, and it was the funniest thing I ever saw. She's pulling the covers off the bed with both hands, and saying something I couldn't hear because they were too far away, and the wireless was playing into a bowl on the table next to the door. And he kept calling her *bitch,* at first I thought it was witch – like we call her – but it was *bitch.*"

Bob grinned, and I was a little disappointed he didn't think it was as funny as I did. "Guess you had to see it for yourself," I sighed, and went back to gnawing the burnt sugar off the front of my shirt, left there from the cinnamon buns.

"Buttin' him in the belly, huh?" He shook his head. "Never heard of that. I know you're s'posed to put it in and wiggle your legs. Christ, it must be really confusing."

"Do you think we're going to have to do that, like you know, with a girl, later on?" I asked.

"Jesus, I think I'm ready now. I woke up with an acher a month ago."

"Jesus, don't tell me it starts this early. Gary says ya gotta pound your puddin' or your nuts get so big you can't even walk."

"Didn't need to," Bob said, "kinda messed up itself."

I could see he was embarrassed so I didn't ask him to explain what messed up meant.

"Did she look like she liked it?" he asked, his interest keened up.

"You know, she had her hands on his ass when she was hitting him with her head, but later she looked like she was in agony when he was wiggling on her, just tearing the hell out of the bed." I paused and shrugged. "It's a mystery to me."

We ate a little... well... I guess half of the cake and cookies. That was because of the lesson we learned from before when we got sick. This time, we would only get half-sick, shortly after we carefully placed the food into hiding – inside the box by the little utilities door to the tunnel.

We didn't fight it this time. We just took turns coughing up the cake and cookies. '*Coughing your cake and cookies*', became our saying for being sick.

We were both laid out on our bunks nibbling on the replacement cookies when a heavy knock came from the door above us. It startled me so badly, my stomach contracted and I leapt from the bed to the shower drain just in time to cough again. Bob slowly climbed the stairs as a second knock sounded.

"Hey." It was Earl's voice that accompanied the third knock.

Bob turned halfway up the steps, his face white, and made his way quickly back to the drain. I passed him at the foot of the stairs, feeling a little better now myself. It was kind of funny, watching him get sick, made me feel better.

I opened the door to the box and peered in just as Earl sniffled. His red eyes looking back at me, seemingly with a little anger.

"Boy, Mrs. Holmgren has been busy for hours cleaning up your mess, protecting your sorry asses."

"What?"

"Jesus, do you stink!" Earl cut in, wrinkling up his nose.

"What?"

"Your breath man! You two eatin' each other's shit or what?"

"Been sick," I confessed.

"Yeah, eating your stolen goodies," Earl shot back.

I looked at him questioningly. How the hell did he know?

"Coal dust," he said, answering my look. "Lucky for you two, Mrs. Holmgren has been washing floors and cupboards since first thing. The Warlock slept in and she got finished cleaning before he came in for his morning tea."

"Coal dust!?" I looked at my clothes. How could I have been so stupid? They were filthy. We just took it for granted that the whole world was the same.

Bob came up and bent down to look into the box at Earl. "What's the matter?"

His breath hit me a second before Earl. We both wrinkled up our faces.

"Phew," we said in unison, and waved our hands to get rid of the smell that assaulted our nostrils.

"We got caught...I got caught," I corrected, "left coal dust prints all over the kitchen."

"She ain't gonna say anything, just don't do it again," Earl said. "You're really lucky she stayed here 'cause of the snow.

"She sleep in the larder?"

"Yeah," Earl confirmed. The Warlock had us put a cot in there for June. She gets the fires going in the morning. Whenever it snows now, Mrs. Holmgren uses the cot and June goes back to the girls' dorm.

That explained the lady's shoes to me.

"Hey, how did you get into the kitchen? Was the door unlocked?"

"You don't know?" I asked.

"No. Mrs. Holmgren didn't say she figured it out. She hasn't said anything."

"It was magic," I said. I wasn't keen on telling Earl how. The word may get around and sooner or later, everyone may know. It wasn't that I didn't trust Earl with a secret, I just wasn't ready to take the risk and let it be found out that we had the run of the building. "I'll tell you sometime."

"Oh come on. I won't tell anyone."

I could see him thinking on it. "I cleaned up the halls," I lied. "Will you tell Mrs. Holmgren thanks for covering for me."

"You cleaned the halls?"

"It's getting close to Christmas, must clean up you know." I grinned knowingly into his face and watched the confusion leave, come back, and then disappear.

He figured he had it. I smiled and put my finger to my lips.

"Neat!" he cried out and sniffed, then turned his head as we heard footsteps on the stairs nearby. The flap dropped into place and I heard a voice sternly ordering him back upstairs.

****

"It's Christmas." The Warlock stood at the opened door not daring to enter, as Bob stood on the first step down from the landing with the key poised in the air. Schlicter dropped the bundle he held onto the landing. "These are new clothes," he said, then bent and produced two pairs of boots. "These are for you as well." He dropped them onto the bundle of clothes. "You may wish to dress and join the rest of us for Christmas dinner."

He looked Bob up and down then searched for me. He found me by standing on his tiptoes and peering over the edge of the landing. I held the board we used for wedging the door. Bob had dropped it to me, as he was the first to reach the door when we heard the bolts being slid back. I was busy taking my turn at stoking the fire when we heard the lock being undone.

"You both should bathe." He said, wrinkling up his nose. "The brothers grime," he added in amusement, as he turned and went away leaving the door open behind him. "No soap!" I yelled after him.

"In a minute," his voice came back from down the hall.

We heard him climb the steps amid the noise from up above.

Bob kicked the clothes aside and closed the door. On his demand, I handed the board up to him and he wedged it into place.

Minutes later, Earl knocked and called while we were in the middle of removing our clothes. I checked him out to make sure he was alone then let him in. He flipped the soap to me as I hurried back down the stairs.

"Man, it's a *feast*!" he exclaimed, as he looked around the boiler room. He sat on the railing and watched us as we turned on the valve to the hot water and stood aside the spout to wash our faces with the soap.

The bar was not the lye soap we had burnt ourselves with before, but had a nice perfumed smell. I looked up at Earl as I scrubbed my lathered face.

"Close the door. Ain't no need for unwelcome guests," Bob added.

After we had washed and dried using our bed sheets, Bob found the boots he picked out – the largest pair – were too big. And I found the smaller pair too small, so we switched. It was the first time we recognised that I had grown passed him. While it was plain to see we were both skinny, we never stopped to realise that we were outgrowing our clothes lengthways. When I finished dressing, I walked over to him in my new boots and stood next to him. He stretched as tall as he could but remained a good inch shorter than me.

Earl chattered away about kids who arrived in the last months and those that had left as Bob and I got ready.

"June got sick and she's gone," he informed us. "Gladys thinks the Warlock was *doin' it* to her when she stayed in the larder room. The Warlock let June stay there 'cause she gets the fires going in the morning first thing. She doesn't have to wake the rest of the girls 'cause she gets up so early. Now Gladys is going to have to do it 'cause she's gone."

Earl talked about the group in his gang and of Barry, whom I never met, who was expecting to be adopted. He played the fiddle really well and a family of *music* people wanted him, Earl finished.

"How's your pal, Gary?" I asked, grinning.

"Jesus, what an asshole," Earl shook his head. "He rats on everything. He got Klause the cane. Two, for running in the halls. Can't say anything around him, he goes straight to the Warlock. You know, he even tried to get one of the youngest to play with his thing. He's always poundin' his puddin' and tellin' everybody about it!"

"How come he's still here?" Bob asked, puzzled.

"He does all the dirty work for the Warlock," Earl responded.

"Christ, he must be almost what now, sixteen?"

"Yeah," Earl answered me.

"Everyone else gets turned out to work and fend for themselves before they get that old."

"They tried that, remember," Bob said. "He got dumped back here in a hurry, twice."

"Like I said," Earl finished, "he's a real asshole."

We checked the room out. It was the first time in several months we were allowed out and it felt strange to go through the door.

It felt even stranger to climb the stairs to the main floor and find the two of us the centre of hushed curiosity. The hall itself was decked with home-made Christmas decorations. Popcorn chains seemed to be the main theme, with green and red angels hanging from the ceiling and pasted to the walls. A long table covered with white paper ran down the room and t-boned another at the far end. The adults, mostly older ladies, chatted away in small groups which became silent as Bob, Earl and I moved along a wall looking for chairs to seat ourselves. The room quieted and all turned to us. Bob and I hurried to find chairs and sit. Earl's gang came to save us from further embarrassment as they jumped up uproariously, and offered their chairs amongst cheers.

I found myself as quiet as Bob was normally. Despite the stomach conditioning we had put ourselves through with the stolen kitchen goodies previously, the rich meal sat heavily in both our stomachs. Bob and I both slipped away before the after-dinner Christmas carols and other events, even started.

Back in the boiler room, we braced the door once again, aware that it remained unlocked, and with great reluctance, threw up our meals.

Then I curled up on my cot and wondered if I would ever be able to eat again, knowing that the awful pain of hunger would be on us again by tomorrow.

Even if we wanted to change things, we knew we never could. The Warlock could never be trusted. He enjoyed hurting people too much, and all my instincts for self-preservation became aroused even at the mention of his name.

Another thing was clear…or maybe clear wasn't the right word. When I sat looking around the room at all the fresh young faces during the Christmas dinner, I realised that Bob's and mine were lined with black. Every crease in my hands remained black with coal dust that had become etched in. All the washing we could do was not going to remove the black in and around our fingernails, eyes, hands and mouth. We truly were boiler room rats.

It was New Year's Eve, nineteen eighteen. Our door remained unlocked, still, we didn't trust the Warlock and continued to use the board it to wedge it closed. Earl came with a basket now, instead of a bucket. He rapped and called out *picnic time*, and sat with us while we ate.

Mrs. Holmgren sent Bob and I all we could eat and our stomachs stopped their rebellions on rich desserts: like bread and custard puddings, and the last of the Christmas cakes. Earl said she had kept these especially for us when she noted it was one of the items I stole from the kitchen.

We also got three cakes of perfumed soap, and Earl told us the Warlock had said we could use the boys' showers.

"I kinda hope you don't," he said, wrinkling up his nose then sniffing, " 'cause I gotta clean them and you guys will leave a hellava mess." He raised his eyebrows and gave a nervous snicker.

"Don't fret," Bob responded, "don't intend to set a foot outside that door. Don't trust him," he added.

"We're okay here," I answered, grinning at him.

"I was only kidding," he sniffled.

We worked tirelessly to keep the coal dust under control, every time a shovel full of coal was moved, a cloud of dust could be seen rolling upwards from the open door of the firebox. Removing the ashes created an even greater

mess. It was a daily chore that Bob took absolute delight in…
when we were through.

During the next month, we hung additional sacks from
the existing ones, right down to the top of the coal bin walls.
We sprayed them with water when a load came in, and again
lightly, before we shovelled into the firebox.

Bob seemed to take new life. He worked furiously at
getting the place clean.

"There, what do you think, Tommy?" He stood with his
hands on his hips and ran his eyes over the room. The brass
gauges sparkled and each valve handle glistened with a coat
of new paint from the cans James had stored in a box under
the stairs. He seemed to be relentless in demanding me to do
even more, far past when I gave up through tiredness or
boredom.

"What's with you?" I asked one day after a week of
cleaning the clean, and polishing the polished.

Bob, standing on the stairs with a rag in his hand wiping
the railing for the umpteenth time, turned and looked at me.
"This is what I want to do."

"What? Clean?"

"James always said that an engineer's sign was a
meticulous work place. That's what he called it *meticulous*,
really clean. No bilge rats, you know." He looked around the
room as he spoke with a look of satisfaction on his face.

"So, if I'm guessing right, you want to be an engineer."

He looked down at me and grinned, "Right!"

It caught me by surprise. Our lives had been taken up
with just surviving day to day while waiting for our Pa to
return from the war to take us away. I had never ventured a
thought of where we were going, or what we were going to
do. For Bob, who was twelve now and almost grown for

work, he had to figure out where and what. I truly hadn't. I just wanted to go to school.

"You want to be an engineer on a steam ship?"

"Don't matter. Just a steam engineer like James was."

"Takes learnin', Bob," I said, wondering how he would take to that hitch.

"James said the navy taught him. Then he served an indenture. That's what I want to do."

"You don't figure it will take book learnin'?"

"Hell no," he shot back, then hesitated as he thought about it further. "Maybe a little more than I got," he finished.

I could see a sulleness spread across his face as he turned away and began wiping at the rail once again. James had been very clear to both of us that without the book learnin', the farm would probably be the only place that we could find work. I felt guilty. I hadn't opened a book for months. Nothing had changed since the Warlock's refusal to let me attend the special school. I couldn't even go to class here at the orphanage. I had already passed the curriculum, but it would still be good practice. All this inactivity was sapping my interest.

"What do you say we do some book learnin' together?" I called to Bob, and watched as he spun to me with an excited look on his face.

"Do you think?" A shadow of doubt clouded over him. "You think I can learn? I almost forgot how to read and write."

"I think you're going to have to, if you really want to be an engineer."

"My numbers are good," he offered, on a positive note.

I walked over to my treasure of schoolbooks as he jumped over the bottom stair rail onto his cot. I reached for the third-grade speller, the last one he worked with, and turned to the middle. I knew it was going to be difficult for him, and me both. We sat together on my cot.

"Okay," I said, "there's a short 'a' and a long 'a'…" We started.

It was somewhat surprising that we worked on the books so well together, but it was anything but easy. Bob could go through a six-letter word, and sound it out letter by letter, then fail time after time to write it correctly. Sometimes he couldn't even say the word after sounding it all out. Bob was anything but stupid, but at times I had to try very hard not to shout at him in frustration. Of course, part of my patience was a matter of self-preservation.

Over the remaining weeks of deep winter, things went very well. Earl brought our basket, and we used the lavs now instead of James's commode. The Warlock never came down, and Earl remained our messenger when our supply of coal dwindled and needed another delivery.

The place was so easy to clean now that we sprayed the dust down, that we could study for hours during the day, and many times well into the night. Bob was learning. Actually, I found he could get through longer words by breaking them down into two or three letters, then joining them together in his mind over and over. His lips never stopped moving, and he always kept his finger on the first part of the word. I found his way of learning confusing, but had to realise that his method was moving him forward at a reasonable pace.

On the numbers, he didn't have any problems at all. He moved swiftly down the page, almost as fast as I could, and sometimes he would beat me in accuracy when we raced. I had trouble with his gloating when he caught me on an error, but it certainly kept his interest keen. He called me stupid when I was wrong, something I would never say to him, but that only made me work harder. I felt the excitement of learning creeping back into my head.

Soon, I had sharpened up so much that I could leave him behind. I was much more comfortable being back on top, but it dampened Bob's interest, and he was losing his drive. I found if I threw a race on occasion, it helped, and in throwing it, I felt better when he called me stupid. I could pass it off with an inside grin. I didn't want Bob to see me grin because he would be really pissed if he caught me.

As the weeks rolled by, the door remained unlocked but we continued to wedge it closed on the inside. I was a little more trusting than Bob, but I couldn't see any reason not to agree with his concerns. The sheer terror of waking up with the Warlock standing over us made it easy to agree to continue with the precaution.

We were never invited to go upstairs, or to participate in any of the everyday activities such as meals, or church – not that we would anyhow. Instead, we were simply left alone, and that suited us just fine. The boiler room became our heart of the building. James's presence never left this space. Neither Bob nor myself wished to be a part of anything outside of the room.

It was about a month after the restoration of our meals that Earl, making a routine dinner appearance, told us that the 66th Edmonton Regiment had returned to Edmonton from the war. Our father was not among the soldiers who came home with the regiment. We were bewildered and disappointed, and so we told Earl to go and bring back Gladys.

Minutes later she appeared with Earl. She had a light blue dress on with dark blue polka dots and her hair was cut short. This was a new look that I didn't recall ever seeing before. It turned out it was she who was informed of the news by Mrs. Haywood. One of the Benevolent Daughters had dropped around and advised her that when the Edmonton 66th Regiment came home, and our pa took us from the orphanage, we would be replaced by four war orphans from Europe. That's the place that had the war. But today, when the regiment arrived, our pa wasn't with them. He had stopped in England and was to come home later, past spring planting.

"He's alive and well, Mrs. Haywood said. He's done something called a deferred discharge and won't be home for a while," she finished quietly.

"What about us?" Earl sniffled. "We gotta stay here?" he answered his own question with dejection.

"I could go out and find work," Gladys said. "Maybe we could find a cheap place to stay, like together, our own family."

"You want to?" Bob asked.

Gladys turned to Bob. "Yes, I think it would be a good idea. June is gone from the orphanage now. I think she's going to...well she started throwing up in the mornings and feeling faint sometimes."

"She's sick," I concluded, wondering why Gladys took so long to figure that out.

"That's how women get when they're going to have babies," she responded shortly, just a little annoyed at my ignorance.

"Oh! Shut my mouth." And I meant it.

"Mr. Schlicter scares me. He wants me to take over June's chores in the kitchen and that's why I had to cut my hair. Mrs. Holmgren doesn't allow long hair in the kitchen. And he wants me to move into the larder where June stayed...away from the dorm."

"That ain't best," Bob said.

I wasn't sure what this was all leading up to, but said nothing in case Gladys got annoyed with me speaking out again.

"I'll ask Mrs. Dannelchuk if I can take you, and we can find a place together until our father gets home."

"Who's she?" I asked.

"She's the lady in charge of the committee that looks after the home for the Benevolent Daughters. She's here a lot. She's really nice. She talks to me all the time."

"What if she says no?"

"Then, Tom, I won't go. We have our promises to Momma, remember?"

"Don't worry about me," Bob said. "I got this place to keep shipshape. I'll be okay," he finished, and turned to me.

"Yeah," I stammered, "Bob and I are okay." Damn, I thought, it's not okay. I was tired of all this and my thoughts were of getting out and going to school.

"We're a family," Gladys said, cutting off any response that may have come from Earl.

"Yeah," Earl shrugged and sniffed.

"I've got to go," Gladys said, and got up off the stair. She looked around, "You boys got this place tidy. Looks clean enough," she finished, slicking a finger over the railing and looking at it for dust.

"I like your dress…."

"Yeah, you look really nice." Bob chimed in.

Bob and I smiled at her retreating figure, but she never looked back and disappeared through the doorway.

"Shit," Earl said, "I want out of this Goddamn place and away from that asshole Gary in the worst way. I hope we can go."

He got up and left, but stopped before the door. "When the Warlock finds out Pa ain't comin' home, you watch the shit fly again. Only reason he and Gary backed off was 'cause of him comin' home."

Less than two days later, Earl was at the hospital getting a broken arm set. '*He fell down the stairs*,' was the first story we heard. An hour after hearing this, our door was locked.

Our food basket stopped arriving and those old familiar hunger pangs pushed us into a rage that was ignited when Gladys came down to tell us that Mrs. Dannelchuk wouldn't let us all leave the home, and when leaving, informed us that Gary had pushed Earl down the stairs. We were so furious that we didn't even ask about our food.

* * * *

"You can relax, they're locked back in."

I recognised the Warlock's voice as I crept along the boardwalk between the electrical insulators that bordered each side. Finally, I could see down to part of the room through the hole left around the wire suspending the light in the centre, of what was now, the headmaster's office.

There was a second man's voice that murmured something I didn't catch, and it took me a moment to recognise that it was Gary's. Even though it had gone lower in tone, the whiney sound remained as a dead give-away.

"Good, they would sure like to have my ass for givin' that little, snot-faced Earl what he deserved." He gave a little snicker.

"Listen young man," the Warlock said, "that was more than a little foolish. Their father will be back from overseas to pick them up one day and I don't want any problems when he's here."

"You said that was going to be six more months," Gary answered. "His arm should be okay by then, shouldn't it?"

"My point is, we're going to need a sound argument in clarifying our actions in dealing with these two."

"God, Mr. Schlicter, we got that. Sneakin' out, fighting with everyone and, well even you!"

"I know, but don't miss my point. What's going on with these two has to be justified."

I tried to see them below me through the hole, but I could only see a small piece of the penalty box. They had to be somewhere between the desk and the door to the Witch's lair.

"Anyway, Mrs. Haywood is out for the morning and we have some time to ourselves," the Warlock said softly.

There was silence, and for a moment I thought they had left the room. I was about to leave when I heard the Warlock's voice.

"That's it," he murmured.

I saw the bottoms of Gary's boots come into view across the white penalty box square on the floor below me. I was puzzled at what I was seeing.

"You like that don't you?"

There was no reply from Gary.

"C'mon," the Warlock said after a few moments, "grab the desk!"

* * * *

"I'm telling you, Bob, he must have been slapping him, that's what it sounded like, and Gary, he's grunting and squeakin' real strange."

Bob sat on his cot with a puzzled look on his face. "Wasn't mad?" he asked, and took a puff of our last cigarette, then exhaling, handed it to me. We didn't know when we would get any more so we savoured it.

"Not like we've seen him mad," I answered, equally puzzled.

He shrugged, dismissing the scene that I had heard, but never saw. "Pa won't be home for at least six months?" he asked, looking at me for confirmation of what I had over-heard the Warlock say, and was blurting to Bob in bits and pieces after returning from one of my, now regular, spy missions.

"Yeah," I confirmed, "and we're supposed to get treated right or leastwise, he has to be able to have a good excuse for giving us a beating or whatever."

"He's afraid of Pa," Bob concluded. "Thing is, he don't have to be. Pa would pat him on the back probably. He was a meaner sonovabitch than Schlicter is. No, when we get outta here, we gotta clear out altogether."

I sat there for a minute running this around in my mind. "I can't."

Bob looked at me questioningly.

"Earl," I answered. "I can't leave. It's a promise." He knew what I was talking about.

"How long d'ya think?"

"What? How long to take care of him?"

He nodded.

"Damn hell, I don't know. Till he's grown up."

"Tommy," Bob said, "that would be another eight years at least."

"I know," I added it up quickly. "He would be at least fifteen. That's grown up here. That's when the orphanage sends them out to work."

"I ain't gonna last that long, Tommy. I guess I'm gonna have to break my promise to Momma."

I couldn't answer but studied him. It seemed inconceivable that he would break a promise he made to Momma just before she died.

I remembered one or two things about Pa. He did give Bob terrible beatings. Bob never showed fear when Pa beat him, and that seemed to infuriate him. He would knock Bob down with a slap across his face that would send him sprawling. Bob would gather himself up and look at Pa in rigid defiance, and the scene would play out all over again until Bob couldn't get up. Sometimes it would be four or five times, after which Pa would storm out of the barn and I would be spared my part of the punishment. I would sit with him until he could walk. We would go to the creek and I would sit under the tree while Bob splashed water on his face. He was six years old then and I was four.

With Bob's declaration of leaving, I was now engulfed in that terrible feeling that I remember so well from when Momma left, then James. But Bob was even closer to me than they were. A chill went through my bones. It was going to happen one day. Bob would go. He would leave and I would be alone, or at least, without him. This was going to take a lot of thinking to get through.

I looked at Bob who was staring at the floor in front of him. "I understand," I said.

He looked up at me and a soft smile lightened up his face.

"We've got a score to settle with Gary," said Bob, changing the subject. "Any ideas?"

****

It wasn't that we really gave a damn that we were locked in again. While it was all right that Earl and his friends could visit at recess and sometimes at lunch time, and Gladys did come down twice to give us news, Bob and I had no desire to leave the boiler room. School was the only thing I regretfully missed, but not the school here with the Warlock looming over you. While the door was unlocked, I ventured into a few classes where it was made clear to me by the Warlock that I was uninvited. I didn't give a shit because they were boring, and he was a lousy teacher. No, it wasn't that. It was the constant picking on Earl and having no way of helping him that bothered us. We knew we probably could, or at least I could get into the kitchen and sneak down to the dorm at night. Bob ruled out climbing the shaft. Even in the dark he was terrified of heights. I had to try really hard to understand why revenge wouldn't be enough motivation to overcome his fears of climbing a few stories in a dark shaft. I started to make this clear when I saw the lightening in his dark eyes start to flash a warning. I gave up with a sigh, knowing that Gary was now too big for me to give the thrashing he deserved.

A few nights later I lay on my cot feeling the pain of hunger and cursing what that son of a bitch was putting us through. He was *hoggin' at the trough* while we got barely enough to keep our energy up to run the boiler room.

I swung my legs over the bed and pulled out the clean clothes that Bob and I had got at Christmas. I kept them stacked neatly under the bed so the dust would not soil them. I hurriedly changed my coveralls, tied my new boots together and swung them over my shoulder.

"What's up?" Bob watched me out of the corner of his eye as he lay on his cot reading a practice in a school speller I gave him.

"I'm raiding the kitchen. No dust," I said, brushing my coveralls. "I'll put them on," I said, referring to my boots with a pat, "in the shaft before I climb. Gladys said the weather is warming up and Mrs. Holmgren isn't staying over night anymore."

He shrugged and put his attention back to the speller, meaning he wasn't interested in coming with me.

After crawling through the small utilities door and into the dark tunnel, I was met with a dozen pairs of beady eyes glowing in the lamplight. I closed the door and went to the end of the tunnel where we had stuffed the insulation around the pipes that were coming in from the alley. Sure enough, the rats had eaten their way through a corner of it in their desperation to get out of the winter cold. While it would soon be spring, I could still feel the cold air from the tunnel below the alley flowing into this one. No sense in plugging the hole now with all the rats on the inside, I thought, and made my way to the lift more than a little conscious of the scurrying around me as I went. I thought of how *Gutless Gary* would panic if he were in my place. I remembered seeing him shake when he encountered one, years earlier, when we first came to the orphanage.

When I got to the screen, there were a few rats trapped against it. Unable to go any further, they turned to face me with threatening chatter. I moved slowly along the wall giving them as much room as I could. One by one, they took the opening I gave them and hurried back into the darkened tunnel.

I replaced the screen behind me to prevent the rats from advancing before changing my boots and starting up the shaft. I moved quietly, as the only noises I could hear were those made in sleep. I stopped at the first vent, the floor vent in the boys' dorm. I remembered the vent slats were easy to take out and it dawned on me that maybe I could fit through the vent opening. I reached up and started lifting the slats out and putting them into the front of my coveralls. With nothing but the frame left, I could easily get my head and one shoulder through the vent. The pocket in the bib on the front of my coveralls caught and prevented me from going any further this time. I pulled my head and arm back into the shaft. *I can do it*, I thought excitedly.

I closed the pocket before my next attempt. I was halfway through the vent when I thought of my boots. They would have to come off. I hesitated, lying under the closest bed to the vent. Gary's bed couldn't be more than ten feet from me and he would be asleep. I could slither that distance on the floor easily, bash the piss out of him, and get away before the Warlock ever showed up.

I heard someone stir and groan, another tossed with a whimper, and like bookends, one at each end of the room snored steadily. I knew one had to be Gary.

I used the leg of a cot to pull myself to a spot between the beds and then stopped. I was going to get caught. The Warlock wouldn't catch me personally, but my secret ramblings around the walls and ceilings of the building would be discovered. The access to the kitchen would also be found out. I lay there on the floor undecided as the minutes ticked by. I was going to need more time to think this out. The consequences ruined the opportunity.

I left the dorm as I found it, undiscovered, and made a clean, successful raid on the kitchen.

Sitting later with Bob, we nibbled merrily on the baking I had pinched while I filled him in on my latest mission. I finished the story giving my reasons for not pummelling Gary, and at the moment, was quite happy with my decision.

"Right inside the room?"

"Ten feet from his bed," I continued.

We chewed quietly, each absorbed in our thoughts. A scratching sound came from behind the little utilities door.

"The rats are back in the tunnel. They chewed right through the stuffing," I said, looking over at the box covering the door.

We looked at each other, and I met Bob's smile with my own.

* * * *

Gary's eyes opened and looked at me. If he opened his mouth to holler, he was going to get the dead rat I held in my hand stuffed into it. Instead, I saw the slight reflected light in his eyes disappear as he closed them and rolled over facing the wall away from me. He let out a large sigh and an even larger fart, but soon began breathing in a regular sleep. I laid the dead rat on the pillow beside his head, then reaching into the sack, found the second one. The rat struggled in my hand and I released it and it fell to the floor and ran crab-like under the bed. It was a surprise because Bob had bashed the two rats against the wall in the sack several times with a baseball bat-like swing. Apparently that wasn't enough. To chase it would be a mistake, I thought, as it would probably chatter and wake up the whole dorm. I left it under Gary's bed somewhere.

I tiptoed back to the end of the bed, and finding Gary's shoes, I fished in my pocket for the small lump of coal and dropped it into one. Then, I crawled quietly under the bed and found the vent with my bare feet, and backed through it into the shaft.

Below, in the lamplight, Bob waited as I put the slats back into place, before climbing down to join him. He handed me my boots and I sat down and pulled them on. I looked up at his smiling face as his hand squeezed my shoulder.

"He looked at me," I whispered, grinning back. "He kinda shook his head in disbelief and went back to sleep."

We closed the screen behind us. We had cleared the rats out of the tunnel the previous night when we caught the two I had just left with their *Uncle Gary*.

"One of the rats wasn't dead. Made me jump when he struggled out of my hand," I whispered.

"Really?" Bob answered. "Christ, I woulda shit."

"Didn't have time, just glad he didn't bite me. He wasn't in the best of shape," I finished, as we climbed through the little door.

Once back inside the boiler room, I hung the sack back up in the coal bin and Bob and I gleefully retired for the night.

I was just about asleep when I sat up in disbelief of the lungpower of that fat bastard. His high-pitched scream sounded like he was outside our hallway door. There was a crashing noise, and a second even louder scream was followed by a pandemonium of shouts for lights. Noises seemed to be coming from every direction now, and amidst all the noise I could hear some heavy footsteps pounding up the back stairs to the top floor.

I looked over at Bob who was by now also sitting up. He looked at me in pure delight, threw his arms out from his body, and flopped back on his bed. Together, we laughed until my eyes could no longer see through the tears.

I had dropped the piece of coal into his boot to let him know we could get to him – if he could figure it out. Seeing my face looking over him in the dark was something we hadn't planned on, but there was a huge amount of satisfaction in thinking about his reaction.

The next morning, just after the fire was stoked and set, we heard the lock rattle in the hallway door and moments later, as we held our positions on the landing, we heard the chain rattle on the steel chute doors to the alley. We waited but nothing further happened.

We didn't get any food or water all day and our bucket remained unemptied in the box in the door.

Later in the afternoon, I went up into the chimney hole. I climbed up above the old classroom but found it empty. The hallways were deserted and so were the lavs. I returned to the boiler room and found Bob sleeping off his hunger. I cleaned the steps and ladder with a rag to get rid of the telltale signs of use before curling up on my cot for some sleep myself. Tonight I would have to pull off another kitchen raid.

Mrs. Holmgren made the raids on the kitchen easier. On the days when we weren't sent any food, she left some by the door of the lift. Gladys told me she didn't want me to get caught in the kitchen and couldn't leave it any where else lest the rats beat us to it. It was a simple matter of raising the door and taking the bag from the other side of it. No fuss, no muss. Unless I went up for extras, that was on my own hook. I didn't do this too often as I really didn't want to dirty her kitchen and really did appreciate her handouts.

A load of coal came early the following morning. The rattle of the chain had Bob and I standing at the ready, just in case. Bob had the grate key and I went up to the landing to fetch the door wedge and returned to the floor beside him. The coalmongers opened the doors and a rush of cool spring air rushed down the chute.

The Warlock's face appeared and scrutinised us from above, then disappeared.

I turned on the sprinklers as the men emptied their sacks one by one. The mist from the sprinklers held the dust in check as the coal tumbled down the chute into the bin, but there was enough dust remaining in the air to taint the sunlight that streamed down through the hole into the bin.

After, Bob insisted we clean everything in the room until every spec of dust was captured in our rags and washed down the drain. For myself, I thought the wetting down of the coal and hanging the extra sacking was supposed to save this kind of effort. I didn't say anything, though I made it clear my heart wasn't in it. He went over my work, inspecting his rag before and after he wiped.

"If you wanted to do it all, all you had to do is say so," I said, watching him from my cot.

"Whyn't you do it right the first time?" he shot back, polishing the brass gate valves that I had just done myself.

"Jesus, Bob, you'd think the bloody King himself was going to view this...this Goddamn hole!"

Within a flash Bob had dropped the rag he was polishing with and was beside my cot. He seized me by the front of my coveralls and lifted me off the cot and onto my feet. I struggled to break his grip but he held fast until I stopped, his eyes blazing up into mine.

"This *hole* is James's place," he hissed, giving me a shake.

I'm taller, I thought. *I'm bigger than my big brother.* Then what he said sunk in and I felt my own anger vanish and a wave of guilt wash over me. I couldn't look at him. "I know," I answered.

He released me with a little push and I fell back on my cot.

Bob snatched the rag up and began wiping again. I watched him for a bit before picking up the rag I had been using and started in once again. Together, we worked the room without another word.

A revelation occurred to me as I polished. I had always thought of James as my friend first. I hadn't really thought about Bob's relationship to him. Bob had worked with James months before I was sent down. Why wouldn't he feel close to him and his memory, I rationalised. Here, I'd always thought I felt James loss first, and figured Bob's sense of loss as second to mine.

I realised something about my older brother I hadn't thought of before. He did care about things. He didn't show it, but if you scrutinised the things he did, you could see, at least I could see now, how he reacted. He pretended to be hard. No, not pretended, he was tough, and fearless. He took on the older boys at the drop of a hat when we first came here, and he wouldn't quit even when he was soundly beaten. He just wouldn't quit and that made him a person not to be taken lightly when the bullying started. And true to his promise, he looked after me. Together, we became toughies because I wouldn't quit while Bob was scrapping. Not because I didn't want to, I know I didn't have near the stomach for fighting that he did.

I glanced over at Bob and found him standing, looking at me. We grinned at each other a little sheepishly, and he went back to work. *I love him*, I thought…even if he was short.

****

"They thought you got out, until they found a second rat dead under another bed. Gary still thinks it was you. You know he pissed his bed when he woke up with the dead rat under his nose," Earl giggled, then sniffed.

I saw his arm hanging down in a sling, as he knelt on the other side of the box and looked under the flap at me.

"How's you arm?" Bob asked, as he looked though the opening on our side, the top of his head against mine.

"Okay," Earl said, then looked at me. "You did it, didn't you." He made it into a statement rather than a question. "I saw Gary shake something out of his boot and it went under his bed. I found a lump of coal there when we smelled the second dead rat near his bed. You know the Warlock thinks now all he had was a bad dream. He said he dreamt you were standing over him, but the dead rat convinced Gary that he wasn't dreaming."

"Someone checked our doors early the next morning," I said. "They tried this door and the coal chute, but we were locked in...at least they were locked," I corrected, and grinned back at Earl.

"How'd ya do it?" he asked excitedly, sniffing again.

"Do what?" Bob asked back in all innocence.

The three of us chuckled.

"No kiddin', how'd ya do it?" Earl asked again.

"Do what?" I repeated. He was just a little too eager and I had thoughts of him telling his gang, and from there, who knew?

"You buggers!" Earl gave up in frustration.

"One day," Bob said.

"I'm putting the lump of coal under his pillow tonight," Earl declared.

"Good," I said, "but don't get caught or you'll get blamed for the dead rats."

Earl giggled. "Hell, it would take a team of horses to convince him it wasn't you, Tommy. Here," he said, turning away, then back with the food basket, "...rollies with jam. Mrs. Holmgren feels it won't make you sick seeing as you're stealing her blind of her baking anyhow." He placed them into the box.

I reached in and pulled them out and unfolded the cloth wrapping them. Rolled oatcakes with red jam oozing out of the ends. They looked delicious. "Who told you that?" I asked.

"Gladys mentioned it when she was making up your basket."

I realised it was just a matter of time before the whole building knew our secret. "Earl, don't say anything to anyone."

"About what?" he sniffed.

"About stealing from the kitchen."

"About what?" he asked again.

"Okay," I grinned, catching on.

"Gotta go," he said, preparing to get up.

"Take it easy," I said, "seriously, …tonight!" I added, to be more specific.

He grinned, sniffed and the flap fell back into place.

****

"I ain't stayin' here no longer."

The words out of Gary's mouth brought a smile to my face. I looked back down into the room through the peephole around the light cord, but still couldn't see either Gary or the Warlock.

After the morning startup was behind us, I left Bob in the boiler room to do his school tasks that I'd outlined for him. He didn't need me there to help him with the exercise questions any longer, so I left to roam the floors and walls of the building. Normally, nothing much happened.

At recess, I could watch the kids come down the stairs and go out into the recess yard, now that spring weather had arrived. I only recognised one or two besides Earl. The rest came and went so often, that they were now all strangers.

It was easy to tell the new ones, they seemed to stay close to the stair railings, hesitant, eyes wide in fear and mistrust, victimised by family disasters that propelled them into this refuge of the damned. After a while, in most cases, they would come around and before long, they too would be highballing it down the stairs hooting and a hollering, eager to get outside into the sun.

Not today though. Today, as I climbed up into the attic on the top floor, I heard Gary's whinny voice, and the Warlock's quieter voice in response.

"I'll tell you what, I'll lock the dormitory door every night until you're convinced that they can't get you. Gary," he went on, "… I checked the doors, both inside and the coal chute. I even propped sticks on them," he hesitated, "…nothing!"

"I saw him. When I woke up that rat was in my nose. Then the lump of coal under my pillow, where else would that come from?"

"Maybe it was Earl," the Warlock offered calmly, trying to appease the near hysterical voice. "Maybe it was just a dream. The second rat was found in the corner. Maybe they got in during the day when the dorm was left open. Maybe there's a hole somewhere, or a vent they could crawl in from. Maybe around the radiator, they can crawl through very small holes you know."

"There was also a chunk of coal in my boot the morning after I saw him," Gary whined, not convinced.

The Warlock sighed. "Where would you go? You don't have a job. Wait! The Hudson's Bay Company is looking for stockboys. I know the manager. Would you like that?"

"Sure."

"You could get a flat somewhere around here. You'd have your own privacy. I could come and visit you."

"When could you talk to him?" Gary's voice rose excitedly.

"I'll do it this afternoon. How would that be?"

"Good," Gary confirmed.

"Now we have time for something." The Warlock's voice became low and smooth. "Here's something for you...yes, that's it," he said quietly after a minute. "Oh my," the Warlock crooned after another minute, "you're such a greedy boy."

I left to tell Bob of Gary's impending departure.

"I don't know," I shrugged at Bob's question. "At first, I thought Gary was getting it for something...the first time," I clarified. "But this time, they just seemed like, well," I hesitated, "...just friends."

"The Warlock said he would visit Gary when he moves out of here."

"Why'd anyone wanna be friends with that jerk?" Bob asked in disgust.

"Beyond me," I answered, again with a shrug.

A rap on the door cut us short, and we bounded up the stairs. Approaching the door, we heard the familiar sniffle of Earl. Bob and I dropped to our knees and I peered into Earl's face as Bob lifted the flap on the inside of the door.

"Guess what?" Earl asked, grinning ear to ear.

"Gary's leaving," I answered.

Earl's smile disappeared and was replaced by a look of annoyance. "Piss me off!" he exclaimed, as Bob and I both laughed at the look on his face. "How'd you know that? The Warlock came into the dorm not more than five minutes ago to tell him he had a job…"

"With the Hudson's Bay Company?" I pretended to guess.

"You two are too damn spooky for me!" he said, and pushed the meal basket into the box before getting up and leaving without saying another word.

Bob and I split the meal and began eating. I looked up and caught him grinning at me. "Spook!" he said, and we both chuckled through the meal.

****

The summer heat almost made travelling the walls and ceilings intolerable, but because of the boredom, and the pure delight of spying, I kept up my almost daily patrols. Leaving after the fire was set for the hot water in the mornings, I sometimes watched the boys rise in the dorm.

I got a kick out of Earl, who now with Gary gone, ran the dorm with few problems. The kids seemed to follow him around and he was good to them.

Once, a new kid spent the night too afraid to sleep because of nightmares. I found Earl sitting up with him before the morning bell, talking in the dark. I stopped and listened as he told Earl of the fire that took his whole family: ma, pa, grandpa and two sisters, in the night. He and one sister scrambled to safety, but she was so badly burned that she had died hours later – long before any help had come from the neighbouring farms miles away. The neighbours said the cold wind had grounded the smoke until midday when the sun had warmed enough to allow it to rise. It was only then that the neighbours decided to investigate. He had stayed with his sister, trying to wrap her and keep her warm until help arrived, but she went to sleep when he was searching for water, and he couldn't wake her when he got back.

I listened as Earl told him about the other kids in the orphanage, one by one. Most of them had become orphans from fires, too. We were all kind of together in this place.

"How old are you, David?" Earl asked and sniffed.

"Six and a half, almost seven," he answered.

"Well," Earl hesitated, "that ain't the best age to be 'cause the babies and little kids get picked first. Probably you're gonna have to wait 'til you're old enough to be farm labour. That's when they come for you to go and live with them during planting, and for sure harvesting."

"Hey," Earl broke off when David started to sniffle. "It ain't bad. You work hard and they look after you, and sometimes put you through the rest of school, and then you won't have to work on farms for the rest of your life."

"Is that a long time?"

"What, working on a farm? Yeah," Earl went on, getting some sort of confirmation I couldn't see. "The older boys, and girls for that matter, leave and sometimes don't come back. But it's okay here now. Most of the older assholes are gone. Mike can be a tit, but he's afraid of my brothers; they're spooks, y'know."

"Yeah, where are they?"

"All over," Earl answered.

"Everywhere," I whispered through the vent.

"Oh shit," Earl said, his voice edged with disbelief.

"What?" David said.

"You hear that?"

"You said, *all over, everywhere*!" David's voice held Earl's concern.

I remained quiet, a little annoyed with my impulse. It wasn't time to share my secret.

"Bob, Tom, are you here?" Earl whispered.

"I really wish you wouldn't do that," David said.

"I didn't say *'everywhere'*," Earl whispered to David.

"Yeah, you did," David cried. "Don't do this okay?" he pleaded.

"Okay, okay! Now shush, you'll wake everyone."

Earl paused and listened to the silence for a minute before continuing. "Anyway, it ain't bad here now that the assholes are gone. Dennis will probably be leavin' this fall to work the harvest. Most of all, remember, don't piss off the Warlock," he finished.

"The Warlock? Is that another spook?"

"No, Mr. Schlicter. He really likes to beat kids for any reason at all," Earl sniffed.

I let myself down from the ladder and carefully avoided the milk cans resting on the lift as I crossed over to the tunnel and made my way back to the boiler room.

Climbing back into my cot, I couldn't help but grin as I settled in for a final hour or so of sleep before Bob would be up. I was looking forward to telling him of Earl's haunting visitor.

My patrols kept Bob and I informed of what was going on in the orphanage. I overheard conversations about the doctor coming for our examinations, the teas and business meetings of the Benevolent Ladies.

I never saw, but often heard personal moments between the Warlock and the Witch when the door between the classroom and her room was left open. Her teasing voice, and tittering about *the big fella*, then the low concerns and demands. "Do it bitch." His voice becoming gruff, telling her what to do, and all the time, calling her '*bitch*'. Bob and I began referring to her as the Bitch instead of the Witch.

****

It was late in the summer, and we could feel the evening coolness creep into the boiler room. It was cool enough to keep us covered in the mornings, under our blanket, instead of tossing them.

Even though we were getting the same food now as the rest of the kids, I still pulled a kitchen raid once in a while. Mostly, it was for the sweets Mrs. Holmgren made up for the teas, as well as some of the Bitch's favourites, because she had a real sweet tooth.

Late one evening, I left for a kitchen raid with my good clothes and boots under my arms. I changed at the bottom of the lift by lamplight, leaving my dirty work clothes stacked on the milk cans.

Quickly and silently, I climbed the ladder in the lift shaft, past the lower and upper vents of the boys' dorm where all was quiet – relatively speaking. I reached the vent to the larder, across from the sliding door to the kitchen, when I heard a door open close by with a soft click of a latch. I froze, my hand on the kitchen slider.

"Gladys, are you awake?" I heard a man's voice whisper.

There was a pause in the darkness. "What do you want?"

"I thought we could talk," he whispered, "you know, about this afternoon."

The door latched shut, and I heard his feet moving towards the vent by my head. I let go of the door and turned the lamp down until it barely flamed – keeping it well below the vent so it couldn't be seen.

"You have a real nice body," he said, in a soft voice that I recognised immediately, for it was the same voice he used with the Bitch, and suddenly it dawned on me – it was the same voice he used with Gary. It didn't quite figure, but now was not the time to try and figure it out, now was the time to get the hell out of here, except I knew if I made the slightest noise, I would be discovered, so I held tight.

"Did you like my hands on you?" he asked.

I heard the brief sound of a mattress creaking under his weight.

"There you are."

He obviously found her in the darkness as I could hear the rustle of bedclothes.

"Beautiful," he whispered, "put your hand up and feel, they're getting hard."

Silence.

"Here, lay back."

The mattress creaked and there was the thump of his knees on the floor by the bed close to the vent.

The sounds of licking, kissing and sucking were soon covered by breathless gasps.

"Oh my, you're a very ready girl already," his voice full of glee at his discovery. "Here," he shifted on the floor, "put your hand on this…that's it, oh you know…" he cooed, in an impressed whisper.

I heard him get up, and clothes fell to the floor with the sharp sound of something metal. The bed groaned under his weight.

"Spread 'em," he demanded.

There was another brief silence before Gladys cried out, "Oh, God, you're hurting me!"

"Shut up." His voice was now low and cold.

"I can't, it's hurmmm…" Her words and scream were muffled.

"Shut up and take it you bitch!" he hissed, in a harsh whisper.

The bed creaked and groaned in an escalating rhythm, each impact bringing a muffled scream.

In utter confusion, I held onto the ladder and stayed absolutely quiet. I knew all I had to do was shout for him to stop, or bang the wall by my head, yet I couldn't. I heard him gasp the same as I had heard him gasp with the Bitch and Gary. The bed screeched as their bodies found a different position. Gladys's muffled cries became open sobs as the bed groaned, and one foot hit the floor followed by the other.

"Here," he said. I heard the sound of a cloth hitting the bed. "Clean yourself up," he ordered.

The door latch sounded.

"Cheer up. It won't hurt or be as messy next time."

I held onto the ladder until Gladys's sobbing finally quit and her breathing became deep and even. My arm ached as I quietly left her and climbed down the shaft.

Something had happened. I lay on my pillow trying to put this thing together. They were doing it – *it!* It was something that the Bitch seemed to encourage from the Warlock.

Yes, she was definitely eager, there was no mistaking that. I had watched them doing things to each other, and it was she who was aggressive. Yet, with Gladys it was different. If she liked it, she wouldn't have screamed and cried. Then there was Gary, whatever that was about…and then there was a pretty blonde, blue eyed Marlene. Marlene, who had given me my first stirrings *down there*, just by looking at me. Her face kept coming into my mind and my stirrings fell from my stomach, and gathered uncomfortably between my legs. I rolled over, pressed my stomach to the cot and felt better. Sleep finally came to end the confusion.

Even before I opened my eyes, I was aware of my sadness for deserting Gladys. I should have yelled or banged on the wall. The jumbled and confusing mess about *doing it* caused me to stumble and allowed the Warlock to hurt Gladys. I would never be able to tell Bob about the matter for fear he would be critical of my behaviour, or lack of it. Of course, the real thing here was that Gladys was in trouble, and so I resolved right then and there, that somehow the Warlock was going to pay for hurting her.

Three days later, I was once again *ratting*, that's what Bob called my secret missions through the building, when I overheard another visit.

I was watching the boys' dorm and was marvelling at how things had changed in their dorm. Gary's departure seemed to drain the last of the tension that I had known to exist there. The Warlock and the Bitch had a little farewell gathering for Gary, and according to Gladys, he was presented with a shaving brush and mug. Not one boy bothered to attend.

Earl appeared to be the natural leader. Every time I came to look down in the dorm there was always a gang of kids on his bed. They were laughing and playing some sort of game using a roll of socks. They tossed it back and forth while another group tried to intercept the socks. They had to touch the socks to the back wall to score, and after a score they would let the other team of kids have a go. For the number of kids taking part, they managed to play rather quietly. They were all aware that any rowdy behaviour would bring the Warlock down on them and result in early lights out – or worse.

A light knock coming from the vent on the larder room door just above my head alerted me. I took another step on the ladder in the shaft to bring my head up even with the larder vent.

"Hello, Gladys. How are you tonight?" The Warlock had that sound in his voice that he used for *doing it*.

The lantern was on a rung of the ladder below me, its dim light safely out of sight, but a light from the cafeteria on the other side of the larder door showed the Warlock's feet in the doorway. The door closed and I saw the feet move from the door over to the bed. The bed creaked in the darkness as the Warlock moved in on my sister.

The sound of the lights out bell startled me as it echoed through the building.

"Don't!" Gladys said to him.

"Shhh, shhh," he said. "You really like that now don't you?"

There was a hush before I could hear the rustling of bedclothes again.

"There, you see, that tells me you like it." The bed groaned under a shifting of weight. "Mmm, you have beautiful breasts." A moment passed. "Here, lay back and spread your legs, I'll show you something else you will love."

I was immersed again in confusion, but I swept it aside. There was no doubt in my mind that he would be hurting her any moment now. I raised my hand to beat on the wall. My ratting days would be over, but I couldn't let him hurt her again.

My hand stopped in mid-air. There was another way! I stepped back down to the top dorm vent. The lights were out and the room had already settled down. That was even better. I climbed down to the floor vent of the dorm and quickly removed the slats.

I was just about to enter when above me I could hear Gladys's voice, faint and breathlessly, "Oh, God."

I started to squeeze through the vent when it registered on me. I hesitated briefly. The tone in her voice confused me. It would have to wait as I was bent on my mission.

Squeezing through the vent, I slid under the bed next to it and out into the aisle. I pulled myself down the aisle on my belly using the legs of the beds for propulsion. I raised myself up over Earl's bed and touched his arm.

"Earl," I called softly. Through the dark I could still make out two huge eyes on a stranger's face appear before me. An arm directed me to the next bed. There was a rustle of bedclothes as Earl sat up.

"Tommy?"

"Shhh!" I warned him, as I knelt on the floor beside his bed. "You've got to do something, fast!"

"What?" Earl whispered back.

Just then the light went on in the dorm. "Oh shit!" I blurted out, as I spun to see the boy who I had mistaken for Earl, now standing beside the door, one hand still on the switch. My concern for the open vent being discovered had to be put aside.

I turned back to Earl. "Go right now up to the Bitch's room and tell her there's a big rat or something making a hell of a noise in the larder. She's got to come quickly...quickly!" I emphasised in my whisper.

Earl got up and reached for his coveralls.

"No, Earl, like you are – fast!"

"In my nightshirt?"

"Go!"

By now the dorm was awake. Heads were popping out from under covers up and down the rows of beds.

Without another word, Earl scampered to the door. It was still locked from the inside, which was customary upon lights out. He unlocked it, and after going through, gave me a puzzled look before disappearing.

I had a dozen or so pairs of eyes looking at me, 'the Spook'. Climbing back into my hole was out of the question. I instructed the boy by the light switch to turn the lights out. As I left the dorm through the doorway, I reached under his little chin and gently closed his mouth. "Catch flies," I said, and smiled at the huge pair of brown eyes looking up at me.

I flew down the stairs to the boiler room door to find the bolts unlocked, so I slid them open. Above me, I could hear Earl banging on the Bitch's door and calling her to open it. For some reason, the door wouldn't budge, then I remembered the wedge. In desperation, I opened the flap to the small box and found the shit bucket resting inside. Removing the bucket, I frantically tried squeezing into the box and found my best efforts were futile. Thankfully, the noise brought Bob to my rescue.

Bob removed the board inside and by the time I got back to my feet, he had the door open.

"What's up?" he asked with concern.

"Something's happening," was all I could grunt, and handed him the bucket.

"What?" he asked, deepening the scowl.

"Back in a minute," I called to him, as I raced down the stairs and crawled through the utilities door. Pulling the door shut, I raced along the tunnel bumping into things in the dark. I reached the turn in the tunnel, bumping headfirst into the wall. It sat me down hard.

I saw a faint glow from my lamp hanging in the shaft some distance off. Struggling to my feet, I hurried to the lift. After quickly gathering the vent slats that lay scattered on the lift, I climbed back up the ladder to the floor vent in the boys' dorm. The light remained off but there was a lot of chattering going on.

I was quietly replacing the slats to the vent when I heard the Bitch's voice above me.

"Gladys," she said, "you'd best get yourself down to the girls' dorm."

I heard Gladys respond, but couldn't make out what she said exactly. I replaced the last slat and crawled up four rungs to the larder room vent just in time to see a pair of slender ankles go through the door.

"We have to talk," the Bitch said after Gladys had gone.

"Sure," the Warlock's voice answered. "Good bed here, want to try it out?"

"Do up your fly, you son of a bitch."

He chuckled as the bed groaned and his feet appeared and followed her out of the room, the door closing behind him.

By the time I left the larder room vent, went down the lift shaft, raced through the tunnel with the lamp, sailed through the boiler room without explanation to Bob, and climbed up the chimney ladder to the third floor, I was breathless. I took my position over the ceiling and peered down through the hole for the light fixture, into the headmaster's office. I couldn't put my eye right up to the hole for fear that they would hear my heavy breathing.

"You're finished here," the Bitch said from somewhere between the desk and the door to her room, her voice hard with anger.

"Don't even pretend to threaten me, bitch!" the Warlock spat back at her. "I'm finished? If I'm finished, so are you." His head appeared briefly under me as he walked towards the window.

"Yes, I suppose I am. I was a fool. Those two boys in the boiler room, locked up for months, living on bread and water. My God, now the daughter...she's only fourteen!"

"Hell, fourteen is marrying age to these ignorant sod-busters," he said contemptuously.

"He's coming here in the morning," she said.

"Who?"

"Their father. The last contingent of the regiment arrived here today. Mrs. Hart had a boy bring me the news. She has four replacements waiting for the bed vacancies. Of course, I can only take two, one for each dorm. The two boys in the basement can't be replaced."

"Why not?"

"Because, I will not have any further treatment like that carried out against children. That was a job you were hired to do. You don't know anything about steam, do you?"

"Didn't have to, now did I? It's a job that was already looked after. You're the one who sent them down there, not me."

"Yes," she answered quietly. "Somehow helping that old gentleman with two problem children seemed like the right thing to do. I wonder how it all got carried away. Locking them in for months, bread and water, oh, my God..."she hesitated, "...Oh, my God! It's your baby! You got that girl pregnant. It wasn't Gary, it was you, you son of a bitch! June is having your baby. Oh, God." She began to weep. "I wanted your baby! Why didn't you give me a baby?" she cried out.

"You have got to be kidding me," he sneered, with a half laugh.

"And I let you blame Gary," she went on, "he's not the slightest bit interested in girls. I thought it was strange," she finished.

"Look Claudia, our problems are really over. This soldier picks up his kids and resumes his life and they live happily ever after. June has her baby and the Unwed Mother's Chapter looks after her. You and I, we can go on right from here."

He stepped from the window and went over by her. "We shall get along fine." His voice softened into that low slippery way when he's doing *it*. "You want a baby? Let's see what we can do, yes?"

"Oh, God, how I wanted that," she said flatly. "Get your packing done by tomorrow morning, or you'll find your clothes out on the street," she ordered. "I've let you ruin a girl's life, maybe two with the Thompson girl."

"Shrug and grin," she said, almost sounding amused, "you are a scoundrel and a cocksman. Get out! I don't care if it costs me everything! You should never ever be near children again, Warren."

"Claudia, now don't be rash or hasty, my love. Think over what I said. I'll tell the family their father is arriving in the morning and try and get them in a friendlier frame of mind. They'll be anxious to see their father, and we'll sew a little forgiveness in the wind. It will be just fine, I'm sure," he hesitated. "If you don't want me or a child, we could parent, or if you don't want this..."

"Stop it!" she cried.

"Let me know in the morning," he responded, and his footsteps retreated followed by a door gently closing.

I heard her crying softly, just for a moment. Then she took a deep sigh. "Never!" she said firmly, and her footsteps faded into another room as the door crashed shut, echoing and vibrating throughout the building.

My knees ached as I crawled along the wooden footpath between the white spools to the ladder. I knew Bob would be waiting impatiently for an explanation to my dashing about.

"Pa's coming tomorrow?"

"Yeah," I confirmed the information one more time, and looked into his empty face. He was not delighted, to say the least, about the immediate possibility of being reunited with our pa.

I had told Bob everything, except of course, Gladys's personal business that I happened to overhear. This, to me, made everything right. It would be up to Gladys to say anything, and yet I still felt bad about the mess. Her breathless voice saying 'Oh, God' still hung in the back of my mind. I made myself set it aside. It was far too confusing for pondering on.

"You don't look excited about Pa finally showing up," I said to Bob, pushing Gladys and the Warlock out of my thoughts.

"You don't remember much about him?"

"Not very much. Wonder why though? You remember more and yet I was there, too. I can't really remember anything but a few times. Trouble times though, the dog, you know."

"I'm gonna miss not being here," Bob said, ignoring the previous topic.

"James mostly," I agreed.

"He's always been here, I know it," Bob said, looking somewhat wildly about the boiler room. "I don't like the idea of anyone working the boilers. Do you think James will stay here or come with us, Tom?"

"I guess we can have him anywhere we want. Sometimes when things happen, I remember…well, he just pops up and I can see his face and hear what he said about whatever. Just about everyday, …well, maybe not everyday, but sometimes. Shit, it gives me the strangest feeling," I trailed off.

We sat there on the side of his cot. Sleep was gone and we knew it might well be our last night here in this place. This place, where we had had so much fun, and yeah, it was fun. Sometimes not, but for the most part, the good memories of being with James seemed to overshadow the beatings and hunger brought on by the Warlock.

Both of us were deep in our own thoughts. Every once in a while we would look at something that would stir up a memory, causing a sigh or a chuckle. Our room for over two years – James's, Bob's and mine. I finally figured out that this was how you said goodbye. We would be leaving tomorrow and didn't know for where. Wordlessly, I left Bob's cot and fell into mine without bothering to undress.

"You're okay, Tommy," Bob said, some time in the night.

"You too," I answered, pulling out of my strange feelings momentarily.

We raised our heads from the pillows and looked at each other and smiled. Both of us were in the same space.

****

"Well, lads, you're off today. Your father is expected this morning and you'll be gone." He smiled down at us from the landing above. His teaching suit was, as usual, immaculate.

I was frozen in alarm. Both Bob and I were out of our cots, and in the centre of the room in a flash, with his sudden appearance. Damn! We forgot to wedge the door after Bob had let me through.

"You," he hesitated, "you're already packed I see." His smile turned to a frown. "How'd you know?" he asked, almost to himself.

For a second I almost told him, but I had found out too many secrets, and a few of those I wanted to keep. It was tempting to reveal all, kind of like giving him the thumb in the bum, but I held back.

"I want you to know you both did the Daughters and the orphanage yeoman duty. Fine job!"

Bob turned to me. "Do you buy this shit?" he asked with a smirk, then turned in the next instant back to the Warlock. "Kiss my ass!"

The patronising smile slipped off the bottom of his face. "It's a shame to see you go. I could have made good soldiers out of you." His eyes blazed down on us.

"Soldiers?" Bob grinned.

"Seems to me your side lost," I laughed. "Kaiser Bill and all that!" I turned to Bob and saluted.

The Warlock turned and started down the steps from the landing. Alarm bells went off in every part of my body, and we both sobered immediately.

"Our pa will be here," I warned, "and he'll kick the shit out of you."

It wasn't true, according to Bob he'd probably shake his hand and say well done. But he didn't know that... or did he? He didn't stop until he was at the bottom of the landing and had cut us off from our weapons. The grate key was hanging on the wall by the furnace behind the Warlock, and my board was back up on the landing by the door.

"I hadn't intended on this but it seems you two should have something more to remember this place by," he sneered, a small smile pulled at his mouth.

There was no mistaking that look. We had seen it before. He was going to give us one final beating for sure. He moved almost on tiptoes, keeping himself between Bob and the key, as Bob moved around to the firebox.

"Our pa will kick the hell out of you!" I warned again.

"Don't we wish," Bob offered, closing in on the truth as he knew it. He didn't take his eyes off the Warlock.

In a flash, the Warlock sprang at Bob and caught him by the strap of his coveralls. Bob tried to get past him, but he held fast, and Bob only succeeded in keeping him off balance. The Warlock was grinning at Bob, now that he had secured his grip.

I flew to the bed, and jumping on it, grabbed the lower railing to the landing and pulled myself up and over.

Behind me, I heard Bob struggling to get away from the Warlock's grip. The Warlock grunted then gave a chuckle of satisfaction, as the sound of a fist hitting flesh resounded throughout the room.

The board we had left leaning against the wall behind the door, was now in my grip. Seizing it, I spun on my heels and glanced back down onto the floor of the boiler room in time to see the Warlock bent over Bob, who was still struggling. The Warlock was reeling him in by the broken shoulder strap, one fist cocked back. I was going to be too late for Bob. I released the board from over my head in desperation. As it flew through the air I raced down the stairs in two bounds. I was on the floor reaching for the grate key almost the same time I heard the board hit, or was it Bob being hit by the Warlock?

Turning, I saw the Warlock in a crouch being propelled head-first into the wall of the coal bin, his grip on Bob's coverall strap still intact; he pulled Bob onto his stomach before his head hit the wall, and he released his grip.

Bob sprang up and picked up the board as the dazed Warlock was struggling to his feet. Bob laid the board across his head with an axe-like swing. The Warlock collapsed, one foot straightened then relaxed. I moved to Bob's side with the steel grate key at the ready.

We stood over the Warlock's motionless body.

"Should I give him one more?" I whispered, the terrible feeling of revenge for all the things he had done to us over the years blinded me, while my heart desperately tried to beat its way out of my body from the fear.

Bob lifted the board and gave him a whack on the ankle. Warren the Warlock was out.

"You got him good," I whispered.

"What the hell are we gonna do with him?" Bob asked breathlessly.

We stood over him for some time waiting for him to move and trying to think our way clear of this predicament.

"Do you think…" I hesitated, then saw a slight rise and fall of his vest. "No," I answered my own question, "he's not dead."

"We gotta go upstairs, Pa and the Bitch will be waiting," Bob said.

"Yeah, and what if he wakes up and…" I saw the Warlock's legs start to move, then his hands. I raised the key.

"Christ, no, Tom, you'll kill him with that. Here, your lick." He handed me the board.

The Warlock silently brought his knees up under him and raised himself, swaying on all fours. I moved over him and dropped the board on his head and he pancaked back onto the floor.

"We can't stand around and do this all day," Bob said.

Giving him a push with the board and finding no response, I glanced up at the wall where the chimney cleaning rods were stored, and nodded to Bob in that direction. "The rope, we can tie him up."

"What if he yells?" Bob asked, as we stood back surveying the bound up body.

"Gag him," I answered.

We looked around and found a stained rag wrapped around a valve, and tied it into place around his head and mouth, then we stuffed his limp body under Bob's bed and raced up the stairs. We were late in meeting with our new pa – new to me anyway.

****

"He looks like a big toad," I said to Bob, summing up our conversation about the meeting with our pa.

"Meaner looking than I remembered," Bob answered, as we sat on my cot.

"Christ, now what are we going to do?" I asked, as I cast a glance at the Warlock wiggling under Bob's bed.

Bob got up and lifted the cot off the Warlock's body. "Have to put him back to sleep I guess." He walked over to the coal bin and picked up the board, then returned.

The Warlock's eyes flashed in anger as Bob stood over him, and without further ado, Bob whacked him again.

I got up and walked over to the limp body of our former tormentor. "How many times do you think we can do this?"

"Without killing him?" he paused, "I dunno."

"I'm not interested in any more of this." I looked at Bob, "I just want the hell out of here. You can bet that we're stuck here for another day at least."

"Yeah, the Bitch was making it pretty clear she wanted Pa to stay over 'cause of the storm."

"Yeah, I suppose," I answered. What I couldn't help wondering was how would the Bitch plan to do it to Pa with the Warlock still here. She must have already made up her mind he was leaving today, come hell or high water. And we had cleared the field for her. The Warlock was not going to cramp her style with new meat on the menu, meaning Pa.

"Damn!"

"What?" Bob asked, startled.

"What if she talks the ol' man into staying longer? Another day or week!"

"The Warlock's gonna have a head that has more bumps than the Rocky Mountains, I guess," he paused, then heaved a sigh. "We've got to get him out of here. Do you think, if we talked to him, you know, no more bumps on the noggin, he would agree to go?"

I looked at him.

"No, eh?" He read my face.

I had watched the gathering storm break through the chips and scratches in the whitewashed windows of the old classroom upstairs. Now the crash of thunder was soon followed by an even heavier downfall that drummed on the coal chute doors as the clouds opened up. Small rivulets of water ran between the crack of the doors and splashed down on the coal.

"Man." Bob looked at the doors. "Guess it was a good reason to stay."

"Yeah, there was a good reason alright," I said, remembering the little 'H' wiggling in the middle of the big 'M', and wondering what Pa might look like in the same position. A *big* 'H', I suppose.

"Holy jumping, Jesus!"

Bob and I both jumped, then heard the sniff and relaxed. Earl came bounding down the steps. "Ya got him!"

he cried, as he ran up to the bound body of the Warlock and
raised his foot as if to deliver a kick, but stopping short of
actually delivering it. Then reconsidering, he let go with a
swift kick to his crotch. The Warlock moaned but didn't
move.

"Nice shot," Bob said.

We looked at each other in agreement.

"Yeah," I responded fighting down the temptation to
give him a kick there, myself, "but now we don't know what
to do with him. We're stuck here until tomorrow baby-
sitting him."

Earl frowned and sat on the bed next to Bob. We racked
our brains coming up with ideas of what we could do with
him, but they were all unacceptable.

"We just have to get out of town for a few days with Pa.
Put some distance between this asshole and us."

"Pa would look after him in no time flat," Earl chirped.

Bob sighed, "Pa would delight in what we done, then
skin us alive for doin' it."

"What?"

"Bob remembers Pa as being meaner than the Warlock
here," I explained to Earl.

"Really?" He stopped for a minute, thinking on it. "He
seemed really nice...to me," he said turning to Bob.

"Pa has something else on his mind at the moment," I
said.

Earl looked at me with a puzzled face. "Oh," he said,
brightening and reaching into his pocket to produce a key,
"we get a whole bunch of new clothes for travelling. The
Bit...er, Mrs. Haywood," he corrected himself, "said to go to
the store room and get new boots, coveralls and coats, and fit
ourselves out. Gladys too, she'll meet us there. I was
supposed to find the Warlock." He looked down at him. "But

I guess we can manage without him, eh? She's gonna be busy showing Pa everything…" he paused, puzzled once again as Bob and I burst out laughing, "…in the building," he finished quietly, slightly annoyed with us.

"You heard how nice she was this morning? Well that's her *let's do it* voice," I finished on Earl's nod.

"No! Really, I thought she was doin' it to him?" He kicked the Warlock's boot.

"Yup, don't seem to matter. He's been doin' it to more than just her, too."

Bob swung around and looked at me.

"June," I went on, "is gonna have a baby, I heard." I swallowed Gladys's name with a mouthful of guilt that suddenly came up and almost choked me.

"Him?" Earl kicked his boot again.

"Could be," I answered. "Anyway, it seems when they, men and women that is, go to *do it*, they kind of signal each other with their voice. Real smooth like."

"That's the way this asshole sounds when he's gonna give you a beating," Bob said, and stood up and gave the Warlock a stiff kick in the ass.

"You know, you're right," I answered, "maybe he likes beating us as much as he likes *doin' it*." I shrugged.

Earl jumped up. "I saw him open his eye. He's awake!"

Both his eyes opened wide as Bob retrieved the board and came over.

"Let me," Earl said. Bob handed him the board.

The Warlock's eyes darted around in terror as he struggled against his bonds.

"Not too…hard," I said to Earl a bit too late.

The Warlock stiffened then relaxed.

"Too hard?" Earl asked, looking up at me and sniffling.

I looked at the Warlock's chest gently rising and falling.

"Guess not. Let's go get our clothes. At least we'll be that much closer to getting out of here."

Together, we rolled the Warlock back under the bed, and locking the boiler room door with a key from the Warlock's key ring, we left for the storeroom.

"How come you didn't get a pair of these instead?" I asked Bob, as I stood admiring my shiny, black, high-top, oilskin and waterproof boots.

"Too fancy." He stood up and adjusted the straps on his new coveralls.

I pulled the stitched straw out of my pillow and put two pairs of boots into the cover, along with my good coveralls that I used for sneaking around and spying. They were still almost as clean as new. Bob's old coveralls were badly torn from his scuffle with the Warlock, and he tossed them into the coal bin.

Bob stoked the fire while I finished off loading as many books as I could into the pillow sack on top of my clothes. I knew I couldn't take them all, but I wanted to. I was stalled at the selection process and started unloading and reloading my sack. These books were all that was left of James and I hated parting with even one. The sack was now choked to the brim with my absolute final selections and I was about to leave when I saw the poems by Byron. The same book I had read to James just before he left. I stuffed it into my pocket.

After finishing, I sat back on my cot and lifted my legs to admire my new boots. "Wonder who's gonna look after this place when we're gone?"

"The Warlock, I guess," Bob answered, as he set the draft and replaced the grate key.

"Nope! He's done here, I figure. The Bitch wants him out of here." I looked under the bed at the motionless body. "You know, I think we've done her a favour. We should charge her a fee like The Gimp would do. He won't do favours for anyone without...Bob, that's it!" I jumped off the bed. "The Gimp would look after the Warlock for awhile, at least until we get out of town."

"Yeah, for how much?"

* * * *

"Fifty bucks! Jesus, all we have is fifty-two, after all the work we've done for you."

The Gimp sat back in his wheelchair. A small smile tugged at the corner of his mouth. "Okay," he said, "you've convinced me...fifty-two. I was just trying to keep it in round figures."

"Okay, fifty," I blurted out. That would leave two dollars for a can of tobacco, 'baccy money', we called it.

"Fifty it is," he grinned. "Rest assured my young friends, you'll get the deluxe package. Y' know, Tom, I was hopin' we could find a permanent job for you here. You're a hellava runner. And with your brains, we could get you right inside the business. We got telephones out to the west coast, and down the seaboard."

"Can't, sir," I interrupted, "we leave with our Pa in the morning."

"Twenty-five a slip?" he raised his eyebrows hopefully.

I shook my head. "Don't think it would be smart to skin out on my pa," I said, as I pulled out the wad of crumpled bills that Bob and I had saved up, and holding back two, dropped them on his desk.

The Gimp leaned forward and scooped them into an open desk drawer, then closed it.

"You understand, I have to pay extra expenses to give your ah...friend, the kind of service you want, and he deserves. You two go back and get your friend into the alley and Igor will do the rest. In the meantime, I'll make a call."

Silently, Bob and I made for the door.

"Oh, Tom," The Gimp called to me.

"Yeah?" I hesitated, before going through the door and into the rain.

"You ever change your mind, you know, things don't work out, come and see me."

I nodded, and with Bob ahead, stepped out of his office, into the dark alley.

We pushed the struggling body of the Warlock up the coal chute far enough so Igor could reach him. The whole time the Warlock sputtered apparent threats from behind his gag. Once Igor had him, he pulled him out of the chute, stood him up, and spun the bound up body until it was facing him. The Warlock looked like a little boy standing next to Igor.

Bob and I scrambled up the chute as Igor gave a small bop on the top of the Warlock's head. The Warlock collapsed into his arms, and Igor walked down the alley carrying him like a suitcase.

"Igor," Bob called out.

The giant slowed and turned back to us.

"Give us our money's worth." Bob put it as a half question, half command. "The deluxe package is what we paid for."

Igor frowned for a split second, then grinned, reaching in his coat pocket he pulled out a fold of baccy, tossed it over to us, and silently nodded his head.

In a small, lit area down the alley, we watched as Igor undid our rope, and pulling on it, flipped the Warlock over and over like a fish, as he unwound his body. He leaned over, and pulling the limp body up, struck it several times before letting it drop. Igor reached into his pocket and pulled out a flask, then emptied it all over the Warlock. He then pulled the body into a sitting position against the side of The Gimp's car and opening the door, placed the Warlock's arm in it. We watched with a great deal of satisfaction as Igor finished the job on the second arm. Placing the Warlock up against the wall, and then wrapping the rope around his own arm, he turned and waved to us before entering The Gimp's office.

He no sooner disappeared than we heard a horse-drawn wagon turn into the alley. We recognised the wagon as it pulled up in the light beside the Warlock. A constable climbed wearily down and went to the Warlock. Picking through his pockets, he found what he was looking for. He picked the money out of the Warlock's billfold and returned it to a convenient pocket, putting the money in his own billfold. Seizing the Warlock, he dragged the limp body with its flopping arms akimbo, around to the back of the paddy wagon.

Bob and I slipped back into the coal chute and pulled the doors closed. We sat there quietly, listening as the wagon drew up, then passed, with the hoofbeats and crunching of gravel from the wheels fading into the night.

The Warlock was gone! We celebrated this by leaving the boiler room door open all night. Standing in the room for the last night, it didn't seem to be all that bad of a place.

After breakfast, we watched as Earl's friends came and said goodbye to him and then waved at us. We gathered our stuff just inside the front door and waited for Pa. Gladys came down and joined us. Across from where we dropped our stuff stood two beat up and bulging leather suitcases with the initials W.S. on them. I poked Bob and pointed to them.

He grinned. "Won't be carrying those for awhile," he snickered.

Pa and Mrs. Haywood made a noisy trip from upstairs to the front door. She seemed in high spirits, and didn't show too much disappointment when Pa insisted we had to leave.

"Have you children said your goodbyes to your friends?" she asked.

We nodded. Only Earl and Gladys needed to, because Bob and I didn't really know anyone. Mrs. Holmgren came down with a basket of food for our trip and said goodbye.

I opened the door, anxious to be on our way, and found a trim middle-aged man climbing the steps.

"Oh, excuse me," he said politely, "I'm looking for Mrs. Claudia Haywood."

The Bitch stepped forward. "You must be Mr. Butler," she said.

"Yes, ma'am, I'm the engineer you called for."

She brushed past us and took his arm, and turning, pulled him into the orphanage. "Come, Mr. Butler, let's go upstairs and discuss your duties," she said, in a soft, syrupy voice.

Pa grinned as they retreated into the hall. Turning back, he stepped outside with Gladys, Bob, Earl and me right smack behind him.

Except for a few riders and freight wagons, the streets were empty in the early morning. A cool, low mist hung over the street. Above, the sky hung light grey, covering the early October sun that promised to burn through. The trees were gold and half-undressed with brown and yellow leaves on the ground encircling them.

I stopped on the sidewalk and looked up at the building as the others walked down the street towards the livery. In the empty boys' dorm window, I thought I saw James standing with a mop handle in his hand, looking down at me. A kindly smile on his face, his white hair with the morning muss, he raised his hand. *No, no, James,* I thought. It will never be goodbye. I won't wave back because you'll be with me always.

I picked up my heavy sack and glanced at the sign in the little lawn beside the walkway. The paint was chipped and peeling, 'DAUGHTERS' was the only word that could be read.

Ahead, Earl stopped and turned back to see where I was. "You comin'?" he yelled.

"I'm coming."

I walked a few more paces before casting another glance at the building. There was the school. I learned right from the beginning to love it. I couldn't wait to get to wherever we were going so I could start going to class. The new classes have started already, but it would be nothing to catch up. The older boys would be in the fields for another week or two until the harvest was finished. I felt a rush of excitement. That, coupled with the need to get as far from this place as possible, put new energy into my steps.

And, James, I thought as I moved as fast as I could to catch up, he showed me what adults could be like. I couldn't help wondering if you had to get old before you became that way. He just talked to us, and I loved him for it. He knew everything, but didn't get pushy by making us do everything. He didn't have to, Bob and I were both eager to do anything and everything for him. He showed us the best way to do a job, and explained why. To think of him put an ache in my chest.

Pa is here now, and in spite of Bob's memories and warnings, I knew he would kinda be there for all of us. That's what pa's are for. I hardly remembered him at all. He was like a stranger, but everyone said he's my pa – he looks like Bob, or rather, Bob looks like him.

I crossed the street to the livery where they were standing just in the shadow of the open door. Pa seemed to be arguing with another man. He held a horse's front hoof and the horse seemed to be leaning on him. He was pointing to the hoof and yattering something to the man who towered over him. With Pa bent over, he was broader than he was tall.

Pa dropped the hoof and the man disappeared into the dark at the back of the building. Carefully, Pa backed the horse between two poles that were lying on the ground, and then began throwing straps and belts around and over the horse.

"Hot damn," I said to no one, "we got a horse."

Bob looked back to me and left the others to walk outside where he stopped on the sidewalk and waited for me. I looked at him, then over to Pa.

"The livery guy didn't feed the horse this morning. Was s'pose to, that's all."

"I guess I'll put this in the wagon." I carried the sack past Bob and into the building.

"Where you goin', boy?" Pa asked, as I passed him.

"Put this in the wagon." I swung the sack up, but it was too heavy, and it bounced off the boarded side of the wagon and fell on the ground before I could control it.

"What the hell you got in there, boy?" Pa left the horse and I could hear his feet approaching me from behind.

"My gear, sir." I read a book on the war, and that's what it said to call my belongings. I thought it might impress him, being a soldier and all.

I turned and found two large, icy eyes on a face masked by angry lines. I smiled at him. "I read it in a book. About the war over there...in Europe...you know, the big one." I finished, with a crack in my voice giving away for sure, my false bravado.

"You were over there, boy?" His body seemed to all of a sudden grow to twice the size.

"No, sir."

"Then I want you to leave the war talk to those that were."

"Yes, sir." God, I wondered if he took my reply as war talk, too. I put my head down and hunkered into myself.

"Books," he said, peering into my sack. "Ain't carrying all them books, boy." He lifted the sack as if it were weightless and dumped everything in it onto the floor. "Put your clothes back into the sack and store it under the canvass. No books," he said firmly.

"But they're my books. They were James's but they're mine now. He gave them to me," I argued.

I felt myself being hoisted into the air as Pa grabbed my coat front and put me in his face. "You got a problem hearing, boy?" His breath smelled like stale booze.

"I'm taking my books," I said firmly into those fearsome eyes.

Surprisingly, Pa set me down.

"That woman said you were a bright boy," he said under his breath. "You want 'em boy, you're gonna carry 'em. Horse's got a load right now and we got a five day journey ahead of us."

Pa let me put my clothes under the tarp. The sack wasn't much lighter as I carried it back to the boardwalk in front of the livery where Bob, Gladys and Earl were standing and watching.

"You think you'll be able to carry those for five days?" Bob asked.

"Got to, I ain't leaving James's books behind."

It wasn't that I thought I could, the sack was ever so heavy, but it was just that I couldn't leave them. I wouldn't leave them.

"I'll take some to carry," Bob said, and fished into the sack at my feet.

"Me too," Earl sniffed, and got in line behind Bob.

"I can help a little," Gladys added.

"Thanks," I said, and lifted the sack with the remaining books and started after the wagon as Pa left the livery.

"Walk'll do you kids good," he said to us, as he pulled by.

I looked back to the orphanage one last time as we started up the road. A milk wagon came onto the road at the next intersection and I watched him move ahead of us. We shuffled off behind our wagon, but again I found myself looking back. I forgot Momma's face over time and I was afraid I would forget where I had spent what seemed to be all my life.

****

The sound, 'oogah, oogah,' snapped me out of my thoughts as I stood there in the middle of the road. The noise came from a motor car as it bounced up the street. Its wheels dropping into holes and splashing water out from yesterday's rain storm. It sent the horse drawing the milk wagon skittering sideways. The milkman, standing on the boardwalk near the wagon, shook his fist at the driver and ran to tend to the animal. I moved to the road's edge and watched as the car went by – the driver fighting the steering wheel with deep concentration showing on his face.

I turned to see where everyone had gone, and for a second, became aware of the warmth of the sun on my face. I took a deep breath, felt the excitement and shivered. I had no idea where we were going, but I was glad it was away from where we had been. Warren the Warlock was out of my life and I felt a settlement in my gut. I figured we had settled the score, maybe not even, but he would have a reminder of us every time he looked in the mirror.

Several streets up, I could see the backs of Bob and Gladys as they walked behind the wagon and the neckless back of our father sitting inside – a puff of smoke swirling around his head from his weed.

The milkman had returned to the bottle-tray he had set on the sidewalk and went about his deliveries. Once again, the wagon moved up the street without him, revealing Earl as he sat on the edge of the boardwalk watching wide-eyed while the wagon passed him by. He shoved off the walk, got to his feet and stood waiting for me as I approached.

"Isn't that the damnedest, Tommy?" he exclaimed, as he fell in beside me.

"Watch, the horse will stop and wait for the milkman. *See*! *See*! Goddamn, isn't that a smart horse. The wagon stopped as the milkman returned from the last house on the street and as soon as he stepped into the back of the wagon the horse began to pull. See that, he didn't even have to say '*git up*'. Are all horses that smart, Tommy?" he finished with a sniff.

"I don't know," I said with a shrug, but I had to admit I was impressed. We crossed the street behind the milk wagon and listened to the rattling of bottles from within as the milkman reappeared from the back with a tray of full bottles.

"Smart horse," I said, as he walked toward us.

"Sure is," he smiled, "Goddamn motor car scared him though. Nice boots," he added, as he passed through a gate and up to the house. I smiled back and looked down at my shiny, high-top, oilskin boots.

"They don't leak," I called to him. He waved and went on to the next house through a side gate.

"I wish I picked them," Earl sniffed.

"You could have picked any pair you wanted," I said.

"Pa picked them out for me, I didn't. Hey, don't you think we oughtta catch up to everybody?"

I looked up to see we had fallen a long ways behind the rest of the family. "Yeah, we better haul ass."

It was only when the wagon pulled up for lunch that Earl and I finally caught up as my limping slowed us down considerably. Bob looked to be tending the horse while Gladys cut vegetables into a pot. The pot hung on a chain suspended from a three-legged stand that was straddling the fire.

Pa was throwing twigs on the fire and glared at us. "You two decided to show for food, eh?"

"I'm sorry, my boots hurt my feet, I couldn't walk faster."

"You had to pick sissy slippers instead of boots. Aren't too bright are you, boy?"

I wanted to tell him how I could read and remember things but a thought also tweaked my mind. He wasn't making conversation, he was baiting me. I kept my mouth shut. Sitting there on his haunches, he reminded me of a picture I saw of a frog sitting on a lily pad, eyeing me like I was a fly.

He looked over at me. "You build the next fire," then looked at Earl, "and you will clean up after we eat."

"Yes, sir," I stood there wondering if he was finished.

"Well, Goddamn it, boy," he spoke softly, "move, get some wood or we'll be here all Goddamn day!"

I forgot all about my blistering feet and scrambled off the road for sticks. The pickings were good and I soon returned with an armful. I went over to the fire and began to place them as I had seen him do.

"I'll be go to hell, what the hell are you playing at, boy?"

I set the wood down beside the fire and turned to him. He leaned against the side of the wagon working three strands of leather into one. "Sir?"

"You ain't never built a fire, have you boy?"

"No, sir. Not a bon fire."

He heaved a sigh, put the leather down and came over to the fire. "Get some twigs like this." He stopped and pulled a dried branch out of the grass at the side of the road. "Now I'm going to show you…only once." He removed the pot and set it beside Gladys and squatted down.

He knelt by the fire and began snapping the branch into smaller pieces. "You build a cook fire so the wood feeds the flame in the centre. You always use small wood for a cook fire, elsewise you'll be here all day. You want all the heat under your pot and fast. It takes too much time for big wood to suck up the heat and catch. Be a mile away 'for that happens, you understand?" He looked up at me. "Big wood's for overnight."

"Yes, sir," I said, and watched as his eyes squinted at me, holding me uncomfortably.

"You do pay attention, don't you?" he said, finally looking back at the fire before getting up and brushing his big hands against his pants. Reaching into his pocket he pulled out his baccy pouch, and with one hand, rolled himself a weed. Then taking a brand from the fire, he lit it and dragged deeply.

I stooped and added the twigs that I had scrounged to the fire. Gladys brought the pot over and squatted beside me.

I took it from her and put the handle onto the hook over the fire.

"We got him, Gladys. He ain't never gonna touch you or anybody anymore." I studied her face as I told her. She was different, older, her eyes didn't shine and her mouth was pulled down at the corners. I thought I saw a trace of a smile twitch across her lips, but only for a moment, and it was gone. She was fourteen now but she brought back the memory of our mother in her tired eyes and face. A deep sadness filled me, and as we sat together and waited for the stew to heat, I told her quickly what had happened.

"You should have killed him," she said, her eyes filling with tears. She got up and moved to the back of the wagon carrying out food supplies, and with her back to me, began putting things away.

"Damn it, boy, I told you to hobble him. Memory serves me right, you never did listen a damn."

Pa stood beside the horse and watched as Bob quickly attached a steel ball on the tether to the feed bag.

"Not there, damn it," Pa roared. "That'll pull the bag off her and she could be gone. Put it here!" he said, as Bob scrambled to unhook it and fumbled.

"Jesus Lord Lightening Christ, boy, you are a cause." He snatched the tether from Bob and strapped it onto the leather around the horse's head, then turned to Bob.

I watched as Bob and Pa faced each other, eyes popping wide and blazing with fire. I was thinking how each of them could be looking in a mirror, when Pa snapped.

"Don't you go looking at me like that boy or I'll shove your head up the Kaiser's ass," Pa warned.

Bob squared himself in open defiance and I knew what was going to happen a split second before Pa's hand flew in a blur of speed and sent Bob cart wheeling in mid-air. He landed flat on his stomach, looking out into the countryside and not seeing a thing. Then, I saw Pa square up and knew what he had in store for Bob if he got up flaming…and he would.

I ran over as he scrambled to his hands and knees then fell forward on his face. By the time I was kneeling in front of him, he had regained his balance and was trying to find his feet. I grabbed him by his shoulders and held him down. It didn't take much, I saw for the first time, a panic in his eyes, and I knew at that moment, he was seized with fear.

He struggled briefly against me, then stopped there on his knees. I watched the fear subside, the fire start up briefly, then go out.

"Okay?" He looked at me, his eyes focusing on mine and nodded. I helped him up. Pa had moved off to the fire.

Earl had left the area but I heard him sniff and I could see him hunched down under a small bush. There was fear on his face as his dark eyes bounced between Bob and I and then over to Pa.

"Get it while it's hot," Pa said, and dished up the steaming food onto one plate, two tin bowls and two tin cups. We ate in silence.

"That teacher says you're the bright one. You'll look after the horse," he said, looking at me, "and you'll build the fires." He glanced at Bob.

He reached over and pulled Gladys's dress up above her boots showing a red, raw line that had etched into her leg. "Both of you change back to your boots and outta those Goddamn barn slippers," he said in disgust.

Pa sent Earl for water from a little stream nearby. I hadn't even noticed when he returned. His duty was to clean up and pack the wagon, but because it was his first time, Pa allowed Gladys to help him.

We all gathered around with great curiosity to see what was under the heavy cover Pa called a canvas tarpaulin. He tossed it back and there was a large, heavy looking, steel machine of some kind.

"Is it a sewing machine?" Gladys asked.

"You bet missy, that's what I did in the war before I was assigned to the medical corps. Make harnesses and the like. Kept me from getting my lungs gassed and my ass from being shot off by the Heinies. She'll sew through a quarter inch of sole leather with waxed thread the thickness of piano wire."

"You're a shoemaker?" I asked.

"Yup, shoemaker, harness maker and...," he reached into the wagon and pulled out a coil of braided leather, "whip maker."

He let the coil unwind to the ground. "Watch," he said, squaring up to a small tree. With small circular motions of his arm the whip arched through the air again and again, each time whistling and ending in a crack as loud as a gunshot. He snapped branches off the tree and sent them tumbling through the air so fast, that he had as many as three flying at once.

Gladys covered her ears, Bob and I watched with our mouths open while Earl made for under the wagon, sniffling all the way.

"Will you teach me?" Bob asked.

"You can earn one first, then I'll show you how to use it," Pa said, as he wound up and placed the coil back in the wagon. "For now, we got to make some miles."

He pulled the canvas cover back into place, and climbed back on the wagon. "You'll be doin' a lotta walkin'. Ol' nag can all but manage this load." He gave the reins a shake. "C'mon gal."

Walking was okay by me. The blisters on my feet didn't feel so bad in my old boots. I looked at my 'barn slippers' and noticed the shiny coating was cracked and peeling already. I figured with a shoemaker for a pa, we wouldn't have a problem for boots anyway, and I chucked them into the bush.

We headed into the farmland towards the east. Gladys walked ahead of us as we followed the wagon past farms with tiny one-room farmhouses and big sheds or barns stuffed with hay. Every now and then, someone working the fields would stop what they were doing and call out or wave. We would wave back, except for Pa, he wouldn't stop or wave. Only the top of his hat showed behind those shoulders as he hunched up on the seat, and I couldn't tell if he even turned his head.

Earl rambled on to Bob about seeing three motor cars. Once a drone in the sky caught our attention and the three of us stopped and gazed at our first aeroplane. It flew so low we could see the head of the man flying it. We waved but the man didn't wave back.

"That's what I wanna do," Earl said, "when I'm all grown up."

It hummed off into the distance and we turned our attention back to the road. Bob picked up a stick and walked with it so Earl and I started looking for walking sticks. Soon we were all walking with them, discarding them for better ones as we moved along.

"Maybe things will be better," I said, looking at the road and flicking stones with my walking stick.

Earl began to whistle, Bob said nothing. I looked at him and noticed the bruise on his cheek from Pa's hand. I was kind of hoping Bob would maybe say something positive, but he had nothing to add.

I wanted to believe we were going somewhere where all the bad stuff in our lives would be over. I wanted an end to all the beatings, the fights, the hunger and the fear that seemed to nest deep in the pit of my stomach. The same fear I saw in Bob's eyes after Pa laid him out earlier. Earl, he just ran and hid while Gladys, she just seemed to live with it. I hadn't put it all together yet, but I knew she had been afraid and hurt.

I felt the warmth of the sun on my back and took a deep breath of fresh, clean air. It was filled with the smells of freshly cut hay, warm, wet dirt, and the slight scent of burning wood from the smoking chimney pipes sticking out of the little farm houses we passed. The sun and the fresh air – two trivial things that most everybody just took for granted, but two things that I, and probably Bob, would cherish for the rest of our lives.

Of course, things would be better, I told myself. We were out of the orphanage, away from the Bitch and away from Warren the Warlock.

We walked for what seemed like forever, ate a cold supper and hunkered down into our blankets – so tired we didn't even say goodnight.

The next morning didn't bring us any joy as the sky was grey and the wind cold. We started another day's journey not even taking the time for breakfast.

We stopped our eastern trek around noon for lunch and set about our chores. Bob and Earl went for water and firewood. Gladys pulled out the pots from the back of the wagon while Pa showed me how to care for Rosy, our horse.

An hour later the pots were scrubbed and put away and I hitched up Rosy without Pa's help. We hit the road again with Pa on the wagon and the rest of us walking behind.

We walked 'til near dark, before we caught up to Pa who was stopped at the side of the road. All of us were hobbling as we sat down for a cold supper of beans and biscuits left over from lunch. We didn't complain. We were too hungry and tired.

After we ate and cleaned up, Pa, who was obviously disgusted with us, but mercifully quiet, threw us our blankets before crawling under the cover of the wagon and settling in for the night.

We huddled in our blankets and slept until the cold made it impossible to sleep any longer. Chilled to the bone and miserable, we sat and listened to Pa's snoring while waiting for the sun to rise. As soon as it was light enough, we gathered wood for a fire, and following Pa's advice from the previous day, set and lit it.

Pa got up when the sun was full but low in the eastern sky, and after plodding into the bushes for a whizzer, came back and broke open a package of hard tack. We each got a square. I ate mine while harnessing Rosy. Pa was eager to be moving on.

We marched behind the wagon knowing full well that if we didn't keep up all we could expect for lunch was more hardtack.

We kept up pretty good, and when we stopped for lunch all of us went about our chores without a word. Pa said nothing as he waited for Gladys to serve up a warm meal of fried oatcakes with molasses. They were delicious and we devoured them all, not even thinking that they may have been meant for that night's dinner as well.

Not far from where we broke for lunch, we stopped at a small, clear stream, watered Rosy and filled our bucket. Bob found a good spot on the bank where we could lie on our bellies and drink our fill.

By mid-afternoon, the farmhouses were behind us and the road became a single wagon track, winding its way through scrub and the odd thicket of skinny trees, whose leaves had mostly fallen to the ground. The sun on our backs barely kept the chill of the breeze from making us cold.

The first inkling we had that someone was approaching was when Pa pulled off the track and stopped. Looking around on the left side of the wagon, we saw another wagon pulling up beside ours.

"Howdy." The driver touched his hat to Pa. Beside him sat two women, one older – near his age, and the second one younger. They noticed us behind the wagon and smiled, lifting their hands in a small wave. Pa touched his hat but said nothing.

"We're on our way to Edmonton," the man said. "Daughter's pregnant, needs to see the doctor. She's chuckin' everything she eats." He spat a black stream of juice from his grizzled mouth then stuck a finger between his lips and pushed the baccy back into place.

"Don' say?" Pa said, looking the young woman over.

"Reckon 'bout day an' a half, nearer two?"

"Reckon," Pa answered.

"Bound for Viking?" the man asked, as he pressed his thumb to his nose, leaned over and cleared his nostril with a splat.

"Yup," Pa leaned over and did the same, "matter of fact."

"Figured. Open wagon, kids on foot, time of year."

"Not to mention," Pa said, "there ain't really much else 'tween here and Saskatoon" He finished with a grin.

"Well now," the man said, returning Pa's grin, "you got near a couple er three days 'fore you'll see it," he said, then cleared the other side of his nose before wiping it on his sleeve. "Guess this must be 'bout half way for both of us."

"Figures right. Track 'pears to be getting skinny. What's left look like this?"

"Nope, she turns south in an hour then 'bout three hours you hit the tracks of the Grand Trunk Railroad. Best keep alert, she gets up to near gallop speed out on the flats. Say, we might be neighbours by the time we get back, what's your name?"

"Thompson. Tom, by given, go by Willie."

"See by your shirt you were in the big one."

"Yup, sixty-sixth. You?"

"Hell no. Too old, flat feet and family. See you got family yourself."

"Yeah," Pa answered. "Let's see, the girl is Gladys, my sons are Bob, Tom Junior, and Earl." We're up from Indiana originally.

Junior! Jesus H. Christ! I thought. The first son of a bitch that calls me *junior* better learn to digest teeth!

We exchanged smiles as the stranger in turn, introduced Penelope and their daughter Beatrice. "Last name is Trechuk, call me Lester."

"Handsome women," Pa said, and tipped his hat.

"Good lookin' kids," the man responded, then smiled himself, revealing a toothless mouth.

"What's your business?" the man asked, looking at the bumps in the tarpaulin behind Pa.

"Everything in leather, from shoes to harnesses to whips," Pa answered.

"Man, you're gonna be run off your feet. Goddamn, we got ourselves a harness maker and a shoemaker rolled into one. Ain't another from Ranfurly to Bruce. Closest is Camrose. Fifty miles give or take."

The younger woman suddenly pitched over the side, and only the speed of the older one who grabbed her, stopped her from falling out of the wagon as she upchucked. The father didn't pay any attention to her.

"Goddamnedest case of preggies I ever saw," he said to Pa.

The girl straightened, her eyes red, as her mother wiped the corners of her mouth.

"Best we move on," the man said, then spat another stream on the ground.

"Good notion," Pa said, and shook the reins.

Rosy moved out, and as we passed, all waved except for Beatrice who hung over the side gripped tightly by her mother as the wheels of their wagon jolted them while finding the worn track.

It was late in the afternoon when we came upon another stream and Pa called a halt for the rest of the day. We made camp and got a good fire going to keep off the evening chill.

Bob and I said we would look for firewood and escaped long enough to have a smoke. I wasn't sure what Pa would do if he knew we had baccy. We decided not to tell him, well actually, I decided and convinced Bob who really didn't give a damn. We finished our smoke, loaded up the wood in our arms, and headed back.

Because Pa stopped when he did, there was still some daylight left for us to do our chores, but cooled off quickly as the daylight faded. We felt the cold, once again, on our backs as we huddled around the fire wordlessly staring into it. After a while, Pa got up and pulled our blankets out from under the tarpaulin on the wagon. Dropping them on the ground, he took his own and unrolled it under the wagon once again.

"Put some of the bigger pieces on the fire for the night and get some sleep. We'll be there soon," he added, as he pulled off his pants, rolled them up for a pillow and crawled into his blanket.

Gladys got up and brought us the blankets as I placed a log in the middle of the fire.

I lay awake under the blanket, looked up at the clear sky and waited for sleep. The stars seemed so bright as they lay scattered throughout the night sky. I had never seen the stars so bright. I could actually see my breath in the cold air by starlight. I heard Pa as he started snoring, deep and heavy. Then Earl's, lighter, shorter. Soon Bob's fell somewhere in between.

I looked over and saw Gladys. The fire reflected in her eyes as she lay on her back looking at the sky as well. Gladys had always been quiet, now she hardly ever spoke, and I wondered if the Warlock had done this to her. Her flat – 'you should have killed him', ran through my mind. It was the most I had heard here say in such a long time. She rolled her head and looked in my direction, and then, still in silence, closed here eyes and went to sleep. In the distance I heard a train moving somewhere to the south of us, the muffled chugging and clattering on steel rails, was somewhat comforting.

Still, sleep would not come as I pondered, with growing anticipation, my new life. There would be school. There was so much to learn, and not taking anything away from Bob, there would be a whole town of people. There would be new friends and games to play outside...outside in this huge country. Even though we'd travelled for almost three days, it was hardly a speck on the map of Canada.

My excitement subsided and I drew in deep breaths of cold, clean air and eventually found sleep amidst the snoring.

Just as I slipped off, I heard a dog barking and howling off in the distance and I snuggled down, pulling the blanket over my head.

I opened my eyes and took a moment to adjust to the early light of dawn. In the direction we were heading yesterday, east, I saw the bluest sky I had ever seen. I looked around, and as the sun peaked over the prairie and reflected on the frost, everything glittered: branches, bushes, leaves and grass, and the world turned into a vast sea of white sparkles.

I sat still as the sun rose and watched it dazzle the prairie. For me, it was beyond anything I had ever experienced or seen. My heart nearly pounded through my chest.

Around me, the snoring had stopped. Apart from the occasional tossing from one of the bundled up lumps, and of course the inevitable gas erupting from all around, all were awake but none moved. It sounded, one time, as if a great naval battle was taking place with backsides instead of broadsides. And Gladys, I thought, pulling my blanket around me to try and keep up the losing battle with the cold, was the ultimate winner hands down!

I rose and placed some smaller sticks onto the embers and waited a moment to make sure they caught, then added larger pieces until the wood started crackling and snapping.

Bob and Earl sat by the fire while Pa and I got Rosy and the wagon ready. After giving Rosy a small portion of oats in her feed bag, I went over and joined them. The two of them sat staring off into space, shaking the last remnants of sleep from their eyes, and I found myself staring at Earl.

"What?" He turned and looked at me, slightly annoyed with my gaze.

"You don't know?" I smiled at him. "Bob look at Earl."

"Yer pissing me off!" Earl said, looking from Bob back to me.

"Look at his eyes. They aren't red anymore." I turned to Earl, "and I haven't heard you sniff all morning, or even yesterday for that matter!"

Earl sniffed. "Hey, you're right, I can breathe! My eyes red?" he turned to Bob.

"Nope." Bob replied. "You think he's gonna be normal?" he asked, turning to me.

"Let's not go overboard."

"You guys never quit do you?" Earl got up and went over to the other side of the fire where Gladys was making porridge.

Bob and I grinned at each other then watched as Gladys studied Earl's face. A minute later he came back.

"Gladys says I must have been allergic to that place."

"Me too," I said, looking over at Bob to catch his nod of agreement.

****

After finishing with breakfast and packing up, it was on the road again. We hit the rail line around noon after travelling almost three hours from our overnight camp and making pretty good time, I thought. This, in spite of the extra weight of my books, which we, in turn, slipped one at a time under the canvas. Pa never said anything, but he must have seen us walking, hands free, as we walked behind the wagon.

Pa was constantly looking over his shoulder at us like we were going to run off into the frozen prairie in some frenzy or stampede. Finally, he stopped and I saw he wasn't looking at us, but at the sky in the west. I turned to look back and discovered a black wall emerging from the horizon. I looked up and read concern in his eyes.

"Wow, looks like a storm on the way."

"It's big," Pa confirmed, "and at this temperature I think we're in for our first snow of the season."

"Still a long ways off," Bob said, studying it with squinting eyes.

"Not far enough," Pa answered, then hawked and spit over the side of the wagon. "Best we move smartly," he said, "it's gonna be a mother, and then some."

He clucked Rosy and shook the reins. Rosy didn't seem to sense his urgency, plodding along at her usual pace.

There were wagon tracks every so often leading off from the track we were following beside the rails. Each time we came to one, Pa would climb the railway embankment and look over to the other side of the tracks, then to the west, before returning to drive on some more.

I noticed the wagon track was almost thinned out and I ran up beside the wagon.

"Are we going to cross soon, Pa?"

"We're gonna have to. Damn pipeline crew's left a soft ditch 'tween the rail and the road. Never get the wagon through unless we find a stand a' trees somewhere and bridge our way over that cut." He spat over my head and continued. "Trouble is, don't know when the train's comin' and we're damn shorta space 'tween the rails an' the ditch... and that ain't helpin'," he said, looking up to the western sky.

The sun hung on the edge of a purple and black sky. The wind freshened and gusted at our backs. The word ominous kept leaping to mind whenever I looked over my shoulder.

"I'll walk up and see if I can find a place," I offered, and started around the wagon and up to the tracks.

"See if you can see the crew up ahead while you're at it. Maybe we can get in front of that damn ditch."

"Yes, sir," I replied, as I scrambled up the rocky embankment to the tracks, and stopping, surveyed the land up ahead. I could see for miles and miles. In spite of the concern, I was literally breathless as I surveyed the land dotted with groves of now mostly naked trees, blue lakes and ponds spread over brown, rolling mounds that seemed endless.

A green track of marsh stood directly in front of us less than ten minutes away by my reckoning. We'd have to cross soon. I studied the ditch which ran down the line and couldn't find a break in it, although miles ahead, straight as an arrow, I could see a series of black dots that sat on the tip. I ran back to Pa and told him. He grunted and we continued to move on. When the rail bed embankment got a little lower, he turned into it and stopped.

Pa pulled out a wheel block from the back of the wagon and set it beside the rail. He then steered the wagon up the sloping block and turned it to line up the other wheel. The rear wheel scraped along the outside edge and finally rode up and over the rail. Pa stopped the wagon and had me fetch the block and set it so that we could get over the other rail. Now the wagon straddled both rails as we carried on looking for a place to get over the ditch and onto the road.

The sun was gone behind the clouds and the wind picked up and became very cold. We pulled our coats around us and fought off the chill as best we could. At least it was to our backs.

We didn't stop for lunch. Instead, we munched on bread and dried beef strips called *jerky*, as we walked behind the wagon. We were allowed two strips with a handful of

bread. The bread was dry but if I chewed long enough, it
went down pretty good.

We were about halfway to the dots, which turned out to
be the pipeline crew, from where I first spotted them, when
we heard the train whistle in the distance. Pa kept moving
and studied the ground ahead for a place to get off the tracks.
The heavy marsh on our left ruled out that side for at least
another mile. Thick undergrowth of briers, brambles and
stunted trees were on our right.

The train blew its whistle as it passed the crew ahead. It
was only minutes before it would be upon us.

Pa flicked the reins and Rosy, ears forward, began to
move faster than I had seen her go in three days. She
certainly sensed the urgency this time.

The train must have seen us on the tracks because it
blew its whistle once, then as it grew larger, it began to blow
its whistle again and again, longer and longer blasts. Rosy
was doing a loping trot and snorting clouds of steam as the
wagon bounced from tie to tie, with the load crashing in the
back. I ran beside Pa on one side, Bob on the other. Gladys
grabbed Earl and moved off the track at a half run then
bounded down the embankment.

Pa spotted an opening before I did and threw me the
wheel block. "Run ahead and set this beside the rail on your
side so I can get over into that patch over there, boy."

I picked up the block, raced ahead and placed it along
the outside of the rail before ducking out of the way. The
train whistled again and again, but never slowed. Pa directed
the wagon wheels towards the block and the side of the
wagon literally flew over the rail. I scrambled back onto the
track, and picking up the block again, raced to get ahead of
the wagon. I set the block against the inside of the other rail
then tucked and rolled down the embankment. Pa steered

Rosy to the outside of the track and the wagon wheels scraped up and over as Rosy headed down into the bald patch. The wagon bounced and cleared the track only seconds before the train roared by. Somehow, Pa, like a bump on a log, stayed upright in the seat of the wagon as it lurched to a sudden stop behind Rosy.

The driver leaned out his window and said something, an angry look on his face, but his words were lost in the roar of the engine. Pa made a gesture back at him by slapping his raised arm.

Bob appeared on the tracks just after the engine and five passenger carriages rushed by, and seeing we were all okay, he picked up a rock and flung it, albeit, far short of the fleeing train. The roar subsided from clacking wheels to clicking, then nothing, as it mounted the gradual rise and disappeared over the top.

Pa climbed out of the wagon and stood beside Rosy, stroking her neck to calm her down. "Horse has to rest," Pa said. "You two start fetchin' the stuff that fell outta the wagon," his words directed to Bob and me.

Rosy's sides heaved and steam blew up from her nostrils as she lowered her head. In front, there was low scrub for a few yards then the ditch, again only a few yards before the chewed up road.

"And see if you can find some trees or boards to put across this cut," Pa said, as he studied the broken ground in front of Rosy. It was only about three feet wide, but as I looked around for trees, there was nothing save for that useless low scrub. "Away you go," he ordered, gruffly.

We headed out in different directions.

"Gladys, come back," he called. "We'll make camp here tonight as soon as we get across." He glanced at the sky which had now closed overhead. The only sunlight finding its way to the ground was miles ahead to the east and it was quickly disappearing. "We ain't gonna outrun this sonovabitch," he added, in a grave tone.

The cut might as well be a hundred feet across, I thought, as I looked out across the Prairie – there wasn't a tree within a mile. I wondered about the work crew. They would have boards, but they were still a long ways away, and I had picked the opposite direction to search in.

It took about an hour, but I had managed to find an armload of fairly stout sticks. Returning, I found Pa had managed to get the front wheels over the ditch, but the back ones were sunk in almost to the axles.

Pa asked me to climb up and give Rosy *a crack on the ass*. He joined the others behind the wagon and at his command, I smacked Rosy's backside as they heaved. The wagon came out of the ditch and I kept Rosy going until I reached the far side of the road.

"Turn her ass to the wind," Pa shouted, as the first flakes of snow began to fall.

I just got her to where Pa said when the wind started to roar and the light grey wall fronting the black clouds became horizontal. The blizzard was upon us and we had to leave Rosy in harness as we leapt about gathering the last of the belongings that fell out of the wagon during our ordeal with the train.

"Get under the wagon," Pa ordered, as he reached under the tarp and drew out our blankets.

We scrambled under with the bundle and each of us grabbed one and wrapped it around us.

"Now line up across the back end of the wagon here and put your backs to the wind."

We did as we were told and found, while it was cold on our backs, at least the snow was not in our faces.

Suddenly, the darkness lit up and a crash of thunder had Rosy in panic. The wagon lurched forward about three feet but the brake held her. We got up, scrambled back underneath and resettled.

"You get out there and calm her boy and hang on to that harness."

Damn! He was looking at me.

"Git boy, 'fore she gets some snow under these wheels and turns this into a sled."

I got up beside the wagon and couldn't even see Rosy. There was another flash, then another. I ran forward just as the thunder cracked again and caught her reins near the bit as she tossed herself up on her hind legs, almost pulling me off my feet. When she came down, she brushed my shoulder just enough to put me on the ground, but I still had a grip on her and held on for dear life. She lifted me back up to my feet with a head toss and swung me clear of her hoofs.

"Whoa, girl!" I tried to keep my voice down so I wouldn't excite her by yelling. I looked at her head and saw Bob's arm lunging up to grab her harness on the other side. Earl and Gladys appeared, but Bob shouted over the wind and angrily motioned them to the back and they slipped away.

The snow was mixed with freezing rain, and before long, we were soaked to the skin. Rosy settled down with one of us on each side of her. Bob, while holding on to her, got on his knees and pulled her head down. I joined him, and together we held her from a kneeling position, our own bodies curled and bowed before the wind and snow.

The storm blew over in about an hour and we asked Pa if we could start a fire to get warm and dry, but Pa changed his mind about setting up camp for the night and decided to move on using the remaining light.

"You'll get dry, just keep walkin', 'sides there's no dry wood here 'bouts anyways."

We got the long rays of the sun on our backs as we moved to the work crews' – now vacant – muddy camp from the previous night. On a slight rise above the camp, we decided to call it a day and all looked forward to a hot meal after our chores.

Bob left to gather wood while I unharnessed Rosy and hobbled her near a patch of grass protruding through the wet snow. By the time I had finished with Rosy and fed her some oats and hay, Bob had the fire roaring so we huddled in close and watched great clouds of steam lift from our soggy clothes. After a hot supper, I left camp and found Bob a ways off in a cop of small trees sitting and enjoying a smoke. I slipped down beside him and took the weed he was offering, dragging deeply.

"Thanks for the hand with Rosy. Man I didn't think she was that strong. She lifted me right off my feet."

"That asshole should have done it. You could have been hurt. Wouldn't get off his ass," he finished, almost to himself.

"You know what else?" He turned to me angrily, then hesitated.

"What?" I asked, waiting as he stared at me then turned away.

"Nothing," he murmured.

We finished the smoke, gathered up the wood and returned to camp to find Gladys folding our, now dry, blankets and tucking them back into the wagon.

The fading light in the west gave way to the night with a huge October harvest moon that gave off almost enough light to read by.

"Gonna be cool tonight," Pa observed, as he pulled out his blanket from under the canvass. "You kids stretch out under the back of the wagon. Here…" he said, "let me show you something. He took my blanket and opened it up on the ground under the wagon. "Gladys, you and Bob wrap your blankets around you and lay on each side of this one." They climbed under the wagon after doing so, and lay down. He then gestured for Earl and I to lie between them. When we were all in place, he doubled Earl's blanket and placed it over us. "That should keep you warm enough."

Thank God, we didn't have beans tonight for dinner, I thought, as I cuddled close to Gladys and fell into an instant sleep.

We broke camp in the dark with the dawn still a ways off. The moon hung over the horizon to the west and a heavy, low mist covered the fields. Islands of trees and taller scrub poked out in countless numbers to the horizon. The freezing temperatures over night made the thin cover of snow crunchy underfoot.

We went silently about our chores after a breakfast of cold beans, stale bread and more jerky. Earl and Gladys packed up the camp, and Bob loaded the wagon, while I got Rosy into her harness and hooked up. I was aware that Pa was watching from somewhere in the dark and wasn't surprised when he stepped out at me when I finished.

"In the dark, quick and right, boy. You learn fast. You got all you could out of those books I'll bet, eh?"

"Yes, sir, thank you," I answered back, pleased and proud. This was the first time I could remember that I heard him say something nice.

By sun up the small community of Bruce was far behind us. The road was better after we passed the area where the pipe line crew had made camp at the end of the line, as it wasn't chewed up by their heavy equipment. Lengths of pipe lay on the ground in an endless procession that lined out to the thickness of a thread before disappearing over the next hill.

After passing over the hill, we came upon a small twisty section of hidden road winding down and around a large sinkhole. Tall scrub filled the gorge to the road's edge. It would be at least an hour, in this perfect place, where Bob and I could slip back a ways and light up a smoke and follow just out of sight of the wagon.

"Tom?"

"What?"

I lit up the smoke, gratefully inhaled and passed it to Bob, making sure at each turn in the road that Pa was out of sight, as we carefully kept pace. "What?" I asked again. Damn! Bob was beginning to annoy me.

"Uh," Bob responded to my prod. "You know that hole beside the road, when uh, we left the tracks?"

"The ditch?"

"Uh, yeah, well, while we were out finding sticks for that crossing, Gladys…" he paused and took a deep breath, "saw Pa throw all your books into it, and that's how he got the wagon over," he finished quickly.

I stopped. Oh Christ, I loved those books so. "All of them?" I looked at Bob hopefully.

"Yeah, I looked and there's none left," he said, his eyes downcast.

I shook with a tearful rage coming over me. I seemed helpless to control it. My books, James's books…gone. All the pieces of him that I had tied to his memory…gone. At the bottom of a Goddamn ditch, buried in mud!

"I hate that sonovabitch!" I blurted out.

The crack of the whip in front of my face stopped me cold. I was faintly aware that something flew from my lips as I wet them with a searching tongue.

Pa was standing behind a tree at the roadside, the whip snaked at his feet. Neither Bob nor I moved and scarcely breathed.

"Who you talkin' 'bout boy?"

I realised he had snapped the weed right out of my mouth. It had happened so fast and I hadn't even felt it. Fear followed my shock, and for a moment, I was tongue-tied.

"You!" I blurted, the pain over my loss of the books pushed me off the edge.

"I could have as easily taken off your nose as that cigarette. You think on that, boy."

"You buried my books!"

"Boy, those books helped us out of a bad spot. Hell, the world is full of books."

"Now hear me boys, you stay the hell out of my baccy, or by God, you'll get the fat side of this." He shook the whip threateningly.

I opened my mouth to shout at Pa as he turned and started back to Gladys and the wagon. Bob's sudden grip on my arm squelched my *sonovabitch* to a faint whisper.

We stood motionless in the middle of the road and waited for him to get back into the wagon and move out.

"Tom, let's go. Let's just turn around and head back to Edmonton. We can work for The Gimp. At least until we can find something else. There's always farm work."

There was a lot of persuasiveness in his voice, and for a moment, I was prepared to turn and run for it.

"We could go to the coast, Vancouver maybe," he added, no doubt sensing I was very close to heading west instead of carrying on to Viking.

I was racked with indecision. It would be so easy. "Can't," I said, and saw a mix of frustration and disappointment.

"The promise?" He made it half question and half statement.

I nodded. "We're a family again. Almost, anyhow. I want to see how it goes. Earl's getting bigger, maybe later." I put my hand on his shoulder and we started walking.

"It ain't gonna change," Bob said, matter of factly. "He's a prick, Tom. I remember, you don't, you just wait 'n' see, it'll get worse than this."

Already I could feel the division between Pa and us kids. Bob and I for sure. Gladys was going to go along. She would. Earl, well, there was no doubt he would make up his own mind. But Momma wanted us together, and I had promised to look after Earl.

There would be other books, I guess. Viking was big enough to have a school and there would surely be books there. The disappointment I felt was for James, for I promised myself never to forget him, and reading those books, just having them near, was like having James around. I felt he was near when I had one of those books open. Then I remembered and reached into my pocket and felt the small book of poems I had placed there days ago. Relief washed over me.

Viking was nestled in amongst cleared fields and was bordered by the railway tracks to the south and a large alkali lake to the north and east of the town. We were like a procession going up the main street after crossing the tracks and entering the town. At the first corner ahead, three boys were gathered and watched us as we headed towards them.

"Wal, lookee here," the oldest of the boys pulled a straw from his mouth and stared at Gladys. "A keeper messed up with three ugly little toad stools." They laughed.

"Looks like they was drug through a knot hole ass backwards," chimed in a second.

As we trudged past, Bob slipped around behind me. I turned when I heard the smack of bone on bone just in time to see the biggest of the farm boys go down. The other two jumped on Bob's back and started flailing, so I left the wagon to help him out.

Seems to me, a dormitory and a town have a few things in common and some parts of life don't change a hell of a lot between them. Bob had tossed one of the farm boys off his back. I followed him down to the ground and stuck my fingers in his eyes. He wouldn't be a problem for a while. Two down, but the third had locked himself onto Bob's back and was pounding his head.

"Turn!" I shouted to Bob, and Bob twisted his back to me. One good punch up between the big boy's legs sprung him loose, right smart like. The boy just groaned and slipped off his back to his knees. Before I could finish the matter, I felt myself being lifted off the ground and high into the air.

"That's enough of that, sonny," a strange voice said from below me.

Then all of a sudden Pa's voice spoke coolly. "Put my boy down, Percy."

I managed to turn my head to get a look at the man who had a grip on me and was holding me off the ground. Bob looked ready to tear into him. Suddenly, Pa was under the man and holding us both off the ground.

"That you, Willie? Well, damn me. Sure, Willie, I'll set him down right like."

I felt his grip relax and he returned me to the ground.

We watched the three farm boys shuffle off while Pa glared at this Percy man. One limped while the second was teary eyed. The third wasn't really hurt but he made a point about not looking back.

"Well, Willie! Good to see you back," the man named Percy said, as he straightened his coat then hurriedly reached to shake Pa's hand. "I see you got the family rounded up. Damn shame what happened, losing the wife and havin' the bank move on ya like that, 'specially when you're off fightin' the war."

"Banker still around?" Pa asked, not taking the man's proffered hand.

"Er... yeah, Willie, that is, the bank is. New banker and the bank put a branch...uh ...well, on your old stand," he finished lamely.

"That so." Pa turned and looked up the street. "Guess I'd better have a talk with this new banker."

"Got the Mounties comin' through here on a regular basis." Percy made it sound like a warning.

"That so." Pa mused, as he turned to squint into the other man's eyes. "You a friend of his?"

"Well, you know, Willie, you don't get very far runnin' against the bank out here. I guess you of all people know that, eh?"

"Well Percy you can do your friend a favour and tell him I'll be in right quick like to clean up some business."

"Lands sake, Willie, don't go an' do somethin' rash."

"Put your shit on the field, Percy. It ain't growin' nothin' here."

"Your pa's up in Ranfurly, Willie. Whyn't you go there for a spell?"

"Cause this was my home," Pa said, anger rising. Then he turned away. "You kids get into the wagon," he commanded, like we had been riding there all the time.

We jumped up on the box and held fast as Pa left Percy, without another word, and we started off down the street.

I guess we had arrived!

THE SAGA CONTINUES...

The author invites you to read THE SHADOWERS.

In this book, the land calls the veterans home where they must pick up their lives and make up for time lost during the war. Willy Thompson has returned to the small farming community of Viking and finds it necessary to send his sons, Bob and Tom, to work. The boys soon grow to resent Willy taking their pay each month and often confront the stranger who calls himself their father.

New to farming, Bob and Tom fight the worst winter in recorded history, along with prairie fires and floods.

Despite the hardships, slowly and inevitably, the Thompson family looks away to distant hills and brighter skies. Each of them dreaming of a better life—each of them unafraid to find it.

Here is an excerpt:

Concentrating on my footing, I almost missed Earl running desperately to the barn from the far side of the field. I yelled over the storm several times before he stopped and looked in my direction. He frantically pointed back across the field, motioned me to go there, and took off again running for the barn. The rain was too heavy to see anything in the distance, but I was concerned enough about his antics to quickly head off in that direction.

I didn't think it could possibly rain harder, but it did. I couldn't hear anything and I wasn't able to see twenty feet in front of me. I came upon the grey outline of horses harnessed to a large gang disc used to break sods. Three of them stood, nervously stamping the ground.

Suddenly, Bob's head appeared, followed by his body, as he struggled out of a shallow depression near the creek. I saw that a fourth horse had fallen into the depression. The disc had pinned the animal, ass high and head down, near the bottom of the swale, out of my sight. I lurched forward and met Bob by the horse.

"What happened?" I shouted in his ear.

He pointed to a cottonwood tree that was broken in two, twenty feet from the ground and still smoking. Lightening. I nodded at Bob, then looked at the horse. The three remaining horses continued to struggle, jerking the disc which was imbedded in the fallen horse's flank. Their frantic motion sent the disc slicing deeper and deeper into the screaming horse's body.

"Hold them!" Bob yelled. "I lost my knife in the goddamn mud. I have to cut them loose. The reins are trapped under the disc."

I seized the bridles and managed to hold on while Bob disappeared back into the swale. I stood watching, speaking softly to gentle the horses. Suddenly, Bob's head poked up and he crawled out with the knife and a piece of leather belt in his hand. Quickly, he slipped the belt through the three bridles and tied it off.

"Hold them for Chrissake!" he yelled. "I'm going to cut them loose."

Freed, the horses wheeled and began to take flight, with me holding on. Bob grabbed the harnesses. Together, we settled them down, but the horses remained skittish with every lightening bolt and thunderclap. We managed to turn them and Bob grabbed one of the cut lines and hobbled them to the discs.

We had no sooner stood up, when the downed horse screamed and thrashed in an effort to get up. Bob and I jumped down into the hole and found water pouring around the horse's head. Bob dropped to his knees and lifted the head up onto his lap. The horse's eyes, wide and wild with terror.

"Earl's coming with a rope and shovel!" he shouted, as another clap of thunder sounded overhead and rolled off into the distance, followed by another…and another.

I climbed out of the hole and saw Earl stumble and fall in the mud as he approached – a rope over one arm and shovel in the other. I ran to meet him and grabbed the shovel. Together we rushed to the edge of the hole.

"Oh, Christ!" Earl said.

Below us, the water from the creek was rushing into the place where Bob knelt and cradled the horse's head to his chest. If he let the horse go now, it would surely drown in minutes. Perhaps aware of its impending fate, the horse quietened.

"Don't fuckin' stand there!" Bob screamed at us. "Divert the water! Get that rope around the discs and get the horses to pull it off!"

I jumped into the water and frantically started digging at the bank while Earl tied the rope to the discs.

We worked furiously, but I could see the mud moving out into the water faster than I could shovel. Earl came to the edge and shouted down that the rope was tied to the discs. I scrambled past Bob, his face contorted with the strain of holding the horse's nose above the water. Scrambling up the slope, I found there was nothing to attach the rope to, except the horse's bridles; it would take far too much time to harness them into the rope. I let it fall and walked back to the hole, just in time to see Bob's head and the horse's nose disappear beneath the water's surface.

I had to make a decision.

ABOUT THE AUTHOR

Author Earl Thompson was born in Edmonton and raised on the West Coast of Canada. He is a direct descendant of the story's principal character. Earl describes this novel, his first completed, as a story that had to be told. Much of the story content was provided during his father's final days, and with his passing, Earl realized that he was now the sole keeper of this rich history. With a penchant for creative writing stemming back to high school, he finally devoted time to his talent and completed his first novel.

Earl lives with his wife, Lea, in the Interior of British Columbia during the summer and migrates to Arizona for the winter. His hobbies include golf, boating, volleyball (old-timers), and hiking in the desert. Along with the sequel to *Shadow*, he is currently working on two other novels.

To contact the author or order additional copies of his books simply e-mail info@earlthompson.ca or visit Trafford Press at www.Trafford.com

Earl welcomes your e-mails and encourages you to read the sequel, *The Shadowers*.

ISBN 1-41205118-5